THE
LIGHT
OF A
BLACK
STAR

AMID THE VASTNESS
OF ALL ELSE SAGA
BOOK THREE

THE LIGHT OF A BLACK STAR

C.S. HUMBLE

This book is a work of fiction. The characters, incidents, and dialogue are creations of the author's imagination or are used fictitiously. Any resemblance to actual events or persons, living or dead, is entirely coincidental.

Copyright © 2023 by C.S. Humble

All rights reserved. No part of this book may be reproduced in any form or by any electronic or mechanical means, including information storage and retrieval systems, without written permission from the author, except for the use of brief quotations in a book review.

Without in any way limiting the authors' and publisher's exclusive rights under copyright, any use of this publication to "train" generative artificial intelligence (AI) technologies to generate text is expressly prohibited. The author reserves all rights to license use of their work for generative AI training and development of machine learning language models.

Cover and interior design by Alan Lastufka.

First Shortwave Edition published June 2025.

10 9 8 7 6 5 4 3 2 1

ISBN 978-1-959565-79-6 (Paperback)
ISBN 978-1-959565-80-2 (eBook)

Amid the Vastness of All Else Saga

That Light Sublime Trilogy

Book 1 – The Massacre at Yellow Hill

Book 2 – A Red Winter in the West

Book 3 – The Light of a Black Star

The Peregrine Estate Trilogy

Book 4 – To Carry A Body To Its Resting Place

Book 5 – San Antonio Mission

Book 6 – The Baroness of the Eastern Seaboard

For Mom and Dad

Thus joyously the band pressed on
    Until the least had won
    And stood transfigured on the mount—
    The children of the sun;
    But soon their brightness waxed too great
    For mortal eyes to bear,
    And Night, in mercy, dropped her veil
    To hide the vision fair:
    But we, who saw that light sublime,
    Hallowing yestereven,
    Joyed in the thought that we had sped
    A little nearer Heaven.

        —M. H. COBB, *THE MOUNTAIN IN THE WEST*

PART ONE

Armies Great and Terrible

"...and there, among the great, reddened stones I saw a city within. A city with towers higher than grand Moncalieri that had once proved the zenith of my youth. Never, in all my years exploring blue ocean and gray stone, did I ever suspect to find anything such as I now record. More than a fortress singular, more than a city. It was a nation, little within the mountain, strangely glowing with its red lamps. A kingdom of scarlet light."

— Ennio Malocello, *Il Regno di Luce Scarlatta*

CHAPTER ONE

Black Wells, Colorado

Doc Simmons pressed a damp handkerchief against his raw nose. The mint extract he had soaked through the cloth did little to cover the rank odor. The body of a woman lay on the pinewood table, almost fully thawed. Lamplight danced across her cold, powder-blue skin. The waves of light and the whipping shadows around them cascaded over the flesh. Flame and darkness roiled over her naked form until they reached the red cliff—the edge where the turgid skin slumped against the abdominal wall.

He hoped this woman had been lucky at the end. Hoped that she had died before the creature had begun to eat her.

The light danced away.

Doc let out a sigh. "Goddamn it, Pete. I can't see if you're halfway across the room with the lantern." He turned his head toward the shivering man.

The lantern's yellow light illuminated Pete's all too many angles, casting his thin, giant shadow against the wall. His eyes were wide and wet. Black curls graying at the roots caught the quavering lamplight, darkening his face with hooks.

"Get on over here!"

Pete didn't move.

Outside, the rustle of townsfolk came in low voices. The murmur of rumor or worse, Doc thought. Superstition. He looked out the winter-frosted window to where blobs of light swayed in the darkness. How many of them had bundled on their winter coats and heavy wool scarves only to pile up and wait in the cold darkness? Too many, certainly. Maybe all of them.

Their concern was the same as Doc's. The woman on the table. Her name had been Suzie Lawrence. And it wasn't so much that they cared that Suzie had died—though Doc was sure at least a few of them did, since she'd been well liked among many of them—it was that they wanted to know what had killed her. The townsfolk of Black Wells, like the rest of Colorado, were afraid that Suzie would wake up again, as others had. Wake up and. . . do the things they did.

And so, the crowd sounded their little rumble of concern, awaiting to hear if Suzie Lawrence bore two distinct puncture wounds on her neck.

His office was an absolute mess. His sterling instruments lay submerged, half-frozen, in his scarlet-stained washbasin, and bottles had spilled across the floor, knocked there when he hefted the body to the table with little help from Pete. But the bundled-up people outside would make a bigger mess if he didn't give them answers, and right quick.

"I know the smell is sharp, but I need more light," said Doc, frustrated.

"It ain't the smell; I was a surgeon's assistant in the war," said Pete.

"Every damn body knows you were in the war. It's one

reason I picked you to hold the light." With trained fingers, Doc examined the peeled flesh running across the woman's abdomen. "So, you do not suffer from a weak stomach?"

"No, sir."

Doc turned sharply to look back at the sunken husk of a man, who flinched. The lantern handle squeaked in his white-knuckled grip.

"She isn't going to jump off the table and get you," said Doc.

"You don't know that."

Doc faced Pete fully. He leaned against the table, sighing deeply. Frustrated. "Christ in heaven, Pete, it's half-past midnight. I'm tired. Can you just get your ass over here."

From outside came a voice. "It shouldn't take this long, Doc. Folks wanna know if Mrs. Lawrence is marked." The voice was Sheriff Childs. A stern, solemn man who Doc had never seen get twitchy in a half-dozen gunfights. But there was no mistaking the faint tremor in his voice now.

Doc hollered over his shoulder. "I am occupied with the post-mortem!" Then, he turned back to Pete and took a deep, calming breath. "I have only two hands. I can't examine her and hold the light and help you search for your balls all at the same time!"

Pete frowned. "Ain't no need to be getting mean, Doc. I'm scared. Nothing wrong with a man admitting that."

Doc shoved his glasses up the long slope of his nose. "Would it make you feel better if you held the lantern in one hand and your sidearm in the other."

"Can I put it against her head?"

Even as cold as it was, pearls of sweat dripped from the man's sharp chin.

"Put it wherever you want, Pete. Whatever will steady your nerves and get that damn lantern over here." The last bit came out more forcefully than he would have liked.

Pete walked over to the table, drew his pistol, and pressed it against the dead woman's temple.

"Doc," Sheriff Childs called again outside. "Folks are cold and anxious for answers out here."

"Tell them to go home!"

"Don't reckon they will."

"I will not be rushed!"

Doc, the weight of the town and all his life circumstance fully set upon him, let his head fall. "Pete," he said.

"Yeah, Doc."

"Do me a favor and shoot me in the head, would ya?" Doc's tone leaned sarcastic.

Pete's face twisted in confusion. "What?"

"Never mind. Forget I mentioned it. Now, let's see. . ." Doc put the handkerchief up to his nose and turned back to the corpse. His fingers fluttered over the red cavity and ribbons of muscle that lay slack against her ribs.

"Looks like a bear got a hold of her," said Pete.

"Maybe."

Pete swallowed. It was a hard, dry sound. "Well. . . is she?"

Doc turned the woman's head, searching her neck.

"Doc?"

"I cannot find any sign or. . ." His fingers, running down the back of her neck, rimmed a deep puncture wound.

"Well?"

He found the second wound, not an inch from the first.

"Doc?"

He had to act quickly to protect his people, and what he had to do, Pete was in no condition to help with. So, he smiled and lied. "Nothing, Pete. No reason to worry," he said, letting out a false breath of relief. "Let Sheriff Childs inside. No one else. I won't have this woman put on display for a raving band of grief tourists."

Pete holstered his gun and started toward the door.

"Leave the lantern on the table, please," said Doc, trying very hard to keep his voice steady. "You did a good job."

Pete set the lantern down on the table and brought himself to his full height. He gave a crooked smile. "Yeah?"

Doc nodded, clasping one set of fingers over his trembling left hand. "I'll be asking for your help more often. That's for certain."

All the color ran out of Pete's face. "I. . ."

"I understand you are a busy man, Pete. I'm sure I could find someone else to help in a pinch."

"R-Right," he said, his shoulders relaxing. He headed for the door and reached for the handle.

A voice, pitched so high and terrified that it masked the speaker's gender, punched through the impatient crowd noise outside. *"What is that!"*

The voice repeated the question, this time screaming.

"Everybody, get down!" Sheriff Childs commanded.

Shrieks and yells came from outside as the rustle of worried townsfolk worked themselves into a wailing, panicked herd.

A gunshot cut the air. Pete pulled his hand back and retreated from the door. Doc watched the blobs of lantern light outside the window scatter like frightened fireflies.

"Run!" the sheriff shouted.

Another thunder of gunfire flared in the night.

From out in the street came an unsettling noise, like a large canvas sheet snapping in the wind.

The shrill cries of the mob outside buckled Doc's knees.

Pete approached the window to look.

"Pete, don't—"

A man screamed. Something blurred through the night. Dark liquid arced across the frosted window, beading red against the light of Pete's lantern.

Pete shuffled backward, away from the window, the

soles of his boots scraping the wooden slats, toward Doc and the body of Suzie Lawrence.

Outside, someone was choking. A blood-soaked hand slapped against the window, groping at the slick surface and finding no purchase. Flesh moaning along the pane, the hand fell out of sight, leaving only wet red streaks.

The braying of human terror outside stopped suddenly, leaving only silence. The wind sighed, cold and lonely. Silence came again.

It was in that desperate quiet that Doc could hear his heart thumping in his chest. His breath, hot and heavy, fogged his glasses.

"D-Doc?"

"I don't know—"

Through the blood-streaked window, the lanterns bobbed slowly, collectively back into view. The lights stretched to form a row, reaching from the eastern edge of one window, across the face of the office, to the western side of the other. They just stood there, uniform and unmoving as a line of soldiers.

"What's going—"

There came a single knock at the door.

Pete yelped and fell on his ass. His lantern clattered to the ground, where its flame died. The office was thrown into almost complete darkness, save for what little light the perpetual eclipse and stars threw through the frosted glass.

Doc stared at the door, hearing only the labor of his breathing.

The spring inside the doorknob squealed. The lever clicked. The hinges sighed as the door opened. A spray of snow powdered the floor, carried into the office on the cold winter wind that had for over half a year been their pestilence.

Three shadows stood in the doorway.

A voice spoke a single word from the shuddering cold and blackness. "Kneel."

Pete rolled over, whimpering in prostration.

Doc obeyed the command, unsure as to why.

The three stepped into the office. One of them, a woman judging by her silhouette, closed the door.

"Do not be afraid." The voice was masculine, aristocratic. Smooth and slick as silk. A voice that compelled. A voice that was felt more than heard, with a power greater than its sound. "Though the world is fearfully changing, I bring you a chance at survival. And more."

The three figures stepped deeper into the office. The center figure turned his head slightly to the person on his left. "Give them more light, Sigurd. That they may see."

Sigurd snapped his fingers.

The row of lanterns outside, carried by the very townsfolk who Doc Simmons had stitched and healed and cared for, stepped into the office single file. Ten of them, their twenty eyes unblinking, wide, and shimmering wet with tears. They formed a circle within the room, illuminating the office and the figures at the center.

The tallest of the trio, Sigurd, was cut in stark contrast. Skin pale as cream against black hair curled in heavy bangs across a lineless brow. His large green eyes blinked heavy and languid. He wore a high-necked black military coat that cut snuggly over his chest. A black cape coat, its interior lined in yellow velvet, hung about his shoulders.

Opposite him was the most beautiful woman Doc Simmons had ever seen. Her dark hair gleamed like spindles of polished iron—spindles that twisted around sapphire eyes burning hot as embers in a forge. Her red dress matched her scarlet lips. Though it was deathly cold, she was barefoot, as if her beauty and internal fire were all she needed protect herself from the winter frost.

When she saw Doc staring, she winked at him.

Doc shuddered at the sight.

"You will understand," said the man at the center of the other two figures, stepping forward, "that what I do now, I do for the safety of us all." His voice flowed like honey, dark and rich. He wore a black suit, with a black cape coat mantling his thin shoulders. The man's dark presence was arresting. He slicked back a brown curl from his eyes—eyes, Doc saw, that were black as crude oil. It was those deep, black circles that captured Doc entirely. Eyes that did not look at the doctor but looked into him. Penetrated him. "You are Doctor Timothy Simmons."

Doc opened his mouth to speak.

"You are the mayor of this town. The leader of these. . . people."

"Y-yes."

"Doctor Simmons, I am Kristian. I have come down out of the mountain, as a measure of my goodwill, to inform you that as of this moment you belong to me. You, the people of Black Wells. . . all of the people inside what you once knew as Colorado."

Pete, shivering on the ground, let out a pitiful moan.

"Hush, little bull," said the woman in the scarlet dress.

"I don't understand," said Doc.

"You are an American, Doctor. Surely you must know expansion when you see it? Manifest destiny, you call it. The sun hides its face at all times now, and, though I do not know why, I will use it to my advantage. The time has come for my kingdom to come out of the mountain. In order to expand, I must maintain my people's food supply. This you also understand. Winter reigns now—a cold such as even I, in my long-spanned life, have never known. With the long cold, your people die, yes? I cannot allow this. Our survival is tied to yours. We drink the life from that which lives, subsisting on humans the best. This has been our way since the beginning."

"Why are you telling me this?" asked Doc.

Kristian sniffed a laugh. "The winter kills the wheat

and your cattle. The famine starves our human herd. So, I am reaching out my hand to bring you under my protection. The people of this town *elected* you." The word came out of his mouth in bitter contempt. "I will honor that election, so long as you understand that you are no longer a people of the United States. I shall allow you, as mayor, to oversee this section of my herd. In return, you will be given food and security, that you might live and continue to breed. Under my banner you will be preserved from all manner of predators and assailants."

Doc, who had served in Lincoln's grand army from Sumter to Appomattox and met the late president not once but twice in his life, grit his teeth. Doctor Timothy Simmons, whose grandfather had fought in the bloody American Revolution, found in that moment the great portion of American resolve that had rested unbidden inside him for many years. "And if I refuse?"

Kristian mournfully closed his eyes, as if fatigued by Doc's question. He sighed and said, "Carmilla."

The woman in the scarlet dress lifted her naked foot and set it on the top of Pete's head. She smiled at Doc and pressed the ball of her foot onto his face, pushing the man's head against the hardwood floor.

Pete cried out, then screamed as his skin began to wrinkle, then to flatten against the ground. With a thick wet crunch, Carmilla's foot smashed through the man's skull, spraying his blood and brains onto the floor in a steaming, red mass.

Doc sucked in a fluttering, horrified breath. A noise he did not recognize escaped his lips.

"Suffering, Doctor Simmons," said Kristian, smiling. "A suffering your kind do not have words for, though we certainly do."

CHAPTER TWO

BATON ROUGE, LOUISIANA

Under a gray blanket of clouds, Carson Ptolemy stood on the sundeck of the *Duke of Natchez*. He was alone. Pipe clenched in false teeth, he leaned against a brass rail, watching thin plates of ice float past the churning steamer like frozen lily pads. They drifted down the cold Mississippi River toward Baton Rouge. Annie Miller and the others were waiting for him there. The business of the Peregrine Estate, or at least what was left of it, was in New Orleans, but word had reached Carson about strange reports from the lower Mississippi region: People going missing for weeks. Their blood-drained corpses found in dark alleyways or on the riverbank, bloated, frozen stiff. It was such blatantly vampiric activity that it gave him pause, wondering if it was too risky to ask his friends to meet him. When it came to Sigurd's want for revenge and the guile of the Red Kingdom, the possibility of a trap was a very real thing. He had considered the dangers. Then, he'd telegraphed his friends, informing them of his suspicions.

It had been six months since the Battle of Chicago. Six months since Sarah Lockhart, Sven Erickson, and Annie Miller had come to Carson's rescue. After making their way back to derelict Abilene on the steam train *Hephaestus,* which had been easy to take considering its former owner had been shot and killed by Annie, he'd spent the next month convalescing. While his body healed from what the Society of Prometheus had done to him—at least as much as it could heal—he spent the time learning what had happened to the Peregrine Estate and the Judge. Annie spared no detail of Sigurd's attack and the many lives it stole: Judge Hezekiah Ellison, Professor Robert Bass, her friend Orrin, and even her own mother. All of them dead at the hands of the vampire knight of the Red Kingdom, Sigurd of Antioch.

Annie told him all that she had done, all that she had given up to come to his rescue in Chicago, and Carson had listened to the whole story without interruption. He hadn't known what to say, but she didn't wait for him to say anything.

"Sarah says you know better than her, or Sven, how to hunt the vampires," she'd said, staring at her hands as she stuffed tobacco into the bowl of her pipe. "How to fight them."

Carson envied the dexterity of her fingers, the indifferent ease. His own hands were skinny and weak, blue and black, every knuckle stiff. "Yes," he said. "Gilbert taught me."

Annie's eyes snapped up, flashing in the parlor lamplight with that deep blue of the Texas horizon. There was something about the sharpness of her gaze that made Carson look away, sending his eyes combing through every ribbon of her auburn hair.

She took a deep breath. "Your father taught you. Now, you're going to teach me."

Carson saw in her the same rage and need for revenge

that had driven him to chase the members of the Society of Prometheus. That desire had sent him down a bloody path, leading to his capture and torture at their cruel hands. He would not allow that to happen to Annie. She had saved his life, and, more than that, saved him from the High Priest, the Black Manuscript, and the pantheon of malevolent creatures they served.

He owed her everything.

Annie Miller could have asked him for a handful of starlight and he'd have found a way to reach up and take it for her. There was nothing she could not ask for. Nothing she could not take.

Carson gathered his bravery and dared to look deeply into her eyes. Behind her cold mask of fury, he saw a glimpse of the girl he'd met in Yellow Hill. Though she had traded the yellow sundress for a leather cavalry coat and black breeches strapped with a gun belt, there was still a softness about her that the world had not yet stolen. It was elusive, but there. Carson saw it. Bore witness to it.

"Well?" she asked.

Carson nodded. "Everything I know is yours to have," he said.

And then he had turned away, unable to further match her gaze.

On the *Duke of Natchez*, the wind rolled over the sunless sun deck. The steamer sounded a docking whistle, its big side-wheel paddle chewing up the river toward the row upon row of Creole river houses and saloons lining the port of Baton Rouge.

The port was overflowing with cotton stacks corseted in heavy hemp ropes. Passengers straddled barrels of wheat and barley. There were men and women smoking or tilting back bottles of whiskey trying to keep warm, bundled in heavy coats. Some hovered above shivering children, sheltering them from the cold wind and cold-blooded cutthroats famous to lurk the river. All waiting for transport.

Beyond them, rising tall above the pastel-painted homes and businesses, was a gloomy castle: the Louisiana state capitol building. It overlooked Baton Rouge and its dark river, a gray, cloud-mantled warden with fire-blackened windows. Hanging from its lofty crenels were flimsy scaffolds dangling on guy-lines. Each scaffold bore a mason, who worked to repair what the Slaver's Revolt had rightfully cost the rebel city.

The steamer's massive wheel slowed, and over its thunderous water-slapping chop came the high cry of fiddles and drums echoing off the black Mississippi and the lily pads of ice bound for New Orleans. Carson smiled at the sounds of people persisting in their gaiety despite the pestilent winter. Their endurance in the face of all this new suffering reminded him that no matter the growing darkness, there was light that would forever remain beyond its reach. Or so he dared to believe.

He went down to his quarters, tucked his pinfire revolver into his holster, and threw on his camel-hair duster, and over that he shouldered a satchel. He pocketed a small knife, curling his fingers around it, just in case any of the riverfolk decided that his limp made him look like easy prey.

He made his way to the passenger deck to disembark, passing through the teeming masses of boat-bound bodies, and tramped over mud-soaked wooden slats laid out in the street. Stepping out of the road, he walked the sidewalk, where he passed smoking blacksmith shops ringing with the rhythm of their farriers. Across the street, a short, ruddy woman bellowed over the heavy traffic, thrusting charms and necklaces high into the air. Chains of silver and gold, glimmering with colored glass, tangled around her fingers that she waved at potential customers waiting their turn at a stained butcher's cart.

Two children, their faces streaked with soot, raced over the wooden slats, almost knocking Carson over, laughing and running, untroubled by the weather and the sloppy road conditions.

"Come on," one yelled to the other. "They're gonna do it in the street!"

They dashed ahead toward a group collecting at one of the intersections.

A narrow-eyed tanner sporting a brown derby looked up from a wide strip of hide, calling after them. "Hey! Who's doing what in the street?!"

One of the children turned back, his teeth a flash against his coal-streaked skin. "Gunfighter's Guild! Both of 'em high ranking."

At those words, the tanner set down his tools, and, wiping his hands swiftly on his apron, rushed down the street as if late for his own wedding.

"Sven," said Carson. Worry knotted in his stomach. Up ahead, he saw a face pass between the heads of two coonskin hats jockeying for a good place to see the action. For the briefest of moments, he saw the auburn hair, the blue eyes. "Annie?" said Carson to no one.

Something small and round pressed against his shoulder blades. Something cold. The sound of the hammer ratcheting back would have shriveled the heart of most men, but Carson found only the calm center of himself, all of him relaxing. One of the riverfolk had seen him limping along and likely slipped behind him while he had been focused on the churning crowd ahead. Though he wasn't sure how fast he was now, what with so many infirmities set upon his hands, still his fingers squeezed the handle of the slender knife in his pocket, the muscles in his arms coiled beneath his heavy coat, ready to whip around and—

"Not on your best goddamn day, Carson Ptolemy," said

the voice behind him. It was a woman's voice. Bright and cheerful, arrogant as hell.

Carson relaxed. "Sarah."

He turned and there she was. Sarah Lockhart—all dark skin and dark hair and big hazelnut eyes wrinkling above a smile. Her teeth as white as the pearl handle of the revolver she spun and holstered. "About time you got here," she said.

"Hurried every chance I got. Natchez was—" Just before he could explain, the crowd at the intersection roared.

"Time for that later," said Sarah. She took him by the elbow and tugged him toward the spectators.

"Number five found him?" asked Carson, half-skipping to keep up with her.

"Shit," said Sarah. "Try number *four*."

"Wait," said Carson, trying to keep up with her as she barreled her way into the crowd, shoving aside the duo of coonskin-capped fellows. "Sven killed number three?"

"Damn straight. Never seen a man more tired of being alive. He was a fellow named—hey, you wanna get the hell outta my way," she said, pushing past a passel of bonneted, doe-eyed girls clutching handkerchiefs to their lips. "Named Death Walks Nearby. Lakota fella. Apparently, he'd been number three for the last six years. You should have seen it, Carson. Since Larry got killed in Chicago, Sven cares about only two things: being number one in the Gunfighter's Guild and doing whatever the hell Annie Miller asks."

Carson nodded, finally hearing the name he wanted to hear. "I thought I just saw Ann—"

"Nah, she ain't here. She's back at the hotel. Got it in her mind to get to New Orleans, recruit the rest of the Gunfighter's Guild, and then make Hell against Sigurd and the rest of the kingdom."

Carson stepped on a woman's foot. He apologized,

then said, "She mentioned those plans before I left. Which is why I advised you all to meet me here on our way to New Orleans. She asked me to teach her how to hunt Sigurd and his kind. Baton Rouge is going to give her a chance at learning it first-hand."

They finally broke through the shoulder-to-shoulder press of people. The crowd was much larger than Carson had initially estimated. Across the intersection, he saw another wall of people near three times as long.

Sarah unhooked his elbow, turned, and smiled at him. "She told me she thought that might be why you had us meet you here. Then again, Baton Rouge is where Sally Scull found us. So, that's on you."

Carson wrinkled his nose. "Who the hell is Sally Scull?"

Like an answered prayer from on high, Carson's question was answered by a loud voice, harkening the crowd unto silence: "Listen up, peckerwoods! My name is Sally Scull!"

The voice came from the thoroughfare near Carson, where stood a big woman wrapped in leathers and a bearskin coat. "I am the four. Here as I live and draw breath, do I challenge Sven goddamn Erickson, the three, within the rules of the Gunfighter's Guild. I challenge him in honor to a contest of the gun." The woman's cruel confidence slanted across a face streaked with long red scars. To the shocked gasps of the crowd, she drew her gun almost faster than Carson could see and whirled it, spinning the ironwood handle and its blued steel in a technical display that sent a wave of awe through the onlookers. Then, with a flick of the wrist, the revolver flipped once in the air and fell cleanly into her holster.

The crowd let out a cheer.

Sally took a showman's bow.

Carson swept his eyes down the street. There, standing still as a mountain, was Sven Erickson. His black hat tilted so that it obscured everything except the grim line of his mouth.

Sally silenced the crowd with her bawdy roar. "I've traveled the perils of an ocean and eleven states to find you, Sven. You've famously killed twenty-seven of our number, but now that streak comes to an end. Sorry to say, you won't be making it to the convocation in dear New Orleans. Do you yield or accept?"

Convocation? Carson had never heard of that.

Every head turned to the big gunfighter opposite Sally Scull.

"Withdraw, Sally. Withdraw while you still have your life and your honor," said Sven, then lifted his chin so that his eyes made a hard line for his challenger.

Sally laughed. "Them eyes don't scare me. The challenge stands."

"Fine. I accept."

Time passed between them. Sven stood there, a pale, calm Goliath. Eyes half-lidded. Hands still. Sally Scull, on the other hand, roiled with nervous energy, constantly licking her lips and wiggling her fingers above the butt of her revolver.

What came next was the quickest, cleanest draw Carson had ever seen. Thunder whipped the air. A single cloud of gunsmoke filled the space between the two pistoleers. Sally Scull spun, arms flailing. She slapped hard into the mud, wailing all the way down.

Sven, without flourish, holstered his gun.

A man standing next to Carson whispered to another. "Sh-She's alive."

"I thought they shot for keeps?" the other whispered back.

The men were right. When the challenge was issued, it was for life and death, sure as blood dried black.

Sally let out another moan as she tried to push herself

to her feet. "You son of a bitch," she howled. "You goddamn smooth shooting son of a whore."

Sven walked the long distance between them, the silence cut only by the jingle of his spurs and Sally's moans. He stood over the woman, and then squatted down with his big forearms resting on his knees. Strangely enough, Sven whispered to the woman. Then he stood back up and turned to walk away. "Guild business is concluded."

Sarah Lockhart nudged Carson. "Sven is smooth as a gentleman's manners, yeah?"

It was true. Sven Erickson's pull had been nothing short of marvelous, but it was the non-lethal shot that puzzled Carson the most. "What the hell was that?" he asked under his breath.

"That," she said, "is someone everyone ought to be awful afraid of."

"Why did he leave her alive?"

Sarah's smile was as wide as the Mississippi itself. "Like I said, kiddo. Because Annie Miller told him to."

CHAPTER THREE

NEW ORLEANS, LOUISIANA

Ashley Sutliff rapped his knuckles against the table. "Hey," he said, using his cards to wave cigar smoke out of his face. "You awake?"

"Don't rush me, buddy," the skinny old man across the table said.

The saloon was warm as the weather outside would allow and throbbing with life. A two-piece band comprised of a tap-dancing fiddler and a claw-hammering banjo player rolled through their rendition of "The Foxhunter."

Ashley hated this goddamn song. Hated waiting. He was starting to hate the old man even more. But the old man wasn't the real source of his frustration, even though his snail's pace of play was infuriating. No, Ashley had been in this town for over a week waiting to get an audience with the highest-ranking members of the Gunfighter's Guild. You would've thought for a group of mercenary gunhands they would make themselves easily accessible to clients, but that was painfully not the case. He had been to every saloon in New Orleans it seemed, throwing around his name to every bartender and noting his desire to meet with them.

The old man slid his fingers through the handlebars of a wispy mustache. His other hand held his cards close to his chest, protecting the secrets they would soon tell.

Ashley cocked his head. "Rubbing that caterpillar ain't going to change those cards, pops."

The old man squinted harder, calculating the possibilities set within the three cards on the table: ace of spades, the jack and five of diamonds.

"I bet. . ." the old man said, taking his time, "two hundred." He leveled his wrinkled, brown eyes at Ashley.

"Call," said Ashley without hesitation, shoving his chips to the center of the table.

The old man frowned, suddenly worried. "Now wait a second. . ."

"Here comes the turn," said the dealer. He flipped another card on the table, face-up. He looked at the old man. "Queen of hearts," said the dealer. "Your bet, sir."

Ashley nodded to call.

The old man leaned forward, narrowing his eyes at the queen of hearts. He let out a long, considering hum and, twisting the hairs of his mustache together, stared a hole into the card. "Let's see." Suddenly, his eyes widened as if sparked by a revelation sent from God himself.

Jesus Christ, thought Ashley. Is that what passed for a poker face in goddamn Louisiana?

"Can I get another goddamn drink?" Ashley waved his hand at the bar.

Across the room, the bartender was slinging drinks fast, but nodded. "Yes, sir, Mr. Sutliff."

"Sutliff," said the old man. "That wouldn't be *Ashley* Sutliff, would it?"

Ashley shook his head. Goddamn bartender was going to scare off all the easy money. "It. Is. Your. Bet," he said.

"I-I don't know. . ." The old man looked at the cards in

his hand, then back to the table. Back to his own cards again. "You know what," he said, "it don't matter if you is him. I ain't scared of some Texas dandy."

The band wended their tune into another lively piece, and when they came to the refrain a group of pale-skinned cowboys hollered a "hey!" in unison.

"Well then, let your courage guide your coin."

"I'm all in," the old man said with a mean grin.

"Fucking finally," said Ashley. "I call." He flipped his aces over onto the table, got up and began to walk toward the bar.

"Sir," said the dealer, "aren't you going to wait for the river card?"

Ashley patted the old man on the shoulder. "My three-of-a-kind beats your queen pair. And even if you catch a third queen, I've got aces. And don't think about taking those chips back. I know how much is there."

"How? Now, wait—"

"I am all fucking done with waiting."

"Jack of clubs," said the dealer. "Trip aces takes the pot."

The old man, disgusted, tossed his cards into the mess of chips. "Goddamn it!"

"Ah, the delightful keening of a man gambling away that which he couldn't afford to lose." Ashley brushed past a saloon girl and winked at her. He had forgotten her name.

"Mister Sutliff," she said, blushing.

Ashley patted her on the rump. "Grab those chips off the table and meet me upstairs in ten, would you, sweetheart."

"My pleasure," she said.

Ashley leaned an elbow on the bar. "It certainly will be," he said to himself.

The bartender slid a mug of beer across the oak bar

with a practiced hand. It slid to a stop in front of Ashley without spilling a drop.

Again, the crowd of cowboys let out a delighted "hey!" at the end of their tune.

It wasn't the drink he craved, but it went down smooth. Ashley wiped the froth from his mustache and sighed. "Earl," he said to the bartender. "When are you going to get a decent band in here?"

Earl smiled, punching a rag into a mug. "The minute you start paying for it. God knows you could afford it."

Ashley finished the beer. "Never pay for anything you can get for free." He turned and watched the saloon girl walk up the stairs to his room. "Not once."

If the band hadn't stopped playing, Ashley wouldn't have heard the boots stepping behind him.

Earl's smile fell into a frown, his eyes going wide.

Goddamn it, Ashley thought. I do not have the time or the patience for this. He drew his gun and whirled.

The old man was standing there, a skinning knife in his wavering hand. The blade gleamed slender and sharp.

Ashley's gun was in the old man's face, and the pisspot's menacing expression melted into panic.

The sounds of the bustling saloon and a dozen conversations died.

"I—" the old man squeaked.

Ashley pulled back the hammer on his revolver. "Need the money? Then you shouldn't have sat at the table."

"My wife... my grandchildren—"

"Are not my goddamn concern."

Earl spoke up, his voice a warning. "Boys, I don't like blood on my floor. Takes too damn long to clean, and the stain doesn't come out."

"Then tell Methuselah here to sheathe his knife, so that he can go live out the rest of his life in poverty."

The old man's lip began to quiver, then his eyes narrowed. "You cheated."

"Aw, shit," said Earl.

An angry fire rushed up from Ashley's belly. "Cheated," he growled.

"Damn right." The old man's cheeks flushed. "I'm saying you cheated. You ain't gonna kill me, Sutliff. I know the killing type, and you ain't it."

"Ashley," warned Earl.

"Therein lies your second mistake, old-timer. You've got me figured all wrong."

The old man's hand was quavering now, either too tired to hold the knife or too scared to do anything meaningful with it. "Now, you listen to me, Sutliff—"

Ashley leveled his cold green eyes at the old man. "The first was you went for your knife instead of your gun. Should've shot me in the back while you had the chance."

"I ain't a coward."

"Shame. Cowards live longer. But, that means you won't mind taking our business out into the street. I'd hate to ruin Earl's floor."

The old man's courage shriveled, his face drained white. "N-name the time, Sutliff."

Ashley stepped in close, letting the tip of the man's knife press into the gambler's brocade vest. "Like I said, I'm all fucking done with waiting."

The old man licked his lips. He nodded slowly, desperation fueling his courage. "All right, you little bastard. Let's do it." He sheathed his knife and turned toward the door.

Ashley let him turn and take one step for the door. Then he kicked him square in the balls.

The crowd let out a collective moan.

The old man collapsed, clutching his crotch.

"Third mistake," said Ashley.

"My balls," the old man cried. "You broke my balls!"

"You weren't using them." Ashley turned away from the shriveled mass on the floor back to the bar. "You can walk away with some busted balls, or do you still wanna fight?"

"God, no," the old man whimpered.

"Someone help gramps to his horse." Ashley picked up his empty beer mug and delivered a disappointed stare into the glass. "No one calls me a goddamn cheat."

"Charlie, Bill," Earl said, pointing at two men at a nearby table. "Would you two be so kind as to help this man outside."

Two men got up from their table, laughing and shaking their heads. They carried the old man out the door.

The voice of the old man gave one final curse from outside, "Goddamn you, Sutliff!"

Ashley laughed joylessly. "I'll have one more before I retire, Earl." Then he turned to the fiddler and the banjo player. "And you two, play 'Young Hunting.'"

The two-piece band didn't miss a beat. With a hard, glorious clap and a "one, two, three," they rolled into Ashley's favorite ballad.

The saloon doors swung open again, but it wasn't Charlie and Bill who came back inside. A short dark man wrapped in a black wool suit and matching felt hat stepped through the doors. He eyed the room slow and patient, like an eagle scanning a stream. A pearl-handled revolver on his hip rippled in the ruddy lamplight.

He approached the bar, put a boot on the brass footrail that ran its length, and took off his hat, revealing a freshly shaven scalp. He set it down between himself and Ashley. "Earl," he said.

"Mister Sterling," said Earl without looking the man in the eye. "Your usual?"

Sterling nodded.

Earl reached over to grab a bottle of rye. Ashley caught the slight tremble in the bartender's fingers. That, like the fancy pistol, grabbed Ashley's attention.

"This him?" asked Sterling, leaning his head at Ashley.

Earl set a shot glass down on the bar. "Yes, sir." He filled the glass to the brim and then shuffled to the other end of the bar, suddenly needing to wipe it down even though it was clean.

Sterling swiveled his body toward Ashley, swinging a leg wide, but did not meet his gaze. Instead, he looked over at the band playing their lively melody. "Mister Sutliff, I presume?"

"Depends."

"On?"

"Well, you don't strike me as a bounty hunter looking for money or a husband wanting revenge."

Sterling laughed. "I am a solicitor. At this moment, a proxy."

"I know. For the Gunfighter's Guild." Ashley locked his eyes on the man, sizing him up. He reached over and took the shot glass in front of Sterling. Never looking away, Ashley drank the whiskey in one slow gulp. Then, he wiped his mustache with the back of his thumb, once to the left, then to the right. "And that's what you owe me for making me wait a whole goddamn week," he said. "You're the Guild's man. Was wondering when I'd finally get an audience. I have a proposal."

"You're a sharp man, Mr. Sutliff."

"Don't need to be sharp to pick one of you Guild proxy fellas out. All formal and self-serious as you are."

"What is your proposal?" the dark man said, reaching over to take the shot glass out of Ashley's hand.

Ashley let him take it. "Not you," he said. "I want an audience. At the Guild estate."

Sterling examined the glass, rolling it in his fingers. "I am afraid that is an impossibility. The Guild is currently—"

"Under the rules of the convocation. Yes, I know. Which is exactly why it is important that I meet with them now, while every single ranked gunfighter is in the same place."

"You wish to appeal to all of the members? Why?"

Ashley grinned. "I don't want to appeal to them. I want to hire them. All of them."

"I had heard you were a funny man. A brigand, though charming. I also heard that you joke to hide your fear or"—he looked Ashley in the eyes, unflinching—"what I am given to understand is an almost ungovernable anger. Your name has a long reach in certain circles."

"And what circles would that be?"

"Gamblers, highwaymen, occultists, and degenerates, such as yourself. The people in those circles say that you are a man to be cautious of." Sterling set the glass on the bar and rapped his knuckles on the wood. "Do you understand how much money it would require to hire every single member of the Guild? To ask them to forgo their game and work unto one purpose? No offense, Mr. Sutliff, but even the most successful gambler alive could not afford that kind of purchase."

"Ain't my money I'm spending but the money of my own employer."

Sterling lifted a curious eyebrow. "Deep pockets?"

"Oceans wide and fathoms deep, Mr. Sterling."

Earl came and filled the empty glass with whiskey, silent as the grave, then shuffled back down the bar. Sterling slid the glass over to Ashley and smiled. "Perhaps if you gave me the name of your employer, it might carry some weight as to how serious I take this proposal."

Ashley had to laugh. Despite the man's priggish sense of formality, he liked him. He slugged the shot. "Fine." He reached into his coat pocket, drew out a folded sheet, and handed it to Sterling.

Sterling opened the sheet, read it. His expression never changed, not even when he got to the signature at the bottom.

Now that was a poker face, Ashley thought.

"It's genuine," said Ashley.

"Oh, I believe its authenticity, Mr. Sutliff. And because of that, I'd like to invite you to take a walk with me."

"It would be my pleasure."

Ashley followed the man out of the saloon, leaving behind the money and the saloon girl in his room. He didn't need either.

Ashley Sutliff was finally done waiting.

CHAPTER FOUR

The Astolat Mountain Range, Colorado

Sheriff John Childs slopped through the winter snow, barefoot, shivering, shoulder to shoulder with a hundred others being driven up the mountain pass like cattle. The long, hot wound running from his shoulder to elbow felt like a branding iron had seared him to the bone. But he walked on, nevertheless, with his people.

John thought it strange that their captors had not shackled or chained those humans who had been selected for bondage. He thought about making a run for it, to try to save his own life, but he couldn't bring himself to do it. He was these people's sheriff. They had elected him as their protector. That may not have meant much to other men, but it meant just about everything to him. And then, just as John had decided to march on and remain faithful to those who had trusted him, he saw movement through the light powder of the blowing snow: two of the huddled townsfolk making a break for the dark timberline. The man ran with arms pumping hard, his hot breath billowing in the cold night. Just behind him, a woman ran head down, leaning into the wind, her arms clutched close to her chest, holding a bundled blanket.

They made it fewer than twenty yards before leathery wings bore down upon them with a speed and strength greater than any other predator that had ever stepped the earth. With a sweeping claw, the one they called Carmilla snatched the blankets from the woman, plucking a newborn child from its mother's arms. The vampire, her long white teeth so clear in the open black sky, carried the squalling mass back to the head of the human herd.

The mother screamed, helpless, and pulled against the strong arms of her husband, who had run with her toward the trees. "My baby," she screamed and screamed and screamed.

The vampires laughed.

The mother broke away from the man and ran back to where her baby lay nestled in the arms of what John might have considered to be the embodiment of evil itself. But even Carmilla had a master, one to whom the winged woman gave absolute deference. And it was that creature, the king they called Kristian, who approached Carmilla and took the crying child from her without word.

"Please," the mother said. "Please give me back my baby. We won't—"

"Shh," said King Kristian. "Bid your man return to his place, and I will show you and your child mercy."

The mother whirled, tears streaming down her face. Veins bulged in her throat, and in her reddening forehead. "Mark! Mark, come back. Please, god, come back."

Mark looked back to the tall, dark safety of the timbers, shoulders heaving. His breath blew out in visible jets from his mouth.

"Bid him," said the king, encouraging.

"Mark! Mark, please!"

What John saw in Mark's eyes was a look he had seen

so many times over on the faces of gunfighters, bandits, and gamblers alike: the anticipatory moment before a life-changing decision. In that moment, Mark's entire life must have flashed before his eyes. All the love he bore for his wife and their newborn, every heart-graven memory weighed against the love for his own survival.

Mark opened his mouth to say something, but only his breath escaped his lips. He ran. Not toward his family, but for the wilderness.

Carmilla took flight. The mother screamed.

King Kristian clutched the squalling infant by the ankles, and, taking it up as a cudgel, destroyed both mother and child.

The press of human chattel let out a collective panic that sent men and women to their knees at a soul-crushing moment that lasted much, much longer than any of them could endure.

John Childs, a man who had taken a solemn oath to protect the innocent and the weak in the name of the law, stood watching, as still as the trees Mark ran toward. The sheriff of Black Wells did nothing. Said nothing. Only watched Carmilla's dark expanse unfurl in the night before she came crashing down on Mark. Bending at the waist, over the downed man, Carmilla wrapped her hands around his face and twisted his head. The body fell out her hands and then out of sight into the tall grass.

"Drink," said King Kristian.

At the command, the entire brood of vampires, all save for the one named Sigurd who had stayed behind in Black Wells, rushed to the place where Carmilla stood in bloody victory, leaving only King Kristian to stand with the herd.

The king of the vampires tossed the obliterated infant corpse onto the heap of its mother's body. He turned to face the herd, this small man whose eyes glittered like black stones in the twilight.

He lifted his hand and, with a silent, invisible oppression, bent every human knee into the snow. "You are afraid," he said, though his lips did not move. "This is your way. In so many ways it is your chief strength. Your fear of each other has given you war, and war made you strong. It gave you primacy in numbers. Made you formidable. But your wars are over. Your ways are over. Let, too, your fear be over. My reign is a gentle thing, so long as you prove masters of your fear. Take heed, children. You need not perish needlessly in this new age."

John's legs, driven deeply into the cold snow, grew numb. His heart hammered in his chest, and hot blood flushed his face. He had sworn to protect these people. Defend them. But what could he do against such strength? If he tried to act, it could mean more people would die. That would be as selfish a sin as Mark had committed. He was helpless to do the work God had placed in him. And that feeling sent a dagger through his aching soul.

When the brood had taken everything from Mark, they came back to the kneeling crowd.

"Your old life is behind you," said King Kristian, lifting his oppression from them. "Come with me, and I will see that none of you shall die without need. . . or without reward. But, when your hearts return to your fear, and return they shall, remember this moment and consider those we left behind—" Suddenly, his head lifted. With a lupine gracefulness, he sniffed the air. "The night beasts," he said, turning to Carmilla. "In the trees. Many of them."

Carmilla's voice pealed brightly like the sound of a great bell. "Protect the herd!"

From out of the dark timberline came a slavering pack of monstrosities. Churning up the snow into a powdery oncoming tide. Their wide mouths flashed with hundreds of needle-sharp teeth, bounding through the tall grass.

The human herd screamed again, falling in behind the semi-circle arc of their new masters for protection. John, huddled in the panicked mass, had seen these beasts in action only once before, and to see so many of them now filled him with the irrepressible knowledge that this moment would be his last. Night had fallen forever, bringing with it the final winter civilization would ever know. John was going to die. They were all going to die.

Though few in number, the vampire throng rushed the pack. Carmilla led them, her great wings unfurling again. The snowbank beneath her blew apart, scattering the icy powder like ten-thousand dandelion tops caught in a maelstrom. Those under her command took to the tall, yellowing grass, fearless, making battle in a fashion that would have annihilated any human force. They leaped as one, arcing high into the air to come down on the pack leader, a great gray beast that stood a head above the rest. The pack turned inward to the center of the melee, but Carmilla, with flashes of her taloned wings, kept them at bay. Howling clear commands in a language that John did not know, the brood ripped and slashed with their long, glimmering claws, revealing a strength never to be equaled by any living man.

The vampire they called Roland, a small hawkish creature, shot out a hand, striking a beast so hard that his hand punched through its throat. He then turned gracefully and threw the bloody corpse into one of its kin. The beast, struck so mightily, groaned and fell to the ground, its clawed feet kicking wildly in final death throes.

But the others were not so easily dispatched, proving at least a close equal to the destructive power of the brood. Roland found himself outside the protection of Carmilla's wings. The wolves surrounded the vampire, and three of their number bounded atop him. Their slavering jaws plunged down behind the grass where the fallen vampire lay. The hungry growls of triumphant slaughter filled the bloody night, where there came the sound of clothes and flesh ripped apart.

"Roland!" King Kristian's voice boomed. His placid countenance vanished.

What happened next defied every natural law John Childs had ever known.

The king of the vampires melted into a vaporous cloud of silver-white smoke that shot forth into the waylay. The cloud expanded, covering the field in a blanket of white thicker than any battery of cannon fire John had seen during the war. So thick that only the roars and echoing cries indicated the carnage of battle. Rising in tempo and ferocity, Carmilla's voice loosed commands in the language of her people.

"W-we should run," a man standing next to John said.

A dull-faced woman next to him agreed. "We will never have another chance—"

"You'll stand right there. Both of you."

"But, Sheriff—"

"There is nowhere to run. Not yet, at least," said John, shaking his head, listening to the sound of supernatural war begin to die. "They own every advantage." He considered the situation deeper still and said words he never thought he would say. "They own us."

"I ain't owned," the man said. "Ain't no one ever gonna own me."

John turned to him. "I'll kill you myself if you endanger these people with your cowardice."

"Cowardice? How can you call it cowardice to want to live!"

"Look over there," said John, leaning his gaze to where the cloud of smoke retained its form, coalescing back into the slender malevolence of King Kristian. "The only life to be lived is the one they allow us to have. At least for now."

Kristian and the other vampires stood victorious in a field of blood-soaked mud. After they ensured that all the wolves were dead, the brood walked to where the one named Roland had been downed. The king knelt in the snow and reached down. From out of the grass, he lifted Roland's body, cradling him. The dead vampire's chest had been torn open, and where his heart should have been there was only a wet red cavity.

"Is he?" the woman next to John whispered.

"Yes," said John. "Which means they can be killed."

King Kristian, cheeks wet with bloody tears, looked up to the black, unknowable object that had for months hidden the sun. The sound the vampire king produced was inhuman but not unlike sorrow.

John looked back at the man, whose eyes were wide with mutual realization. And with grim hope in his voice he repeated, "They can be killed."

CHAPTER FIVE

BATON ROUGE, LOUISIANA

Annie Miller lit her pipe and let out a long, deep sigh. The hotel parlor was quiet. She sat alone, watching the flames chew through the wood in the fireplace. A whip-crack sound sent a flare of embers into the flue like a cloud of frightened fireflies. Georgie had loved fireflies, but she couldn't remember the last time she had seen one. Would she ever see one again? Had the unrelenting winter put to death fireflies, butterflies, and all the wondrous creatures of spring? Perhaps they were wherever her brother was. But that thought gave her no comfort, only a deeper grief.

She shook the thoughts away and took another drag off the pipe. The heat of the smoke bit down into her raw tongue. She kept smoking anyway.

The bell above the hotel lobby jingled.

"Natchez Under-the-Hill was already bad," came the voice of Sarah Lockhart. "Always has been. But cannibalism? Shitfire."

Round the corner of the dividing wall of the entryway Sven and Sarah walked into view.

Behind them trailed Carson Ptolemy. His hair had grown out, black and curly, swooping across his brow and those big green eyes of his. Annie knew he was ashamed of his false teeth, rarely showing them to strangers, but when he saw Annie, he smiled big and wide, brimming with confidence.

She let out a breath she hadn't known she was holding.

"Look what we found down by the river," Sarah said, heading to the fire to warm her hands.

Annie rose. Grinned with her curved pipe clenched between her teeth. "They run out of barbers in Natchez?"

Carson combed his fingers through his hair. "Lost track of how long it's gotten. Gilbert would have scolded me something fierce."

"I like it," she said, hugged him hello.

"Jesus Christ," Sven Erickson groaned. He passed the two of them and plopped down in one of the chairs. He reached into his vest and produced a flask and took a long drink. Sven had taken the death of Larry Cornish very hard, and none could blame him. His husband had been the singular point of light that guided the Swede's every action. Now, without that lighthouse to guide his way and his purpose, well, when he wasn't fighting, he was drinking. Both of which Sven seemed more and more eager to do.

Annie and Carson went and sat in opposite chairs near the fire.

"The four?" Annie asked the big Swede.

"Alive. Probably on her way to New Orleans after she sees a surgeon about the bullet in her arm."

"Good," said Annie, giving Sven a nod. "That's where we need her. And where we need to get to. I'm thinking we make passage there tomorrow, now that we're all together."

Carson shook his head. "Maybe. We've got business here tonight. And I don't know how long it will take."

"What business?" asked Sarah.

"When I was in Natchez, I got word that bodies drained of blood have been discovered here in Baton Rouge. It's why I asked you to meet me here, before we traveled to New Orleans. There is a member of the Red Kingdom here, and I mean to find them."

"Sigurd?" asked Annie, eager.

"Possible, though I believe it unlikely." Carson laced his fingers together, massaging the knuckles. "Sigurd is a creature of subterfuge. These attacks follow a pattern: a body showing up every couple of days. My guess it's a vampire that's just eating on a regular basis and isn't bothering to hide it."

Sven moved the flask away from his lips. "Could be a trap. Lure us out into the open and overwhelm us. Hell, we already know that Sigurd wants you dead something fierce. For killing his wife, no doubt," he said, his eyes falling on Carson. "That vampire bastard murdered a whole goddamn town just to get the drop on the Judge, all because he thought you might be there."

Annie remembered that night in Abilene all too clearly. She played the memory over in her mind, as she had done almost every night since. The details were still so clear. Sigurd's cold, luminous eyes. How quickly and easily he had overwhelmed them at the dinner table. How he had, with such indifference, pierced Tabitha's throat with those long, black talons. She remembered the terror that shot through her upon seeing her mother's eyes go flat. Her life snuffed out quicker than a candle. Annie gritted her teeth. Her fingers squeezed into fists.

"I've considered that it might be a trap," said Carson, looking back at Annie. "Doesn't feel like one to me, but if it is, they won't be expecting all of us. Trap or not, we have an obligation to put this thing down before it has the chance to take one more innocent life."

"Good lord," said Sven, rolling his eyes. "You talk, and it's like Gilbert's rising from the grave."

"He's right," said Sarah, who moved to stand by Carson's chair. "These people aren't equipped to handle a vampire, especially one like Sigurd." She looked over to Annie. "What do you think, boss?"

Annie narrowed her eyes, considering. After a moment of thought she said, "Where would we start looking?"

"Saloons and brothels," Carson replied. "Places where folks entertain with the specific purpose of letting down their guard. Places at the edge of town. Places where, if things go bad with the kill, escape is easier for the predator."

Annie pushed herself out of the chair. "Then we should get started as soon as it gets dark. We're leaving tomorrow, so we don't have a moment to waste."

"It's a big town, Annie," said Carson. "Unless we get lucky, this hunt could take near a week. Maybe longer."

"New Orleans is a hundred miles away, and the Gunfighter Guild's convocation ends in three days. I'm not missing my chance to speak to their leadership and hire them," said Annie, who then turned her back to head upstairs and grab her pistol.

"Are you saying that if we don't find this killer tonight, we'll just leave?" he asked. "Leave these people to suffer further?"

Annie didn't turn back as she said, "Everyone is suffering, Carson. I'm not in this for one vampire. I'm in it to see the earth rid of them."

* * *

Night fell. The four of them pushed out of the hotel together into the eclipse-lit Baton Rouge evening. A fresh snowfall dusted the muddy streets like powdered sugar on chocolate cake. A lonely lamplighter, thin and tall, shuffled along the street, setting alight oil lamps for the small crowds populating the thoroughfare as he went. Annie stared at them, thinking again of Georgie, and her mother, and the marvelous gas lamps that her brother had considered such a marvel.

"Annie?" Carson was closer to her than she had realized. "You all right?"

They walked along the street in pairs, Sarah and Sven trailing behind them.

"Yeah," Annie replied. "Just thinking about Georgie."

"I always wondered what it would be like to have a brother or, come to think of it, a sister." His words left his lips in clouds of vapor in the cold.

Annie smirked. "Nothing else like it. Georgie was something else, too. Momma always doted on him because it made him happy to be doted upon. And when Georgie was happy, it made everyone happy. Sometimes, it's hard to remember what he looked like, but I can always hear his laughter. It was loud and unashamed. Full of life." Annie shook her head, remembering. "When he died, his laughter left. Part of my happiness left with it. Sometimes, I wonder if I'll ever be happy again."

Carson wrapped his arm over Annie's shoulder.

Annie, in reflex, wrapped her arm around his back.

"There wasn't much laughter with Gilbert," said Carson, as they walked down the snowy sidewalk, a cool wind on their faces. "We were always so focused on the business of the Peregrine Estate. It seemed like every conversation held a lesson or a critique. He used to say that life was the anvil, and the father was the hammer. The child between them was a billet that required shaping. He believed that God had set us upon the earth to do a purposeful work and that if I wasn't hardened and molded properly, I wouldn't be ready when God's will for my life came calling."

"I remember you telling me that," said Annie. "You mentioned it while you were mending in Abilene."

"Oh, I did?"

"Yeah," she said, squeezing his waist. "But I don't mind hearing it again. I like it when you talk about him."

"He was a hard man, but loving in his own way. Sometimes I wonder what he'd think of me now. If he'd be upset by what I allowed the Society of Prometheus to do to me. Ashamed. Or disappointed."

That was new, thought Annie. Carson had told her about what life had been like on the trail, hunting monsters of all sorts and kinds, but he rarely, if ever, spoke this way about his second father.

She patted his waist. "My mother told me that he was a very decent man and that it was clear to her, from the moment she met him, that you were the most important thing in the world to him. So, I don't think he would have been disappointed at all. I know I'm not."

Carson turned his head to look away, as if he'd spied something interesting across the street, but there was nothing there that Annie thought was strange or worth noting. Just a group of men hooting and hollering up at a bare-chested whore singing her siren song.

Carson turned to look back at the sidewalk ahead of them.

"Carson?" asked Annie.

"Keep walking," he said, his tone shifting entirely.

"What is it?"

He didn't say anything for a few more paces, until they came to a set of saloon doors. "In here," he said, turning abruptly to guide her inside.

Annie almost stumbled over his boots but managed to turn just in time to keep her feet. "What did you see?" she asked.

He led the group to one of the hardwood tables at the center of the saloon that allowed a clear view of the street. Keeping his eyes low, he focused on the hollering men outside.

"You going to let us in on what's got your attention?" asked Sarah.

It was Sven who answered the question. "So, you didn't see him?"

Sarah wrinkled her brow at the big man. "See who?"

"I didn't see anyone either," said Annie.

"Fella in the alley behind the brothel," answered Carson, his voice low. "He's still there. Just watching from the shadows."

Annie went to turn her head but stopped short of looking out the door when Carson put his hand on her wrist.

"Don't," he said.

His hand was winter cool on her skin.

"I've got eyes on him," he said, "and near as I can tell, he hasn't seen me yet."

"Could just be an opportunistic thief, yeah?" asked Sven.

Carson ignored the question. "Annie, I want you to take a look now, slowly, out of the corner of your eye. In the alleyway. Tell me what you notice about him."

Annie did as Carson said. She traced a finger around her ear, pushing her hair out of her line of vision. The man was short, his hands tucked into his pockets, leaning up against the side of a general store. He didn't look malicious to her. Just a man, minding his business. She tried to perceive what Carson wanted her to see, but she didn't see much of anything about him. "I'm not sure what you—"

"Look at the men he's watching," said Carson.

They were cowboys, drunk by the look of them. One of them, a Mexican, clasped his hands together as if in supplication to the woman and her swaying breasts in the cold night air. When he called out to her, the vapor of his breath caught the lamplight, then dissipated. And that's when she realized what Carson had seen. The thing she had missed.

"He's got no breath," she said.

"Close," Carson said. "He's breathing all right, but that breath is as cold as the world around him."

"How do you want to play it?" asked Sarah.

"Two of us are going to slip around the brothel while Sven and I come at him from the front. We'll pretend to be interested in the woman. That'll get us close enough to close the net without him knowing we're on to him."

"We can't just shoot him down in the middle of the street," said Sarah.

"The fuck we can't," said Sven. "We'll plug that leech with silver shells, and there'll be nothing but ash."

"What if someone sees us?" asked Annie. "Sees it happen?"

"Then I'll tell them to move their ass along." Sven's impatience was rising. "If we don't act now, one of those fellas—maybe all of them—will be dead."

"Sven." Carson's tone was as hard and cold as the iron on his hip. The word was a command.

Sven looked at Carson, his eyes widening with indignation. "Careful with that tone, pup. Man who speaks to me like that, friend or no, will find himself picking his teeth out of his ass."

"Sven." Annie said it calmly and kindly. She and the Swede had forged a deep friendship in the time since Chicago, and she had learned how to blunt his ever-sharpening edge.

He shook his head. "The time to act is now." And with that he stood up. "Come on, kid. Let's kill this bastard and be on our merry. We've got other shit to do."

They split into pairs. Annie and Sarah exited the saloon first, giving no attention to the drunken cowboys or the alleyway. The two women passed the brothel, traveling a piece before they began to circle around toward the dark alley.

"When you going to tell him?" asked Sarah, voice low but blunt.

Annie looked at her, confused. "Tell who what?"

"Carson. When are you going to tell him how you feel?"

In the shadow of the brothel, Annie blushed. And denied what she knew to be true. "I haven't the foggiest idea what you're talking about."

Even in the dark of the evening, Annie saw Sarah roll her eyes. "You're kidding right? Smartest person in the outfit when it comes to planning, but goodness do you have a lot to learn about yourself, sweetheart." Sarah shook her head. "Word to the wise: don't ever let a good thing get away. Truth be told, I was in love with that boy's father, and that damned fool used to say that we'd have our time together. He'd say, 'Nothing good gets away, Sarah.' But he was wrong."

"You were in love with Gilbert?"

"Sure was," she whispered, placing her back against the brothel wall near the end of the alley. "That man made me feel something I never found again. I don't suspect I ever will. If you feel something, anything for Carson, you should let him know. If you don't, and something happens, it'll haunt you like no ghost ever could."

"I... I had no clue," said Annie. "About you and Gilbert, I mean."

Sarah lifted a finger. "You can open that book on me later," she said, drawing her pistol. "I hear our fellas getting rid of those cowboys."

Annie drew her gun too. She focused her hearing, listening to the posse of drunkards laughing and expressing their illimitable devotion to the woman who called out to them. Then, she heard Sven's voice, but she couldn't make out the words. There was silence for a moment, and then suddenly came the sound of the men breaking into a run. The whore barked in protest.

It was easy to make out Sven, who barked back, "Whatever you say, Juliet."

Annie chuckled. "A real charmer that one."

Sarah peered around the corner, then looked back at Annie. "He's still there, but now he's watching our boys. Now's our chance."

Annie mimicked Sarah, who crouched low and began to step lightly down the alleyway. Then, she saw Carson, who was exaggerating his limp, step into the alleyway with Sven nowhere to be seen. And like she had seen in the Peregrine Estate half a year ago, the vampire snatched Carson by the collar and dragged him to the ground. Carson struggled, but the vampire overtook him easily. Then, he began to pull Carson deeper into the shadow of the alley.

The trap sprung, Sarah rushed the length of the alley. Placing the barrel of her pistol against the back of the man's head, she said, "Let him go, or I'll burn you down."

To Annie's surprise, the predator-turned-prey looming over Carson lifted his hands into the air as if being robbed. He stood up, turning to face them. The man was pale-skinned, black-haired. The snarl on his lips shimmered with long slick teeth. His eyes glowed cougar-like even in the low light.

"We know what you are," said Sarah.

Sven appeared from around the corner and helped Carson to his feet.

The vampire looked left, then right, obviously assessing the possibility of escape.

Sarah thumbed back the hammer of her revolver. "Your kind is fast, but not faster than a bullet."

Annie saw something she did not expect in the vampire's eyes. Something she had not seen before among the dozen of his kind she had met: not in the one that had killed her mother nor the others that had killed her best friend and the whole town of Abilene. There was fear in his eyes. And uncertainty.

"What am I?" The creature's voice was high-pitched, nasally. The question was genuine.

"A goddamn plague is what you are," said Sven, shoving the vampire deeper into the alley. "And we're the cure."

The vampire shook his head, sorrow masking his face. "Please," he pleaded, "I don't understand. I only know. . . this thirst. Thirst and pain of the daylight. Please, help me."

"Help you?" asked Annie.

"A woman. . . no, not a woman. Something else. She promised me immortality. Promised me power if I would go to Colorado and fight for her. And she lied. . . she made me this. . . whatever I am. And when I ran away from her. . . she only laughed."

"What woman?" Carson snapped off the question.

"Carmilla. Her name was Carmilla. I am Arthur Mangold." Arthur shot his hands out faster than Annie could see, grabbing Sarah's pistol by its long barrel. He didn't try to snatch it away but rather jerked it against his forehead. "Please, I don't want to be—" He began to sob, though no tears fell down his pale cheeks. "I don't want to live like this!"

Before Carson could do anything, Sven's silver-edged knife was plunging into the vampire's back, through his heart, and out his chest. A flash of blue fire blinded them.

Then, there was nothing left of Arthur but his simple clothes and a pile of ash and bone.

Everyone had just stood there in shocked silence as the big man sheathed his knife. "Ask and you shall receive," he said, then spat on the vampire's ashes.

"Why did you—" Annie began.

"Do you realize what we could have learned about them?" Carson boomed. "Do you realize what you've just lost us?"

"Damn it, Sven," were Sarah's final words on the matter. There was understanding in the chastisement though.

CHAPTER SIX

Carbon County, Wyoming Territory

Cyrus Culliver examined the powder burn just above the dead man's singed eyebrow. It was hard to tell what was gunpowder and what was coal dust, but even in the low light, Cy could discern the difference. He looked up, squinting hard against the dark yawning mouth of the mineshaft ahead. Drifts of snow fell before the cross timbers, swirling in and out of the aperture, as if the white flecks themselves didn't dare the darkness. His eyes traced a distinct series of tracks. Tracks that told him the story of comings and goings.

Behind him, five riders waited quietly, though he could hear several of the horses whinnying, impatient. Chopping the ground. Ready to move on.

Cy looked back at the dead miner, the powder burn, and the neat dime-sized hole punched into the skull. He dared to slip off his glove, weathering the cold only for a moment as he slid his pinky finger into the dead man's head. The man's brains were still warm.

"Hmph," Cy grunted and wiped his hands on the dead man's shirt.

He rummaged through all the man's pockets. There was a watch, a pocketknife sharp enough for whittling but too short for much protection, a half-full tinder box, and a tobacco pouch. No rolling papers. No pipe. No pistol.

Cy took in a slow breath. He had planned to shoot this man. His plan, however, had also included taking the deed that the late Mr. Charles Makes always carried on his person as a point of pride. At least, others had reported he did. And so, Cy Culliver considered the two possibilities regarding the identity of the dead man staring back at him.

"Well," came the frustrated voice of Surly Bob Brown. Surly Bob was as impatient as the horses. A big, rough man unburdened by laws or morals crafted by human institutions or the divine. By Cy's estimation, there were few more skilled with a fighting knife and even fewer more mean. None more vicious. "Is it Makes or ain't it Makes?"

"Likely is," said Cy.

"What's that?" came a holler just behind them. Katie Jessup had joined them just after that unfortunate dust-up in Arizona. She was one of the few meaner than Surly Bob, a cold and cruel woman, and twice over a widow. Katie, honest as you please, would happily recount for anyone who asked just what happened to both her husbands when they each came to her asking for a divorce.

"He said it's Makes," Surly Bob rasped against the wind.

"No," said Cy. "I said it's *likely* him." He cinched his hat to his head, turning his eyes to the gang of five still sitting astride their horses.

"He got the deed on him?" asked Katie. "If there ain't no deed, then it ain't no Makes."

Surly Bob snapped at her. "He wouldn't have the deed if he were shot and robbed, you ignorant mule. The thief likely took the deed and run off with it."

Cy strode back toward his horse. "Two-thirds of that pie is likely, Surly Bob. The final slice, however, is objectively wrong. See, this man, who may or may not be the deed-carrying Charlie Makes, is certainly dead, but he ain't been dead so long as yet to freeze solid." He slid his shotgun from the leather sleeve on the saddle, broke it open, and eyed the shells. "And the person who did the shooting more than likely went into the mine for safety from this fast-approaching blizzard. Or for other purposes unknown. But the track tells the tale. Makes came out. Someone approached. Shot him dead. Sought cover."

"So," said Katie, pointing her finger toward the sky, ticking it back and forth as she considered Cy's meaning, "the person who shot the man who may be Makes is probably in the mine?"

"Spot on," Cy said, smiling against the cold. He snapped the shotgun shut and thumbed back the hammers. "I want shotgunners holding lanterns in the front with me. Bob, you and Katie walk just a few paces behind, steady in the gaps with your pistols. No one shoots lest I say so."

Every member of the group did as Cy commanded, trailing through the snow, stalking like a pack of wolves in brown wool coats. They passed under the cracked timbers into a cold, dark shaft.

Spears of yellow light slanted against the throat of the shaft, shining a cosmos of stony refractions. Lamplight brought into view the rivulets of water trickling in heavy drops from spindles of sparkling stone. Their breath clouded the beams of gloomy light as they slid their boots along the wet bedrock.

Further into the mine, the shaft began to narrow, drawing the six of them to within arm's reach of one another. The wind howled behind them, a storm whipping up outside.

"Should we call out?" said Katie, keeping her voice down.

"And relinquish our element of surprise? Not a chance," said Surly Bob.

Thomas Caine, a knobby man slim as a river reed, spoke from his position next to Cy: "I don't like this, boss. We're too bunched up. If whoever came in here has a scattergun, we're all at risk of getting peppered."

"There ain't nobody in here," said Katie, her voice now echoing off the slick stone. "If there was, we'd have been able to see their lamplight by now."

Just as the echoes of her voice died, there came a high whistle—a bright piercing sound that could not have come from the baritone storm howling at the mine's entrance. It was a sing-song tune. Something familiar, but Cy couldn't place it.

Katie and Surly Bob ratcheted back the hammers of their pistols, pointing into the void. They held that position, eyes wide, peering.

Cy felt something tugging at the back of his mind, the kill or run instinct that he had learned to suppress over the many years of a life spent within a maelstrom of hazard. He narrowed his eyes against the shadow and there, set deep within the darkness, were two pinpricks of light. At first, he mistook them for refractions slanting from the jagged rocks, but when he saw that they were two lone lights set right next to one another, his hair stood up on his arms. Those weren't reflections of stone from the lamp light; they were lamplight reflected off eyes. Eyes that he somehow knew, instinctively, had seen him long before he had seen them.

Cy, a man hardened by frontier living, who had survived Alabama knife fighters and Texas rangers and all measure of sons of bitches that had tried to come between him and the riches destined to be his, didn't run at the sight of the eyes gazing at him. He did what any tough, sensible man with a shotgun would do: he aimed the weapon and demanded submission. "Don't move," said Cy.

The sing-song tune fluttered through the mine again.

Cy swore to God he knew that tune. "Quit that whistlin'."

The eyes glimmered, unblinking.

"What's that," said Katie. "Who's he talkin' to?"

Thomas's voice cracked. "Someone is standing there. We can't see 'em, but they's there." He tried to call up his courage, barking at the shadowy figure, "Hey, you, come over here, into the light!"

"Easy, Tommy," said Cy, then pointed his voice back to the darkness. "Listen, whoever you are, we don't care that you shot Makes. Don't care *why* you shot 'em. But, if you took what I think you took off his person, well, I do care about that. Only because I'm paid to care about it. And because of how much I'm paid, I care a great deal. So, you have a choice. I reckon you don't need me to tell you what your options are. My name is Cyrus Culliver, and I am a man of my word. If you hand over the deed you took, I promise—"

"You *promise*," the voice slashed out from beyond the veil of shadow, echoing harshly along the shaft. "You promise me what? My life? Coming from you that is no promise at all. I've paid my debts, Cy. And he that dies pays them all. Time for you to pay yours."

That voice, Cy thought. It sounded familiar. "Name yourself and your intent, friend. Or by god, we'll cut you in half."

Their answer was a low, predatory growl that rolled up into laughter. "You've come a long way from Arizona, Cy. So have I. But I see that not much has changed with you: still a dog leading strays."

Cy squinted, leaned forward. "Who is that? Come on out of the dark. Past acquaintance or not, I have the authority of the Union Pacific behind me. Those are powerful men, and they've charged me to procure this land. And if you don't come into the light, with the deed and nothing else in hand, I'll blast you sure enough."

"Okay, Cyrus," said the voice. "I'll come into the light."

The man's form materialized into the lamplight. Cy saw the scar on the man's cheek, a puckered pink mass, six slashes forming a star. "Wesley? Wesley Burrows?"

"You left me in Arizona to die, Cy. But I met someone there who showed me a road back to you. And now I'm going to give you what every dog needs. A master."

Thomas Caine lifted his shotgun. "Who the fu—"

Before he could finish his sentence, Burrows moved so fast that his whole form lengthened. Before Cy could make sense of the speed, suddenly, impossibly, Burrows was holding Thomas by the throat, lifting him high into the air. Thomas struggled and kicked, his hands trying to pry loose Burrow's grip.

"I have use of you," Burrows said. "My *king* has use of you."

Cy, without any remorse or thought to the man dangling between him and whatever Wesley Burrows now was, gave the command to fire.

None of them hesitated.

They fired round after round through Thomas Caine at Wesley Burrows. The shaft flared to life with a devastating battery of bullets and gunsmoke.

Over the ear-splitting cacophony of lead, Cy watched Burrows toss Thomas's mutilated body to the ground.

The eyes of Wesley Burrows flashed, and suddenly it felt like someone had reached inside of Cy's skull and taken a firm grip of his brain. The sound of gunfire echoed as if from down the long, dark mineshaft. Though he fought against the power now seizing his every action, he was incapable of doing. . . doing anything. All he could see now were the hot pools of indescribable color glowing in the sockets of the thing before him.

"Are. . ." Cy's voice caught in his throat. "Are you going to kill me?"

Wesley Burrows found that question somehow amusing. As if it brought a fond memory back to the surface of his mind. "Sadly, only once, Cyrus," he said, and began to stalk forward. "Only once, and never again."

CHAPTER SEVEN

ABOARD THE STEAM TRAIN *THE JUDGE*, EN ROUTE TO NEW ORLEANS, LOUISIANA

Carson was the last to enter the main passenger car aboard the steam train that had once been dubbed the *Hephaestus*. Annie had seen the brass plating removed and replaced with a name that suited both the train's new purpose and its passengers. *The Judge* she had named it. No longer a vehicle of the Prometheus Society, it would, for so long as it rolled across America, live in memory of the Peregrine Estate's late founder Judge Hezekiah Ellison.

Carson scraped the mud from his boots outside the train car, angry as a swarm of hornets.

An argument had erupted in that Baton Rouge alley between Sven and the rest of them. Annie, Sarah, and Carson had all spoken over each other, making different arguments that Sven clearly felt no need to address.

He'd only looked at each of them, stone-faced, and when the silence returned to the alley, the big man turned and walked away.

Carson, angry as a bull, went to go after Sven. He'd

make the gunfighter understand how much they could have learned from the vampire. Tell him that kind of impulsive, selfish behavior would not be tolerated. But Sarah snatched him by the elbow. "I admire the courage, kid, but you don't want whatever he's ready to give. Not right now."

"There's nothing for us in Baton Rouge," Annie said, placing a hand on Carson's shoulder. "We should leave tonight. The sooner we get to New Orleans, the better."

Carson jerked back from both Sarah and Annie. "What the hell has gotten into him since I left?"

Sarah's eyes widened, as if Carson had insulted her. "Same thing that got inside of you when the Prometheus Society killed your pa. Surely you, of all people, can appreciate the sensibilities of a man who has lost the person most important to him." She was so close that Carson could smell the whiskey on her breath. "The pain. The want for revenge." Sarah's eyes flared. "Or have you forgotten how we all ended up in Chicago in the first place?"

Carson wanted to say that it was a different situation. Different circumstances. But, deep down, he knew the woman's words were true. His shame only made him angrier.

"Sarah," said Annie, trying to lower the tempers flashing white hot in the frosty night.

"Nah," Sarah replied, stepping around Carson's cold stare. "He knows I'm right. Let him stew on it bit."

And stew on it Carson had. He'd walked, wordless, seething, all the way back to the hotel, where they gathered their things in silence. That silence had followed them to the trainyard. All the way to *The Judge*.

And now, standing near the landing, Carson took out his anger on his muddy boots, cussing to himself as he scraped off the mud in two thick curls.

He stepped on board. Annie and Sarah were sitting in

the lush chairs, conversing, while Sven mixed himself a drink at the bar. But they weren't the first thing he noticed: the first thing he noticed was the dark bloodstained wall at the far end of the car. The bullet holes had been patched, but the blood was still there.

He squeezed his knotted, aching fingers on the hands that had once made him fast and accurate. Dangerous to his enemies. After what the Baroness's men had done to him, these hands would never be dangerous again. His father had given him his pistol, his pocket watch, and the gift of the quickdraw, but the Baroness and the goddamn Prometheus Society had taken all three.

Sarah's words in the alley had cut him to the quick, and seeing the tapestry of his own revenge so clearly painted before him brought the shame back, too. That feeling led him to where Annie and Sarah were sitting.

"I'd like to talk to Sven in private, ladies. If you'll indulge me."

Sarah looked at Annie.

Annie looked back at her.

Sarah shook her head, disapproving. "Go on and kill each other. See if I give a good goddamn."

The look that Annie gave Carson was a wary one. But there was something else there too, something he could not piece out.

"Sven?" Annie asked over Carson's shoulder.

"I can drink and listen at the same time," the man said, refilling his whiskey glass.

Annie and Sarah stepped out, leaving the two men alone.

Carson turned and faced the colossus behind the bar. Sven's eyes were big and serious, and he was squeezing his whiskey glass so hard, Carson thought it might shatter in his hand. He wondered if the man would even feel the shards sink into his skin.

"I'll have what you're having," said Carson. He sat down.

Sven slid the decanter of whiskey along the bar, then set a glass down next to it. "Pour it yourself."

Carson looked him right in the eyes, giving as good as he got with the stare. He took in a deep breath and broke the tension with a truth. "I can't," he said, his words hard. "And I'll be damned if I try and pour it with both hands like a child in front of you. My pride won't have it."

Sven's countenance diminished slightly at that. He nodded and poured Carson's whiskey. "Fingers still don't work right, I take it."

"No," said Carson. He picked up the whiskey glass, concentrating. The glass trembled, but he managed to lift it in the air toward the Swede.

Sven crooked an eyebrow at him in confusion.

"In my family, we always toast. Gilbert taught me that."

Sven's cold demeanor cracked, if but for a moment. The corner of his mouth twitched with an emotion he desperately wanted to hide. He lifted his glass.

"Here's to not getting killed," said Carson, remembering—always remembering—the words from his first toast with Gilbert Ptolemy. The first, and the last.

The glasses clinked and the men drank in unison. The bourbon went down smooth and warm.

"He also said that there are things in this world, both human and inhuman, that require men of their time to take action."

Sven's shoulders bounced with an unhappy chuckle. "That old goat sure thought he was some kind of Black Shakespeare."

Carson's eyes hardened on him.

But the big Swede put up his hands as if in defense. "Good lord are you an emotional creature. It's not an insult. The man could turn anything into a goddamn soliloquy. I loved that about him. And I didn't say he was wrong."

Carson relaxed. "I can appreciate it as a man, but shit-fire did I hate it as a boy. Now though, I'd give anything just to hear his voice again. I feel like he'd know what to do." He stared into the cut glass, examining every distinct line. "He had a clarity about him that I did not inherit."

"That was one of his best tricks, kid. His tone might have been as sure as a sunrise, but he was doing what all of us are always doing, what we think is best in the time we have to discern it."

Carson took a sip of whiskey. "And you thought it was best to end Arthur's life before we had a chance to question him."

Sven nodded. "I did."

"Didn't feel the need to consult the rest of us?"

"No."

"Help me understand why."

Sven shifted his shoulders, then leaned his elbow onto the bar. "That *thing* killed four men, one woman, and a girl. Those are just the ones we know about. He didn't do it because he was a killer. He did it because of the gnawing hunger only a vampire can know."

"That doesn't answer my question," said Carson.

"I did it because I *am* a killer. Been one since I was thirteen years old. I did it partly because I was compelled by the creature's suffering, but mostly, Carson, I did it because it had to be done. He wanted it, and I was the only one who realized that it had to be given right then. Right there. You got a name from him. Carmilla. You ever hear of her in your travels?"

Carson shook his head. "Sigurd and his wife were the only ones I ever got names from."

"And that name Carmilla was all we were going to get from him. You might be a decent vampire hunter in your own right, kid. Judge told me all about it. But you have to understand that I've spent time in Black Wells. I've seen the mountain pass they use to head underground when the sun was ready to rise. I've studied their habits. How they think. Wouldn't you figure that, in all that time, I'd have tried to question some of those bastards to get information?"

Carson took another sip, trying not to give away that he felt stupid for not having considered that Sven had been stationed in Colorado at the Judge's behest.

"You've got lots of Gilbert's good qualities, kid. I see most of them living on in you. But you've also got a few of his infirmities."

"Care to illuminate me?"

"You think only of what *you* can do when assessing a problem. You think your knowledge and your pain and your losses are the only ones stacked up in the world. Lot of us have been fighting the Judge's war since before you got hair on your peaches. And almost all of us have lost people. . ." Sven's deep voice caught in his chest. "Lost the people we love the most. And I lost the man I loved best. . . all for the sake of saving you."

Those words made a hollow of where Carson's heart should have been. Sadness filled that empty space: sorrow and shame. "I know," he said.

"This is the loss I carry, Carson. You carry it too. Where I come from, these shared losses, along with our mutual purpose and love for those who share that purpose. . . it makes us family. A family made up of orphans and widowers, and all manner of saints and killers."

Carson, his eyes welling with tears, looked back at Sven. "I am sorry about Larry."

Sven shook his head. "No. You will not apologize. I won't have it, and neither would he. My husband died unto a glorious purpose. A purpose I believe in as strongly as he did. Strong as your pa did."

Carson, drowning in the dark, bottomless well of regret, asked, "What are we fighting for?"

"The same thing any family fights for, Carson," said Sven. "For each other."

Carson shook his head and the tears fell from his eyes.

Sven wrapped his big hand around Carson's wrist, dwarfing it. And he lifted the young man's glass next to his own. He clinked the glasses together once again and said, "For each other."

The two proceeded to get good and drunk, Carson indulging himself in the warmth of liquor and renewed friendship. When their drinking had run its course, he headed for the dining car to look for Sarah and Annie, assuming they were enjoying a dinner together.

He passed through the passenger car, stepping into the howling wind and biting cold for a brief moment, and pushed open the door to the diner car. To his surprise, he found only Annie sitting at one of the booths. She was looking out the window.

"Mind if I sit?" he asked.

She smiled. "Sure. Something on your mind?"

"I'm all talked out," he said, returning the smile. "Just thought I might sit with you a while."

They sat there for a long time, both of them quiet.

The Judge plowed through freshly fallen banks of snow. Though they could not see much of anything beyond the line of track outside, they watched snowflakes rush by. From time to time, Carson stole looks at Annie's placid face. Those little moments were far more calming to him than the patter of snow on the window.

"All our success depends on what happens in New Orleans tomorrow," said Annie, breaking the silence.

"Right."

"Everything I've done over the last six months comes to a head. All the planning. The selling of every Peregrine Estate asset to try and fund the hiring of these gunhands. I took everything Hezekiah built and sold it to whomever would buy it. All that is left of his legacy are crates of silver bullets, the guns that will fire them, and this train and the people on it." She rubbed the tiredness from her eyes with both palms and took a deep breath. "And I'm not even sure it'll all be enough."

"Does Sven think you have enough?" Carson asked. "To employ the Gunfighter's Guild, I mean?"

She shook her head. "I don't mean enough money. I mean us. Even with the full strength of the Gunfighter's Guild behind us, I'm still not sure that we'll have what's required to destroy the kingdom."

Of course that was what she meant, Carson thought. And he felt rather dumb for missing the point. Doubt was painted all over her face, a face that looked much older than her nineteen years. "Well," he said, "you managed to take down the Prometheus Society with nothing more than a few gunfighters and a mean disposition. I've yet to witness anything that hasn't gone the way you've willed it to."

She laughed, but there was little humor in the sound. "You're drunk."

"I'm not drunk," he said. "Well, I am, but that's not the point. The point is that you're a woman of incredible strength and determination, Annie. You've made two of the most experienced Peregrine agents listen to you. Gained their trust, and, more than that, captured their deference. That's something that only Judge Ellison accomplished. You've shown capability where others shrink. Courage where most everyone else in the world would buckle."

Her eyes swayed up to meet his. Where other women would have blushed and shied away, Annie grasped the moment. "Do you have feelings for me, Carson?"

The words hit him like a slug in the stomach. His mouth opened. Nothing came out.

"I have feelings for you," she said, so matter-of-factly.

"If you don't share those feelings then that's fine. But. . . Sarah said something to me. Something that made a lot of sense." She took another deep breath, almost frustrated. "Those months we spent in Abilene, I grew close to you. And when you left to go to Natchez, I found myself afraid that I might never see you again. I hated that feeling. It twisted me up inside every day."

Carson knew the feeling she was describing. He had felt it too. Had felt it for the first time standing on the porch of the Peregrine Estate when she had confessed how scared she was. He'd been scared too, but when she wrapped her arms around his waist, it changed his feelings. It wasn't that the fear was removed from his heart; it was that a different kind of fear—something other than a fear of dying—had replaced it. It was a terror that he might fail Annie. Or worse, lose her.

Losing her would feel like losing everything all over again.

The whiskey-dulling of his mind began to melt away. Right now, in his life, there was only right now. There was no coming war. No Red Kingdom. No memories of torture. No memories of the great god's eye he'd seen inside the pages of the Black Manuscript, the way it stared back at him, all encompassing, lidless.

There was only Annie Miller.

And in that moment, in the right now of right now, in an uncertain world, Carson Watts Ptolemy was certain of this: Annie Joy Miller was precious and irreplaceable.

Her gaze fell away, taking his silence as a refusal.

"No," the word spilled out of him.

Her eyes shot back up, frustrated. "Well, you don't have to be so adamant about it—"

"No," he interjected. "I do have feelings for you, Annie."

Her shoulders relaxed, relief passing over her.

"I just never understood them. Not until you said. . . well, said what you said." He was stumbling all over himself. And he wondered if falling for someone felt an awful lot like feeling like a dipshit.

"Listen," she said, "I've never had much need for men. In my experience, most of them are manipulative bastards at best, absolute villains at worst. But you... you've always been kind to me. Sweet. And I like the way it makes me feel."

For the first time in years, ever since Annie had kissed him on the cheek in Yellow Hill, Carson Watts Ptolemy felt himself blush. He was unsure of what to do next though. Was he supposed to leap over the table and embrace her? Kiss her?

He didn't have a goddamn clue.

So, he said the only thing he could think to say. A question. "What are we supposed to do next?"

Annie laughed. She laughed so loud and hard that her almond-shaped eyes wrinkled. "I don't have the faintest idea, Carson."

Carson stared deep into the blue pools of Annie's eyes that captured in such a small expanse all the wide-open spaces of Texas. She brandished them, without effort, like a weapon. "What would you like it to be?"

She tilted her head at the question. Her smile widened. "I don't think I'd mind if you sit next to me for a while. Just sit in the quiet for a bit."

And that's exactly what he did. He sat next to her, and she relaxed into him, resting her weight against his chest. And together, their fingers laced, they watched the snow blow through the darkness. And though that moment stretched out for much of the long evening and into the early morning, it passed much too quickly for him.

CHAPTER EIGHT

Black Wells, Colorado

Wesley Burrows, now the master of four newly sired vampires, walked through the streets of Black Wells, Colorado. The young vampire strode, his head held high, and the brood followed. Sigurd had educated him in the ways of the dark gift, and he had used it to take his too-long-awaited revenge on Cyrus. The former menace of the West was now nothing more than a slavering creature that would, until the end of time, obey Wesley's every command.

The sensation was delicious.

But Wesley was still under the command of Sigurd, and so, with his revenge accomplished, returned back to Black Wells as his master instructed.

Human's cast sideways glances at Wesley and his brood from where they toiled. He paid them no mind. Cyrus tried to slake his virginal bloodlust on one of the young women cutting wood in the street. A word from Wesley was all that was required to bring Cyrus to heel.

They went without further incident through a picketed

fence and up a series of short steps leading to a former Methodist church. The two-story, white-washed building had seen all its religious icons removed.

Two oak doors parted before Wesley, and he entered the candle-lit sanctuary. The pews had been removed, but the altar remained. And standing before it, looking up at a golden stained-glass window, was Sigurd of Antioch.

Upon their entrance into that once holy place, Sigurd, arms clasped behind his back, turned his head to look back at them. Though the vampire knight was possessed of an age older than a millennium, he looked no older than forty. His black hair shone like river stones in the moonlight, and the one eye that turned to assess Wesley glowed bright and green.

"Wesley," said Sigurd. The name passing over his lips was sweet in Wesley's ears.

The young vampire inclined his head, proud and eager. "I have returned, as you commanded."

Sigurd turned to face the open sanctuary, his eyes assessing Wesley's brood. "Yes. Robed in your vengeance, you return with four of our kin beneath your wing."

Wesley felt his master's dark influence expand, the invisible pressure rippling through the sanctuary. Lifting a blue-black eyebrow, Sigurd said, "You have dominated them completely. They retain nothing of their former selves."

Wesley smiled. "I could not have done it without your guidance, Master."

Sigurd's countenance wrinkled. "You disappoint me."

Wesley furrowed his brow. "But I—"

Sigurd put up a hand.

Wesley froze.

"Your first taste of power, and this," said Sigurd, gesturing to the brood, "this is how you use it. I gave you a chance to make allies, and you bring me slaves. I gave you a gift, and upon first use, you cheapen it."

Fear rushed through Wesley. Disappointing Sigurd came with a great cost. He had learned this for the first time when he had been told to kill all the remaining members of the Peregrine Estate. He had killed them all... all except the girl. That failure was one his master did not quickly let him forget.

Sigurd descended the steps of the raised platform near the altar. "How should I return this slight, hmm?" From out of the depths within the vampire knight, the invisible weight of darkness went from ripples to a torrent, throwing itself over the sanctuary in a malevolent flood. Its power—no, *his* power—unfurled fully, dwarfing anything Wesley could have ever hoped to hold for himself in a hundred lifetimes. The sheer pressure of it shattered Wesley's hold on the four freshly sired vampires standing behind him. And just like that, with this minute expression of his will, Sigurd took from Wesley his most prized possession.

And those possessions moved with impossible swiftness, their power amplified by Sigurd's influence. They were on Wesley, their talons unleashed, clutching him by the arms and around the waist. He struggled against them. Commanded them to release him. But, though he had a hundred kills and more under his fang, their young strength was still too great.

"Release me!" he barked, unleashing his own inner dominance toward their minds. But his own will, his own dark power, crashed into Sigurd's, and when they collided, Wesley's was annihilated. Fear shot through him, and he cast his eyes up to his master.

"I-I don't understand." The sound of those words coming from his voice made him sound very young and very afraid. Worse, they made him sound weak.

"That much is clear," said Sigurd, approaching slowly. "You have acted like an animal, and so, like an animal, you must be *made* to understand."

Suddenly, Cyrus buried his fangs into Wesley's shoulder. And with a thirst that only a new vampire knows, he began to drink deeply. The pain, like a lance, shot from Wesley's shoulder, piercing his heart. He could feel Cyrus draining him, pulling the reserves of blood from deep within. He howled. He bucked and writhed against them. But even with his great strength, it was nothing to his thralls turned assailants.

"Please, I only did as you commanded!"

Sigurd shook his head slowly. "Hush, Wesley, and hear. When you took too greedily from these humans and did not allow them to retain their minds, when you made them brainless slaves, you made them susceptible to another vampire's will. And so, they can be turned against you." The vampire knight's voice was calm and cool, serene. "Are you so quick to forget my words? I told you to make your enemies *as I made you.*"

Sigurd passed his hand through the air, and Cy extracted his fangs from Wesley's shoulder, sending cold ribbons of blood into the air. Cy let out a deep, satisfied groan.

"I gave you a chance to have ultimate revenge, but your error is that you allowed your revenge to have you instead. But do not despair. I, too, have known the pain of this error in my own way. Do you understand now?"

Wesley was dizzy, his vision blurring. He opened his mouth to tell Sigurd that he understood, but no words escaped. His throat was too dry, and his lungs were on fire.

Sigurd was close now, as close as he had been upon their first meeting: the night Sigurd had taken Wesley for himself. "Let me educate you further, child. We are the people of the Kingdom. We have not survived for thousands of years because we were more powerful than the humans. We survived because we are more cautious, more cunning than they are. You too must find your own cunning. I could have a thousand brutes under my command, Wesley, but I did not make you a brute. I asked you to be my friend. To help me in the coming conflict."

Wesley could feel the roiling power inside of his master, and that power bent him at the waist. Then, it folded his legs beneath him, so that he found himself kneeling before the vampire knight. "The war," said Wesley.

"Yes." Sigurd let the sound linger, then slowly die. "Word has reached their government that we have taken much of Colorado for ourselves, but they are possessive creatures—creatures of destruction. And they will come to destroy us. They will try to take from us, and from our king. That, we cannot allow."

Wesley trembled, the thirst coming upon him as it had not since his first night after being sired. "No, master, we cannot."

And like that, Sigurd's seemingly illimitable will receded. He reached down and placed a gentle finger beneath Wesley's chin. Lifted the young vampire's eyes to meet his own. "Oh, desperate and thirsty as you are, wash your fangs with blood. Renew your strength and then return to me. For I have much I must entrust to you before our enemies come and try to reclaim what they so foolishly thought was theirs. And when they do, then, I will teach you how to take revenge."

CHAPTER NINE

New Orleans, Louisiana

The *Judge* whistled, spraying hot steam into the cold perpetual gloom of New Orleans. Annie Miller, stepping off the back end of the caboose, lifted her head at the unmistakable sound of music. A stirring carnival of sound that could not have more deeply contrasted the depressing night. Horns bellowed, bright and clear. Drums thundered. Cymbals crashed. And the electric hum of human voices filled the streets.

Annie looked back at her companions filing off the train, wide-eyed and wondering. "What on earth?"

Sarah Lockhart stepped off the train, that grin of hers practically touching both ears. "It's Marti Gras."

Carson followed behind her. "Can't be. That's in March. We're into July."

Sarah shook her head at him. "You obviously don't know anything about folk from New Orleans. They're a people of celebration in the face of devastation."

"So they started in March and just kept it going?" asked Annie.

"And they always will," said Sven, who for the first time since Annie could remember, smiled. "Used to come here with Larry in days gone by. Best city in the world. The kind of place I wish I had been born."

Carson looked over at the big Swede. "Where *were* you born?"

He shook his head. "Someplace you've never heard of, across the Atlantic. A place a lot duller than this."

The four of them plodded over cobblestone streets wet with snowmelt, shoving through a teeming, stamping throng whose spirits were hot though the winter assailed them. The walkways of New Orleans were ramparted with laugher and singing, fiddles and drums. People danced and drank, wearing diabolic masks of all sorts and kinds. The misty night was perfumed with jasmine and smoke.

With Sven leading the way, they crossed Bourbon Street, where a circle of shirtless men stood under a banner of gold, green, and purple, watching two Black pugilists slither in the clench. Half of the motley cried out in ecstasy when one of the men knocked the other to the ground. The other half bellowed in sorrow, bracing their hands on their knees.

Annie shook her head in disbelief. All the sadness that had poisoned the rest of the country was absent here. There was so much life being lived. Life and revelry and thousands of hot hearts thundering blood through the veins of a city that would dance until the final night of the world.

A fat, topless woman, her pale breasts slathered in sweat and beads, burst out of the crowd. "Welcome to New Orleans," she bellowed as she wrapped her meaty hands around Carson's face, pulled him into her, and planted a wet kiss on his lips. Carson's eyes widened to the size of dinner plates.

Sarah and Sven burst into laughter as the woman

pulled away as quickly as she had come, sucking on Carson's bottom lip.

Annie took the woman by the wrist and yanked her around in a spin that brought them face-to-face. "Excuse me!" Annie's tone was furious.

"Oh," said the woman, half-surprised. "I'm sorry, honey." And then she planted a big kiss on Annie, too.

The young woman jerked back, all her anger melting into a laugh.

Sarah Lockhart, almost toppling with laughter, threw an arm around Sven's shoulder to keep herself upright. Sven laughed right along with her.

"I'm at the Cooper House," said the big woman, her cheeks and nose flush with drink. "If the night gets too cold for ya." She grinned, revealing tobacco-stained teeth.

Sven patted her on the back. "I'm sorry, madam. I'm afraid we have pressing business."

"You'll change your mind," she said with a wink, and then began to twirl round and round before disappearing into the writhing mass of bodies.

Carson looked at Annie, a disbelieving look on his face. "Well, the people here sure are friendly."

Annie furrowed her brow and reached into her mouth. To her horror, she fished out a chewed-up kernel of corn that absolutely had not been there before. "I'm gonna be sick."

Sarah wiped a tear from her eye, her brown skin reddened with laughter. "Goddamn do I love New Orleans. It's a Fat Tuesday that'll go on until the sun rises again."

They continued on, their boots clacking along the slick stones. After walking for a good piece, they came to a three-story estate house surrounded by an iron fence three times as tall as it needed to be. Alabaster pillars ranged across the edifice, tall behind a pair of immense sentinel oaks. A lamp-lighted trellis, bearded with dark ivy, spanned the front of the estate. A dozen glowing windows illuminated the front porch, their golden light stretching and dying along the long yard toward the guarded gate, where two armed men stood.

Sven flashed the silver pin under his coat. The guards nodded and let them pass by without question.

They followed a wending pebble path up to a pair of great red doors.

Sven turned to face his companions. He removed his hat and gave a little bow. "Let me welcome you to the House of the Gun. There are a few pieces of etiquette we'll be expected to follow."

"I'm guessing it's more than just wiping our feet before we go inside," said Sarah.

"Correct," said Sven. "Firstly, you are a guest in this house, an extension of myself. Any attempt to engage in any kind of contest will be met with extreme displeasure."

"What kind of idiot would challenge a house full of gunfighters?" asked Carson.

"You'd be surprised," replied Sven. "The Guild considers this place to be a solemn location. Blood is very rarely shed, and respect is always given. Secondly, every man and woman inside this house represents over a hundred years of tradition. The convocation is a rare event, one that takes certain precautions to protect the Guild members inside. I'm sure you can guess my meaning."

Sarah pulled her pistol from the holster. "Means no iron."

"Correct again." Sven collected their pistols, tucking them into the waistband of his belt. "One more thing. . ."

"How many goddamn rules do you people have, Sven?" asked Annie, mockingly frustrated.

"Just this last one. The three elders of the Guild are identified by golden pins, and they are to be treated with the utmost respect. They're the ones Annie will need to convince to let her hire the entire Guild. The Silver Pins do as the Gold Pins say. And the Gold Pins make sure that

Guild law remains equal among the silver." The big Swede reached out for the doorknob then paused. "One more thing. The Gold Pins will also be the only ones armed."

Annie rolled her eyes. "Well, that's comforting."

"All right, now you know the rules. Don't break them."

"Sure," said Sarah unconvincingly. "Best behavior."

"So, my friends, let me formally invite you into the House of the Gun." Sven turned the doorknob and swung wide one of the great red doors.

Where the streets of New Orleans were all shouts and primal delights made manifest in the night, the House of the Gun thrummed with the sound of measured conversations. The floor, like the staircase, was black-and-white checkered marble leading to a multitude of rooms. Framed portraits decorated the long hall and white sable rugs ran the length of the floor.

Past the foyer, a bald, somber attendant stood behind a bar. The old, amber-eyed vulture of a man lifted his eyebrows. "Ah, Mr. Erickson. You are most expected."

"Boris," said Sven.

"And three companions. If you would please, sir," said Boris, flourishing his hand over the wooden bar before him.

"Of course." Sven set their pistols on the bar top, and Boris began collecting them one at a time, sliding each one into a slotted section of the wall behind him.

"Any news?" Sven asked.

"Indeed. The Gold Pins have received guests as early as yesterday evening. One of them has proposed quite the offer, the details of which are to be discussed tonight."

Annie didn't like the sound of that, but she hoped the Guild would still give her a chance to request their help.

Sven was already ahead of her, though, on that front. "Well, my patron has an offer of her own to make."

"Ah, yes. As I said, you and your patron are expected. The Gold Pins, along with the rest of the current membership, await you in the drawing room. Oh. . ." The man's venerable countenance lilted, and his eyes suddenly became very kind. "My deepest condolences for the loss of Larry Cornish."

"Kind of you to say," said Sven. Then, without further word, the big Swede led Annie and the others down the hallway of portraits toward the drawing room.

Annie did not recognize any of the names stamped into the bronze plates below the frames, but she did notice that every single person in the portraits bore a golden pin.

They entered the drawing room, where two dozen men and women dressed in their finest clothes had gathered. There were dandies in wool suits, skinners in slick buckskin leathers, and a dark-haired beauty wearing a black velvet dress that matched her black gun belt. She wore a golden chain that plunged down her neckline. A ruby, fat as a sugar cube, hung from the chain, and just below it, a golden pin rested against her pronounced bosom.

The woman inclined her head in greeting and smiled. She touched the shoulder of the man next to her. His long gray hair lay in curls across his shoulders.

He turned to look at them—a pair of cold, gunmetal-gray eyes above a thick handlebar mustache—and when he locked his gaze on Annie Miller, the power residing within threatened to buckle her courage. There was fire there, the eyes of a killer.

Annie broke her own gaze away from his, pretending to scan the room, just as Carson walked in front of her, his shoulder brushing her own.

"Carson?" she asked.

"Ah, shit," said Sarah. "Sven."

"What is—" the Swede started. "Kid, don't. . ."

Carson approached two men standing next to one another. One of them, a fancily dressed Mexican, smoking a cigar. The other was a white man with the eyes of a basset hound and, just above the cigar in his mouth, a long, jagged scar.

"Roger Combs," said Carson, his voice terse. "And Jorge Reyes."

The hardened gunfighters looked at Carson, giving him a once over. "Well, I declare," said Combs. He plucked the cigar from between his teeth. "Look who it is, Jorge."

The Mexican smiled. "Would you look at that. It's the kid from Chicago."

"Teeth are still fitting nice," said Combs. "You must be here with—ah, yes, there's Sven Erickson. And by my stars, that's Sarah Lockhart."

"Fuck you, Combs," said Sarah, her voice sweet as honey. "How's the shoulder, Reyes."

Reyes's cool brown eyes hardened. "Got winged yourself, as I remember, bitch."

Annie stepped up beside Carson and placed a hand on the small of his back. She intended to say something soothing to him, to try and cool the tempers flaring in the small circle of growing tension, but Combs cut in.

"You're lucky to be under the protection of the convocation. If we met out in the street—"

Sven put his massive frame between his friends and the two gunfighters. "And what if you met *me* instead, Combs."

Over the big Swede's shoulder, Annie watched some of the color drain out of Combs's face. But he managed to steel himself. "Problem's not with you, Erickson. But in time, believe me, it will be."

"Still number nine," said Sven, the words a rebuke. "I doubt you'll climb any higher than that. And Jorge, hell, I'm surprised you're even still alive, slow as you are."

Carson stepped around Sven, coming almost nose to nose with Combs. "You have something that's mine. I want it back."

Combs laughed him down. "Oh, you mean your iron? Fine piece it is. I can see why you'd be sentimental. But I'm afraid there's only one way you'll get it back. You might have been dangerous once, you little shit, but after what we did to them hands of yours, I *highly* doubt you'll be up to the task."

"I wouldn't worry about it, Carson," said Sven. "Eventually, one way or the other, Roger here will find his way to me, and then the pistol will find its way back to you."

"Piss on you, Erickson," said Combs, pointing his smoldering cigar in the Swede's face.

Sven laughed humorlessly. "When the convocation is over, you come find me Roger. I'll make an exception for your challenge."

"Count on it, you mother—"

A female voice cut in over Combs. "I trust everyone is enjoying themselves?"

It was the woman wearing the gold pin. She had eyes that were a storm of green and blue. Her black hair was pinned around her ears, crowning the smiling wrinkles of her face.

"Young man, this is a party." Her voice wielded authority gracefully, an authority she directed at Carson. "*My* party, to put it plainly, and it would deeply displease me to learn that one of my guests was not enjoying themselves. My name is Belle. Belle Starr. Tell me, what is your name?"

But before Carson could answer, she swept a hand past all of them. "Better yet, Sven, why don't you tell me. Who are all your friends?"

Sven nodded with absolute deference. "The red-faced youth is Mr. Carson Watts Ptolemy."

"Oh," said Belle, clasping her hands together just below her chin. "You must be Gilbert's adopted boy. Tell me, how is he?"

"Dead," said Carson flatly.

Her mouth formed a delicate circle. "My goodness, I am so sorry to hear that. He perished doing the late Judge Ellison's work, no doubt." She gave Carson no chance to respond, placing a hand on Sven's shoulder. "How do you know these two beauties, Mr. Erickson?"

"Allow me to introduce Sarah Lockhart, a deft gunhand and friend of mine for many years," he said, then gestured toward Annie. "And the new head of the Peregrine Estate, Annie Miller."

"Annie Miller," said Belle happily. "Yes. I got your letter. You have business you would like to discuss with the Gold Pins."

Annie didn't hesitate. "Yes. I'm seeking to hire the Gunfighter's Guild, whole cloth."

"So your letter plainly indicated. I like that kind of directness, you know. And I'm certain that you've amassed a great fortune to make such a request?"

Annie nodded. "I have sold everything under the estate's holding, save the supplies my purpose requires."

Belle clicked her tongue against her teeth. "I would most certainly have loved to hear your purpose, Miss Miller. But I'm afraid that the Guild cannot meet your request."

"Will you not even hear my full offer? I am also willing to throw in my own personal train as payment as well, should the bill require it."

Belle smiled again. "You do not seem to understand. There will be no bill to pay, Ms. Miller."

Her heart sank. "But I was told I would get an audience in order to—"

"Yes. And I am that audience, Miss Miller." The words were a proclamation.

It was Annie's turn to turn red in the face. She felt the flush of her anger roiling up inside her. Her heart began to beat quickly. "How can you deny me, without even hearing the totality of my offer?"

"Because I've already purchased the whole of the guild

for myself, little Miss Blood and Thunder," came a smooth, confident voice from behind them.

Annie turned, knowing the voice but disbelieving. Standing there, brandy glass in hand, dressed in a dapper black suit and paisley tie of gold and green, was Ashley Sutliff.

"Ashley!" the word exploded out of Sarah Lockhart's mouth.

"Hello, Sarah. Sven, good to see you're still alive. And just look at you, Carson. You were but a sprout the last time I saw you. My condolences for your pa."

Carson regarded the man, saying nothing.

"Ah, Mister Sutliff," said Belle, "I had no idea you were acquainted with Miss Miller. But I suppose that makes sense. You are a member of the Peregrine Estate, are you not?"

"No," Annie snapped. "He isn't. He quit on the outfit less than a year ago." She leveled her eyes on the man. "How in the hell did you come up with the money to hire the Guild, and to what end?"

Ashley opened his mouth.

"I need the Guild," Annie said, cutting him off. "And you know *why*."

"For a pretty girl, you've sure got a pair of balls on you," said Ashley, smiling playfully.

Annie stepped close to him, remembering how in Fort Worth, less than a year ago, Sutliff had refused to help them in the effort to rescue Carson. "Bigger than yours, you goddamn yellow bastard."

The man's gambler smile slid off his face, revealing the dangerous man beneath. "Careful," he threatened.

"Or what," Carson shot in.

Ashley smirked at the young man. "Considering that I now have in my employ the twenty-five most dangerous gunfighters alive, and the full backing of the president of the United States—its goddamn commander-in-chief—I guess I'll have you blown straight to hell. When you get there, you can tell your pa it was me who gave the order."

"What are you talking about, Ashley?" asked Sarah Lockhart. "Why would President Grant be backing you?"

"Sounds like bullshit to me," said Sven. "Sounds like a trademarked Ashley Sutliff bluff."

"He's not bluffing," said Sarah.

"As ever, Sarah, smartest of the bunch. You know me better than that. Bluffing only works when you know your enemy—know how they think and what their tells are—and if you think I'd waste my time knowing your mind or your tells, Erickson, well then you have an over-estimation of self-importance."

"Enough of the bullshit, Ashley. Spill it."

"Annie, you're about to fall in love with me," he said. Then, he took a long, satisfied sip of his whiskey. "See, I was hired by President Grant to do the thing you've been wanting to do since you watched your momma die in Abilene."

Annie, seething with anger, cut a word through the air. "What."

"I've recruited the Guild to join my own personal army and head up to Colorado to make war. Not just on Sigurd but on the whole lot of them. And the only reason I stayed behind for this little party was to make sure you and I ran into each other."

"Why," said Annie, heart hammering. "So you could gloat?"

Ashley shook his head. "Not one bit. I stayed behind to ask you to do the thing I did not do seven months ago. I want you, all of you"—he nodded at the Peregrine agents behind her—"to come with me to Colorado and destroy the goddamn Red Kingdom."

CHAPTER TEN

The Red Kingdom

Once, and only once in his life, at the age of twenty, had John Childs fallen in love. Her name was Mary Elaine. She was the only thing in life that John had ever wanted. Truly wanted. More than wealth and luck, or the happiness they bring, John wanted to be hers. He courted her for years, but no matter how hard he tried, Mary remained her own woman, never once saying to him the words every man hopes to hear from the one he loves best.

The hardest day of John's life was when Mary, standing before a peach gold sunset, looked into his eyes and said she's chosen another. Worse, she'd chosen his chief rival: a sleepy, dullard of a man who had inherited a vast fortune from his cattle-baron father. Her words were simple. Sweet, even. Making it plain that while she held many deep feelings for John's passion and humor and strength, his rival could provide security. Safety.

John promised to provide her those things.

With a smile, she disbelieved him.

Three weeks after that sun vanished behind the hill where he and Mary had made love for the first time, John was marching for Manassas as a member of the Union army. The Slaver's Revolt changed John as much as it had changed the country. He wrote Mary at every post, letting her know where he was, what he was doing. Lying in every letter with the words, "I hope your husband is doing well."

Mary never wrote him back.

John often wondered if his letters had all been delivered but remained unopened, but he dared himself the fantasy, each and every night, that Mary would open his letters in secret. He imagined her reading paper made gold by a roaring Rhode Island fire, the flames shimmering in the tears he hoped would be falling down her face.

He would never know. And part of him didn't want to, because the dream of her longing had become such a comfort.

And now, marching up the snowy pass through the sweeping, unnamed valley running out toward Black Wells, he needed that comfort more than ever. Comfort not only from the biting cold but from the dispassionate cruelty of the creatures his townsfolk now called masters.

Their tramping up into the jagged, unforgiving stone of the Astolats went on without further hazard from the great beasts that had ambushed them. But the weather and the hard marching had been too much for some of them, and those the vampires drank dry. Not for sustenance but to make clear what would happen should any human lack the vitality required for such a climb. John helped as many as he could. Some survived. Others were swallowed up.

The night, like a malicious god, lorded over them the entire way. However, had he known what awaited them deep within the mountain pass where they were forced into the cleft of the rock itself, John would have gloried in the night.

What began as a slender gap, widened only a little. The

press of bodies squeezing between the walls of stone. The vampires showed no difficulty in gliding through the gap, while the townsfolk were forced to slide their aching feet along the stones. And then, all at once, the passageway opened unto yawning black.

In that vast darkness, John heard the voice of King Kristian. A voice as ancient as the stones that repeated his words. "Welcome, my children."

There was a flash of red light that illuminated the expanse of dark and dripping stone. The light was agony at first, burning John's eyes, but when his sight adjusted, he could make out dozens of massive glass sconces hammered into the cavern walls. They burned with fires blood red, illuminating everything in their sanguine glow.

Standing on a platform of limestone, King Kristian, with his palms upraised, addressed the trembling townsfolk. "Consider yourselves fortunate, sons and daughters, for you have endured where others could not. You have seen what the weak among you shall never see. Only the strong are welcome within the walls of my home, and now, thus proved, you shall pass through the gate of appointment. There you shall be divided. Selected for the work that best suits your talents." He gestured with his left hand, saying, "Those with a trade, and veterans of your Civil War, shall avail themselves to the left, and with you, take your families. I am kind and never will I split blood from blood. Those of you who bear no skill or craft, or able mind for battle, you shall take the right path. There, your purpose shall be provided."

A man's voice rushed up from the human herd. "I am a farmer. But I can't work here, underground."

Kristian regarded the man with a strange kind of pity. "The days of agriculture are over, my son. But do not worry. My progeny will give you a labor even you will be able to accomplish."

The man's bravery must have instilled courage in

another. A woman spoke up: "Will we get to go back home?"

At this, Kristian did not answer; he only smiled. Then, he turned and stepped deeper into the cavern.

The herd of humans were driven deep into the mountain, following the massive red lamps that lined a long shaft cut into the stone. The sound of the people's feet was all John could hear. He kept himself at the rear, helping others if they tripped over stones or collapsed in exhaustion. In the eyes of the fallen, he could see their utter defeat—a complete hopelessness. Lives over. Dreams shattered. In their faces was a kind of dismay that he had only witnessed in the eyes of wounded soldiers at the precipice of death. He had failed them. Failed to provide that which Mary knew he could never give. Safety. Security. Protection.

Ushered through cloven stone walls, they came to a great archway, where the one named Carmilla stood a dark censor. Behind her, over a short bluff, was the most incredible thing John had ever seen. A city of stone that must have rivaled Rome and Babylon before it. The limestone city, bathed in red lamps innumerable, was a marvel. Buildings like skeletal fingers stretched from cavern floor, reaching to the top of the dome itself. Though he hated the truth of it, he knew that it was the most beautiful city he would ever see. Likely, the last.

Carmilla portioned out each fate dispassionately. And when John, the final among their number, came to her, she looked at him.

"Trade or skill?" she asked.

John looked up at her, stiffened his voice with pride, and said, "Sheriff."

Bored and unimpressed, she replied, "To the right, *lawman.*"

John passed through the gate of appointment, turning as he was told to turn. Down a precipitous stairway carved into the bedrock John went, down into the red city where, among the bustling streets of thousands of humans toiling, he saw human and vampire walking the same streets, existing in a way that the Black Africans and their white slaving masters had existed. One in utter bondage, the other in absolute primacy.

John was filled with an inconsolable rage. The same rage that had guided his hand and signed his name to volunteer for the Union ranks years ago. The whipping flame, always burning for human abolition from oppression. For justice. And, in seeing the multitude of humans reduced to property, John gained what so many men failed to achieve during the span of their long, little lives. Purpose. He came to understand, in that moment, the clear vision of why he had been placed upon the earth. While he had once thought that purpose was to love and court, marry and cherish Mary Elaine, he now knew the truth.

John Childs was put upon earth to be placed into bondage in the grandest city the world would never see, so that he could be the man that would burn it to ashes.

PART TWO

The Vampire War

"I watched from a distance. One thing was singularly true of that impossibly lighted city. There were slaves and there were masters."

– Ennio Malocello, *Il Regno di Luce Scarlatta*

CHAPTER ELEVEN

The Judge, en route to Fort Scott, Kansas

The swiftness with which Annie accepted Ashley Sutliff's offer took Carson by surprise. She did not consult the others in the party. Did not hesitate a single moment, despite her displeasure for Ashley himself. At his impassioned suggestion of joining forces, Annie extended her hand, only saying, "We're in."

Annie offered *The Judge* as a means of transportation, making it clear that any route via horseback would be unacceptable. Plans were then made to acquire passenger cars from what remained of the New Orleans railyards. Ashley Sutliff, though he had the entire financial backing of the United States government, balked at the idea of paying for the cars. Instead, he used his letter of authority to 'conscript' the railcars into commission of the US Army.

"Never pay for anything you can get for free," the gambler-turned-American-agent had said upon successful acquisition.

Carson watched Annie's face twist-up in frustration. "We should pay them."

Ashley shook his head. "Sweetheart, if we fail, they ain't gonna need the money anyway. Hell, if you're so bent over backward about it, you pay 'em with the money I saved you by buying the Guild."

Annie had scowled at him. They all knew that despite the considerable fortune she had amassed, she would have bankrupted their funds with such a purchase. Besides, if they succeeded and survived, they would need that money to re-establish the Peregrine Estate and continue the work. The Red Kingdom was the most dangerous threat to humankind, but it wasn't the only one.

With the railcars attached, *The Judge* pulled out of New Orleans, leaving behind the teeming streets of music and drink and celebration that served as a constant reminder of what Carson and his friends were fighting for. This endeavor was not just about revenge, though that was certainly an element of their drive to succeed. But more than that, they were making war on the Red Kingdom for all the things that made life worth living. The passion of life to its top that every human being deserved.

They would need to travel nine hundred miles from New Orleans, through Arkansas, up into Missouri, then west toward Fort Scott, Kansas, where the bulk of Ashley's forces were waiting. Carson was dead set on spending as many of those miles as he could with Annie. In the short time since their proclamation of their feelings to one another, Carson found himself thinking about her more often than he had in Abilene. Even more than when he had made his lonely trip to Natchez. He hadn't even thought that was possible. But, the more time they spent together, the more time he wanted. It was as if his capacity for her company expanded, each minute becoming a craving for more.

"Nothing good gets away," his father had told him near four years ago in Yellow Hill. The man had been right about

so many things, but this was the one that made Carson the happiest to find to be true.

Carson thought about these things, lying in the seat of his cabin. He wondered if Annie was thinking about him too. He got up, determined to find out.

It took him much too long to get dressed, not because of his physical limitations but because he wanted to look his best when Annie saw him. He dressed in a simple black suit and a green puff tie half-hidden beneath a matching paisley vest. Freshly shaven, hair slick with pomade, he stepped out into the passageway, feeling clean and sharp as a blade.

Annie wasn't in her bunk, where he had hoped to find her. But he spied her through the transition-door glass, sitting in the diner car at a table with Sarah and Sven. Most of the tables were full with members of the Gunfighter's Guild, though Ashley Sutliff was nowhere to be seen. Good. All that bastard did was frustrate and complicate every situation he belonged to. Carson opened the door, making sure to shut it loud enough to get Annie's attention.

She saw him. And, much to his satisfaction, her blue eyes widened.

Seeing Annie's expression, Sarah turned back too, and the dark woman let out a whooping sound that would have made a preacher blush.

He made his way toward them, doing his best to hide his limp.

"Well, well. Who is this dashing rogue I see?" said Sarah. "Why, that couldn't possibly be Carson Watts Ptolemy. Sven, could that be him?" She elbowed the gunfighter.

Sven smiled, playing along with her. "Can't be. I know Carson Ptolemy, and this man, who looks as crisp as an autumn apple, must be an imposter."

Carson shook his head, happy but embarrassed.

When he came to the foot of their little table, Sven said, "Who are you and what have you done with our friend?"

Carson ignored the question, looking down at Annie with his most sincere smile. "May I sit with you?"

"Been saving this seat for you all morning," she said, patting the chair next to her.

He sat down. Sven gave him a knowing look and lifted the carafe of coffee to fill his friend's cup, saving Carson the embarrassment of having to struggle with it himself.

Carson looked around the thrumming diner car, electric with morning conversations between Guild members. "It was smart of Sutliff to hire a cook for the trip," he said.

"If there is anything I know about that old gambler," said Sarah, "it's that he refuses to travel without accommodation. I don't think he even *knows* how to cook. Hell, he also hired two more engineers."

"Speaking of, where is he?" asked Carson.

Sven started explaining, but Carson missed most of his words when Annie slid her hand onto his knee beneath the tablecloth. Carson placed his own hand over hers. He liked her forwardness. And holding her hand felt like a secret made known to the world.

". . .he's quickly becoming hated by his employees. Taking all their money when they dare sit down to play in the bar car."

"He'd better not win too much," said Sarah. "One of these Guild members might shoot him dead."

Sven scoffed. "A mercenary gunhand never shoots the billfold. Besides, no one made them sit down at the table."

"You spoke with him?" asked Annie.

"At the table last night. A fifty-dollar conversation," said Sven over the lip of his coffee cup. "Goddamn gamblers."

"No one made you sit down either," said Sarah.

"Did he tell you how he came into the employment of the government?" Annie asked.

"Apparently, after he left our company in Fort Worth, he made his way up north to live out his days in lavish comfort. But he was approached by a man who recognized him. Said that man took him right up to the White House, into the office of President Grant his own damn self."

"How did they know who he was?" asked Carson.

"Ashley Sutliff has been in the game a long time, kid. His reputation as a gambler, which is substantial, is dwarfed by those who know what he did as a killer of all sorts of weird shit in Virginia and South Carolina. He was one of the Judge's most prominent and trustworthy agents. Word like that gets around. So, when Grant learned of what was happening in Colorado, he brought in people like Ashley to deal with it outside of the public eye."

"What kind of people?" asked Carson.

"People like us. The Peregrine Estate is not, and has never been, the only enterprise of its kind. Ashley says he's accumulated other allies; they'll be at Fort Scott too." Sven's brow raised, remembering something. "Oh yeah, he said he wanted to talk with you," he said to Carson. "Sorry, got drunk and forgot."

Annie squeezed Carson's hand.

"With me? About what?"

"No clue. Said it was important though."

Carson didn't like the idea of leaving Annie to go talk to some drunken gambler about God knew what. He just wanted to enjoy her company during what, he suspected, would be the last little measure of peace before the war began in earnest. "I'll catch up with him later. If it's so important, he can come find me."

"He was rather insistent," said Sven. "Said it should just be the two of you."

Carson did not like where this was going.

"You should go see what he wants," said Annie, smiling at him.

He rubbed her fingers with his thumb, trying to let her

know that he did not want to go anywhere out of her reach. "But—"

"We'll be right here, handsome," said Sarah. "All of us. There's time."

Carson, resigning himself to their points, got up from the table. He looked at Annie. "I'll be right back."

"If I'm not here, I'll be in my room."

Carson's stomach folded over. He didn't quite know what her words meant, but he certainly enjoyed the invitation.

He made his way to the south end of the northbound train. At the end of the diner car, Roger Combs was cleaning his revolver at one of the booths.

Not *his* revolver, thought Carson, my *father's* revolver.

Combs looked up and, seeing Carson's eye on him, smiled and nodded. It wasn't a greeting. It was an open challenge. A 'come and get it if you can' look.

Carson passed him by without word.

Through the train he went, passing through cars he had once made a battleground. In the bar car, Ashley Sutliff sat at a round table with three others.

"Mr. Ptolemy," said Sutliff, laying down his cards.

At the sight of his reveal, the occupants of the table groaned.

"What is that, Sutliff," said a woman all dressed in buffalo skins. She tossed her bedraggled hair back. "Six hands in a row?"

"Seven." The man next to her sighed, his head leaning heavily against his palms.

"And with that, the table is closed," said Sutliff. "I'm awful appreciative of your donations. Let's play again tonight." As the other players began to rise, he added, "Don't be shy to bring a friend."

The players, grumbling among themselves, exited the bar car.

"You wanted to speak with me," said Carson.

"Have a seat." Sutliff eyed his chips, stacking them into color-coordinated piles.

Carson sat.

"So," Ashley said, giving him a glance, "what in the hell happened to you?"

"What do you mean?"

"You know exactly what I mean."

Carson stared at Ashley, wordless.

Ashley stared right back. "It's like drawing blood from a stone with you Ptolemys. Last I heard, you were on a killing spree. A one-man war against the Society of Prometheus. You killed Barron and Tanzer, I hear. The Martin brothers, too."

Still Carson sat, looking at the man. There was something about Ashley he had never liked. It wasn't his gambler's shine or the oily charm. It was something else. Something about the man's face that made Carson want to rearrange it for him.

"Now, look at you," continued Ashley. "Teeth all knocked out. Fingers knotted up too bad to sling a gun. And you try to hide that limp, but you ain't foolin' anybody that's got the sense to pay attention."

Anger flushed Carson's face. "I got caught. The Society paid back in full what I'd cost them."

"Nah." Half a grunt, half a laugh. Ashley shook his head knowingly. "I've dealt with that group of lunatics before. The torture, that's them, for sure. But they wouldn't have kept you alive. No, there's something else."

"Annie, Sarah, and Sven got to me before they finished the job," said Carson, shifting uncomfortably in his chair. "What does it matter anyhow. They're all dead."

"That what you figure?" Ashley tried to stare a hole right through him. "What happened in Chicago, Carson?"

He ignored the question. "Are you telling me the Society is still active?"

"I asked first."

Carson swallowed hard, anger slithering through his guts.

Ashley must have seen it. "We're on the same side. And I need to know what happened. Call it a professional courtesy between fellow Peregrine agents."

"You quit, as I hear it," Carson snapped back.

"You don't get it, do you?" asked Ashley, somehow finding a way to further relax in his chair. "You can't fluster me. I'm the one running this goddamn outfit. I'm not a player. I'm the house money and the dealer. You and yours are lucky that I waited in New Orleans to let you in the game. If it weren't for me, you'd have arrived at the House of the Gun only to find locked gates and darkened windows."

That was a lie. And Carson saw right through it. "Now who's telling half a story?"

Ashley smiled. "Tell me about Chicago and you have my word I'll tell you everything."

"You know, every time you give me a guarantee, I can't help but be reminded of something Annie told me. Something her father said. Never trust a gambler or a politician. They both play the same game, one with cards and the other with lives. You're the former, working for the latter."

"Jesus, are you stubborn. Just like goddamn Gilbert—"

Carson backhanded Ashley Sutliff across the mouth. His hands were busted, sure, but his reflexes were still lightning quick.

Ashley's eyes flared wide, the mask of a maniac.

"Say it again, gambler," said Carson.

Ashley's eyes flared and he opened his mouth to speak. Then stopped. He took a deep, calming breath. The man shook his head, his face flushed with frustration, trying to decide his next action. Eyes welling, he ran his tongue over his bottom lip, tasting for blood.

"Go ahead. Say it," said Carson through gritted teeth. "Say my father's name again."

Something shifted behind Ashley's eyes. He laughed. "Christ in Heaven, kid. It's like trying to talk to a haystack. I just want to know—"

"I'll tell you what happened in Chicago," said Carson. Maybe just because he just wanted a break from the man's voice. "What happened to me at the hands of the Society and why you should be on your hands and knees, like I was, thanking God that Annie Miller is in the world." He went through the events, sparing no detail. He recalled his capture at the hands of the Baroness, the torture that was put upon him. Clara Van Horn's cruel experiments. The insane High Priest and his connection to the Black Manuscript, and the connection he and Carson shared. The god's eye that almost drove Carson insane. And how Annie Miller, by arriving just in time to save Carson, had saved every other living person from the ritual that would open the way for the Nine.

Ashley listened, never interrupting.

Carson then explained all that had happened right up until the moment they caught up with Ashley at the House of the Gun.

The gambler let out a long sigh. "Shitfire. So, you're the reason the sun's been hidden for half a year, but you're also the reason we're all still around to complain about the darkness."

Carson nodded. "I am what remains of the conduit that connects the Nine to our world, yes."

"So. . . if you die, what happens? Does the ritual complete and we're all up shit's creek without a paddle? Or, when you shuffle off the mortal coil, does everything go back to normal?"

Carson swallowed hard. He had parsed this question over and over in his mind, but only Ashley Sutliff had ever raised the issue directly. "I don't know."

"I'm guessing the answer is in that black book of theirs."

"Possibly. But both copies I know of have been lost or destroyed."

Ashley shot a dismissive look over to the window, where the cold snowy night rolled by. "It will be in our best interests for you to figure out what route we are to take with your life, Carson Ptolemy. Learning how you're connected in all this will tell us what course we should take: whether we should protect you at all costs or. . . well, you know. The other thing."

Carson tilted his head, reading the gambler. "You've got a copy of the manuscript." His tone was harsher than he had intended.

"Not me," said Ashley. "One of the people I have hired does though."

Carson stood up, his chair flipping over behind him. "You son of a bitch. That's how you know the Society of Prometheus is still around. You've employed them."

Ashley stayed cool as a cat lounging in the sun. "This campaign against the Red Kingdom and their king will determine the fate of the human race, Carson. I was told to bring all the strength of our people together. The Society of Prometheus represents a portion of our occult knowledge. And our power. When we get to Fort Scott, you will be provided the last remaining copy of the manuscript, and you will read it. And by God, you will inform us of what we can do to make things right."

CHAPTER TWELVE

ABOARD *The Judge,* THE ARKANSAS AND MISSOURI BORDER

The knock came at what must have been noon, though Annie didn't check, because it didn't matter what time it was if it was Carson behind the door. To her utter delight, it was him. But he did not appear quite as happy to see her. His pallor was milkier than usual, and his eyes looked as hard as stone in the wavering gas light.

"Annie," he said, the word coiled with tension.

"Yes," she said, her own reply coming out strange.

"We need to talk," he said, nodding politely as a request to enter her quarters.

Annie shuffled back and took a seat on one of the quilt-covered coach benches that had been her bed. "What's wrong?"

He sat across from her on the opposite bench, not beside her where she had hoped. What could Ashley Sutliff have said to Carson to so quickly unman him?

His fingers laced together, unlaced, then slid over his

knees. "There's something I need to tell you. I was too afraid to say it before. I'm still scared to say it now."

Annie smiled at him. "It's okay. Whatever you have to tell me, it'll be okay."

"It's about Chicago. About me. Listen. . ." He smoothed the wrinkles out of his trousers. "When I was taken by the Society, something was made clear to me. I'm connected, in some way, to what is happening to the world—to the persistence of the winter and darkness. And I do not know if I can disentangle myself from it."

"Because of the manuscript?"

"Yes," he said, then shook his head, frustrated. "Maybe. I don't know. The High Priest of the Society said something to me. He said that he and I were connected, and that we were both conduits: a kind of connection point between the Nine and their pathway into our world. It may be that me being. . . being alive is what's allowing the perpetual cold and the night."

"But we saved you from—"

"Please, let me finish." He took a long, deep breath. "The priest and I were meant to be sacrificed together, so our blood would be taken in by the strange orb you saw. You saved me from that fate, and for that I am grateful, but I am afraid that we didn't stop the ritual; we just left it in limbo. What if, so long as I am alive, that ritual will continue to allow this blizzard and the monstrosities to remain? I don't know what to do with the possibility that me being alive means the suffering of everyone else. But I don't know if dying will complete that ritual or end it. I only know that I can still feel the void that event put inside of me."

Annie's spine stiffened. "Well, I don't know about any of that, but I know this, Carson. You are not allowed to die to test that theory."

Carson rocked back on his heels, shocked at her directness.

"I don't give a good goddamn about the Nine or the Society. Piss on them all. They can't have you." *They can't have you because I picked you, and I'm not losing anything else,* was what she wanted to say.

He leaned forward, slid his scarred fingers across the entirety of his brow. Pressing hard as if the pressure would soothe the anxiety in his mind. "If I'm the reason for all this—"

"You're not. I refuse to believe it. One person's life can't mean the end of the world. One person can't save all of it, and one person can't mean its destruction."

"Why not?" The question sounded genuine.

She shook her head, frustrated. "Because. . . because it's not fair. You didn't choose to be made the center of all this."

He looked deep into her eyes. "Neither death nor grace have any fairness to them, Annie."

"No," she said, tears welling in her eyes. "No, goddamn it. Promise me. You promise me right now, Carson Ptolemy, that you aren't going to die in pursuit of this insanity."

"You want me to promise that I won't die?"

She shot out a finger, pointing at him. "Yes. That's exactly what I am telling you."

"I can't promise—"

"Yes, you can," Annie said, standing up. "Yes, you will. I'm not losing anyone else." She had finally said it out loud to another person. She'd finally put words to that feeling burning inside her since the night Sigurd stole her mother. "I lost my father. My brother." Her bottom lip began to tremble. "My mother and Judge Ellison. But not you. Not Sarah and not Sven. I won't have it. I won't *allow* it."

Carson lifted the flat of his hand, a calming gesture.

"Don't," she barked. "Don't you dare try to shush me. You make this promise to me, Carson. You make it, and you damn well better keep it."

His hand fell into his lap. He thought for a long time,

looking out the window and into the utter blackness of night. Then, he stood up. And there, standing in the smallness of that space, Annie was given a gift. A gift she had not, until that very moment, known in life.

Carson took her hands into his. Hands that felt so much stronger than she had suspected they might.

"I promise, Annie," said Carson, vowing the impossible.

Unafraid, she kissed him.

At its quickest pace, a long time passed.

Annie's arms curled around his waist. His encircled her shoulders. He gently ended the embrace, pulling back slightly.

"I have wanted to do that for a long time," he said.

"First day we met?"

He nodded.

"Please stay," said Annie, resting her cheek against his chest. "Please, just stay."

They held one another, neither of them knowing they had just crossed over the Arkansas state line and were now in Missouri. What Annie did know, down in the secret places of her heart, was that she had crossed over into something she had never known before.

"Have you ever been to St. Louis?" asked Carson.

"No," said Annie, closing her eyes to listen to the sound of his heartbeat.

"A barber once told me that it was the most beautiful city in the world. Ashley says we'll need a half-a-day layover for timber and coal. While we're there, would you go with me? Help me see if that barber was telling the truth."

Annie squeezed his waist, then looked up into those big green eyes of his. "Just the two of us?"

"Yes," he replied. "Just you. Just me."

* * *

Annie asked for some time to rest and get ready for what she called their 'night on the town.' And though he wanted nothing more than to stay, he kissed her gently on the cheek and, as *The Judge* rolled through the Missouri darkness, made his way back through the bustling cars to his own bed.

He undressed and tried to sleep, laying his clothes out so they would not wrinkle. His head hit the pillow, but staring at the ceiling was all he could do. His heart and his mind raced in the remembering of the kiss. The feeling that lanced through him, the sweetest wound. Though he looked at the ceiling, all he could see were her eyes. Pressing his fingers against his own lips, he tried to simulate the pressure of hers.

Carson shook his head, laughed. "Nothing good gets away," he said, hoping that wherever his father was, he could hear him. The woman had, with one gesture, made him the most ridiculous man alive. Had he really promised another human being that he wouldn't die? That probably wasn't the most intelligent promise he had ever made, but to say it felt right. Felt true.

He would *make* it true.

Somehow, sleep took him for a time. He did not dream of Annie Miller. What came were rabid visions of his torture at the High Preist's command, the reading of the Black Manuscript, where he again fell into the pages and found himself drifting before the great lidless eye of one of the Nine. There, he heard the strange song that he had tried so hard to forget, but there was no erasure to be had. The discordant melody rolled through him like a winter wind, cutting to the quick of his mind.

But, in his dream, Carson somehow knew it was just that. A dream. And against the song of a cosmic titan, he took hold of his dreaming and compelled away the terror and maleficence brooding within him. In its place, he painted a summer sunset overlooking a green hill, where the warm light washed over his and Annie's faces as they held one another in the shine.

This was what he wanted, and in this place he could have it, at least for as long as he could will it. He did not know if it could be more than a dream; he only knew that the dream was worth having. Worth striving to make it a reality. Their reality.

He woke to the blast of the train's whistle, and the wheels complaining to a stop. He dressed quickly and made his way back toward Annie's cabin.

When he got there, he found Sarah Lockhart leaning against the door, one boot set against it.

"There he is," said Sarah, turning to look at him. "I got here just a few minutes ago. Seems I was a bit too late."

Carson smiled. "Too late for what?"

"Wanted to see if my friend here would like to get a bite to eat while we holdover in St. Louis, but she tells me that you've claimed her for the evening. I am given to understand that the great courtship has begun in earnest." She pushed off the door, rocking onto both feet. "I'm glad for the both of you, Carson. I really am. If your father were here, I'm sure he'd have some kind of man-to-man with you, tell you about how to treat a woman, all that bullshit older bucks like to say to the younger ones. Trying to help them avoid the mistakes they made in their youths."

Carson bristled a bit at that, but he calmed himself. This was Sarah's way.

"Don't whet your horns, kid. I don't mean anything mean by it. I waited for you because *I* wanted to give you two things. The first is my own little piece of advice. Don't let her have her way all the time. She's good about getting it with that attitude of hers, but no relationship lasts long that way."

Carson nodded. "All right. What's the other?"

She stepped in close to him, her eyes serious. "You be good to that girl. She's my dearest friend. And if you break her heart, I swear to God I'll geld you myself." She leaned forward, their noses almost touching, and whispered, "And there's not a person alive that'll be able to stop me." There was no smile.

Carson blinked. "Well, let's hope it doesn't come to that."

She pulled back and patted Carson on the shoulder. "Now, go. Have fun. St. Louis is a real gem of a town."

As she walked away, Carson turned and knocked on Annie's door.

The cabin door slid into the wall on its rolling hinge.

And there she was.

She wore a green satin dress. Her hair was up, the auburn curls bundled up high on her head. The smoothness of her alabaster neck peeped between the folds of an emerald-green scarf. And when he saw the sky blue of her eyes shining like sapphires, he felt his shoulders slack. His heart toppled from its perch, tumbling.

Annie smiled a smile meant only for him. "I take it you like the dress?"

"I... I love it."

"Sarah's. She let me borrow it. I've never bought a dress or had much need for them, but after I saw you dressed so fine, I thought I might make us a matching pair."

Carson extended his elbow to her. Annie slid a gloved hand through the crook of his arm, her fingers resting ever so gently on his forearm.

They made their way out the back of the train, down the caboose steps, and through the train station. It was cold out but not as uncomfortable as it had been. The arches of the station exit were all powdered with snow. There was little wind. The calmness of the night was a welcome relief.

Just outside the station were carriages and buggies waiting patiently for cargo or passengers. Carson picked a carriage and, after helping Annie inside, looked up at the driver.

"Yes, sir?" said the driver, his voice a pinched, whistling sound. He was a little man and bundled in black wool, much of his features hidden behind a wide-brimmed hat pulled low.

"Take us to the best section of the town," said Carson. "Best place to see. Best place to have a meal. We're in no rush."

The man's hat bobbed up and down. "That'll be the south side, near the Eads."

"The Eads?"

"New bridge they been working on. A marvel of engineering, they say. New York is calling it the eighth wonder of the world. You've never seen anything of its like."

Carson nodded. "Perfect." He stood on the rail, bringing him closer to the driver. Lowering his voice, he said, "Look, this might be the most important night of my life, so don't feel the need to rush."

The driver laughed. "I saw the girl. I understand your meaning entirely, sir."

Carson passed the man a silver piece and then joined Annie inside the carriage.

"Where are we headed," she asked, sliding close to lean her weight against him.

"South is all I know. I've put my trust in the driver to show us the sights."

And what a sight St. Louis was, with its long, black roads rowed with snow. The whole city, lighted by the sodium glow of gas lamps, was so clear and bright that the snowbanks sparkled like rolling waves of crushed diamonds. The driver, never rushing, wheeled through parks filled with arched pavilions and empty picnic tables. The grounds were teeming with riders and strollers alike, populating the walkways.

They watched as a trio of children rushed away from

their parents, wading into the powder to laugh, so innocent and so free of all the fear only their parents could know. Their happiness came in tumbles of cheers, rolling unashamed through the night over crystalline carpets of white. In their little hands they balled projectiles, throwing them at one another.

Annie giggled at the sight.

Carson couldn't remember ever hearing that particular sound come out of her. It was young, unscarred.

"Look at them!" she said.

"Looks like fun," he said. "You ever have a snowball fight?"

"No. It would sometimes frost over in Yellow Hill, but never snow like this. You?"

"Never had anyone to throw snowballs with."

"Georgie would have loved this," said Annie, pressing her weight deeper into him. "I think Momma would have loved it too. She hated the Texas heat. Come to think of it, I think she hated everything about Texas."

"Living in West Texas will likely do that to you. But it has its charms, I suppose. Every little corner of the world does."

"You've been all over the states. What's the best place you've ever been?"

Carson thought about that for a time, looking out the window at the grandeur of St. Louis with its great buildings of brick and white mortar looking fresh and sharp in the gas light. Then, he said, "I can't imagine any place better than this. Certainly not a better feeling than I am feeling right now."

"Guess that barber was right," she said.

"You?"

"Well, aside from the circumstances, Chicago was bea—" Her eyes widened, and her hand shot out to point. "Look at that!"

Carson followed the strong line of her smooth arm and looked.

Though it reached only three-quarters across the black Mississippi, there stretched a bridge longer than Carson had ever thought possible. A trio of arches supported the work of iron and stone. "That must be the Eads," he said.

"How on earth do they set the foundation? The river must be so deep here."

It was hard to believe that it was real. Hard to believe anything so glorious could withstand the dark and powerful Mississippi. If such a thing could exist, master such a force, then perhaps Carson could find a way to master the darkness rushing through his life. Maybe there was a way to bridge the gap between the life he was living and the life he wanted to have.

They rolled past the Eads, astonished at whatever work of man had made it possible, and into South St. Louis, which bustled with little shops and eateries, hotels and saloons. Though the people of St. Louis did not carry the same fervor as those in New Orleans, there was ostensibly a sense of calm persistence—a resistance that could not be overtaken—telling the timeless story of the human race: of a people who, even when assailed by all the world's circumstances, could make the very best of subsistence. Living as best as they could in the times they were drawn into.

The driver pulled to a halt, centering the carriage window before a wooden sign reading 'Picadilly's.'

He got down and opened the door for them. "Welcome to Picadilly's," he said. "If there is a better plate to be had in St. Louis, I do not know of it."

They stepped off the carriage onto the sidewalk. The driver tipped his hat to Annie with a courtly bow, going so far for another tip that he went to the double doors of Picadilly's and, with a grand flourish, opened the way for them. Carson rewarded him with a five-dollar piece.

The interior of the restaurant was, in a word, opulent. All brass and red wood surfaces, rugs and drapes tasseled in fine gold thread. There were only eight tables to the whole place, each of them adorned with crystal goblets turned upside down on golden tablecloths. A man in a tuxedo, who stood as stiff as the lectern in front of him, tilted a tight smile at them.

"Bonne soirée, and hello, good evening and, above all welcome, *madam* and *monsieur* to Picadilly's."

"Quite the introduction," said Annie.

"Evening," said Carson.

"I can hear the sound of Texas in your voices," he said, wagging a finger before them. "You are visitors to our fine city and so let me be the *first* to welcome you to the jewel of Missouri, St. Louis. I am guessing from the lady's ravishing attire that we are on an *escapade romantique*, yes?"

Carson opened his mouth, unsure of what to say.

"But of course. You are here for. . . let me guess, an anniversary?"

Carson and Annie, both smiling and shaking their heads, looked at each other.

The man barreled through their missed opportunity to answer him. "No? Then we shall say that tonight is the first evening that shall *become* an anniversary. The night that madam and monsieur became intertwined," he said, lacing his hands together tightly in front of his chest. "Yes!" His smile widened. "Yes, of course. This is that night!"

"Jesus Christ," said Annie, cursing with laughter. "Can we sit at a table, or should we read the vows and have the ceremony right here and now?"

Carson shot a sharp look over at the man in the tuxedo.

He let out a proper giggle of an apology and, with a loud stamp of his foot, shot out his hand. The napkin wrapped around his forearm waved with the gesture. "Most certainly, madam. For you, our very best *offre*." He guided them toward a table at the center of the restaurant, turning back once to introduce himself as Alphonse.

Carson sat, allowing Alphonse the courtesy of sliding out Annie's chair.

"Tonight," Alphonse began again, the flair of the theater more evident than ever, "tonight you shall enjoy our finest. A five-course meal. A complete culinary delight that is—to use a raw, frontier idiom—soup to nuts, the very best French cuisine has to offer." At this, Alphonse laughed. "But first, the wine. The wine is the beginning; and not since the Word was first spoken in Genesis has there been a greater beginning than our Spanish red. Made not from one grape, but from *deux!*"

Carson placed a hand gently over the napkin upon Alphonse's arm. "That's fine. All of that will be fine. The very best is what we would like. But also, too, I would like the share of our own company, as much as we can."

At this, Alphonse was not hurt but emboldened in his duties. "This, at Picadilly's, is no problem, monsieur."

And the waiter was true to his word. After the wine was poured, Annie and Carson were able to focus on each other without interruption.

Their conversation went this way and that. The courses came slowly, one at a time. And it was not until after dessert, when there was only wine and their laughter left at the table, that the conversation swayed from sweet to serious. Annie, of course, brought up the Red Kingdom and the inescapable battle yet to come. Carson sighed at the thought of sharing this evening with any talk of calamity and death. Those conversations had canopied the entirety of his life, and he didn't want them anymore. At least, not tonight. So, he looked at Annie, who was trying to discuss the amount of silver they had cached in the train, and he shook his head.

"You don't think we have enough?" she asked.

"There's plenty of silver. It's time I don't want to run

out of, Annie." He swallowed hard. "You are very beautiful."

"Carson, I—" she said, blue eyes burning above the flush of her cheeks. "No one has ever taken me anywhere like this before. Talked to me the way you talk. It feels like a gift. I'm not sure what to do with it. I mean. . ." She laughed.

The notes of her laughter the sweetest song.

"I've never given it before. There was never a reason. . . not before you."

Her lips trembled. She swallowed, placing a hand over her heart, eyes wet.

"Annie?"

"Yes, Carson."

"I don't know what is going to happen after tonight. After this moment here with you. I only know that I don't want it to end. That's how I've always felt about you, since we met in Yellow Hill. When you came out—you were wearing a yellow sundress ringed with white flowers—and I remember losing myself for the first time, falling. . . somehow falling outside of myself. Into someone else. And I remember looking at you as Gilbert and I rode away, and I made a vow: I swore that it would not be the last time I saw your face. And before I got back to Abilene, I wondered, Does this girl know what she did to me?" He clenched his jaw, looking up from his wine glass into her eyes. "And did I make her feel the same way?"

Annie's eyes were a constellation of candlelight and tears. "I didn't feel that way in that moment, Carson."

He looked to the table.

"But I feel it now."

He looked at her, seeing everything.

Annie reached the hand she had rested over her heart to lay upon his. "And that makes *me* wonder, Carson, does this man know just how important he is? Not to the Peregrine Estate, not to the world, but to me."

CHAPTER THIRTEEN

ABOARD *THE JUDGE*, EN ROUTE TO FORT SCOTT, KANSAS

It was nine in the morning, the sky darker than pitch. Lamps posted along the railyard illuminated a lone iron serpent. *The Judge*, furnace roaring, burdened with lumber and coal, was finally ready to make the push from dark St. Louis to Fort Scott. The whistle screamed. White blossoms of steam billowed from the black, snow-powdered stack. Ashley Sutliff, wearing a navy suit, stepped up onto the train, shook the snow from his coat, and made his way to the passenger cars. Business concluded and telegrams sent, he decided that now was the perfect time to get the deck of his employees shuffled into the diner car. Though he hated waiting, it had its purposes. But now it was time to discuss strategy, tactics, logistics. He had things to say, things they needed to know.

If things went the way he planned, the Vampire War—as some of the gunfighters had begun to call it while drunk and running their mouths—would be the shortest campaign in American history. The attack would be all out. Sudden and brutal. Twelve thousand soldiers, many of them Union holdovers from the Slaver's Revolt, would have their names stamped into the chronicle of history for the second time in their lives.

And the plan *would* work. Ashley had seen to every detail, just as he had during the Werewolf Campaign under Judge Ellison. However, he had already decided this would be the last campaign of his life. After this, he was all through with fighting.

Walking down the passenger cars, he banged on doors. "All late risers up," he said, voice booming. "We're all meeting in the diner car!"

About halfway down the car, he went to bang on a door just as it slid open and almost slapped Carson Ptolemy on the forehead.

The young man looked at him, his eyes widening. His coat was draped over one arm, his shirt wrinkled, tie dangling loose around his neck. His hair tangled wild as a bird's nest.

Before Ashley could peer inside the compartment, Carson quickly slid the door shut behind him. "Sutliff," he said, then cleared his throat.

Ashley gave him a devil's smile. "Mr. Ptolemy," he said, taking his time with the name. "If I recall correctly, your quarters are back down that hallway there." He pointed toward the caboose end of the train.

"I— Right."

The young man looked down the passenger car.

Ashley shook his head, trying not to laugh. "Dipping your wick in the midnight oil?"

"Now wait—"

But the gambler had no time for that. Ashley leaned forward, mockingly polite. "If I could just reach past you here. I need to. . ." He cleared his voice, savoring Carson's embarrassment." He reached over Carson's shoulder and knocked on the door. Raising his voice, he said, "Ms. Miller, we're meeting in the diner car for an important strategy discussion. I'm certain you'll want to attend."

Silence.

Carson furrowed his brow, his embarrassment fading into frustration.

Ashley cleared his throat, this time speaking louder. "Ms. Miller?"

"Yes," came Annie's voice from within her room. "Yes, *thank you*, Mr. Sutliff. I will be there presently."

He gave Carson a wink. "You can come, too, stud."

Carson glared.

"If you aren't too wore out, that is."

"Piss off, Sutliff."

Ashley made a little flourish of his hand, a mocking goodbye. "Better than being pissed on, Mr. Ptolemy."

He had teased Carson, relishing in the young man's fluster, but in truth, Ashley was a little more than surprised to see Annie with him. He found Carson to be stiff-necked, self-righteous at times. Even unlikeable. Just like Gilbert had been. Still, a part of him was deeply pleased to see the two of them come together. Carson would need Annie and that deep fiery strength inside her. And all at once Ashely found himself thinking about the young woman. How much she had survived. Just how strong she must be to not only live in such a time but to lead. He might even have come to admire the woman if she weren't so goddamn ornery. They would make quite the pair, he thought, as he strode up the rest of the passenger cars telling folks there was a meeting.

He got to the diner car, passing by several gunhands breaking their fast, and poured himself a cup of black coffee. A little sugar cut the bitter, making it palatable. Easy to swallow.

Five minutes passed. Five long minutes, where his loose, easygoing demeanor began to coil viper-tight with each passing second. People piled in, took seats at the booths. When the booths were all gone, and the tables full, the rest of the gunfighters were forced to stand, hats in their hands.

"Are they all here?" he asked Sven, who had come to sit next to Sarah Lockhart.

"All but our two."

"Well, I'm done waiting." He raised his voice, his tone razor sharp. "Your attention, if you would, ladies and gents. I've called everyone here because I want to make a few things clear about what is going to happen the moment we step foot off this train in Fort Scott."

A beady-eyed, heavy Mexican, Reyes they had called him, took a deep breath and opened a half-grin to say, "Yeah, we're gonna—"

"Mister Reyes here has something he wants to say," said Ashley, his voice cold and sharp. "Something he thinks is funny, but it's not going to be funny. It's going to be even stupider than the look on his stupid fucking face." He took a sip of his coffee, let the insult suck all the air out of the car. "We're nine hours from Fort Scott, and I've let things run pretty loose since you all piled onto this train. I've commissioned every comfort for you: you've had the finest food, and the finest booze, all at the expense of my patron. Good for you all. Enjoy it while it lasts. And I'm given to understand that, by reputation, you Guild members have a tendency to run fast and loose with the rules and expectations of your other employers. That is because each of you tend to get results. That's also good. I'm a results-oriented kind of man. But, I am not like your other employers, and this is not like any other employment you have ever known."

He took a breath. "Some of you may wonder how a gambler, even one as good as me," he said winking, "was able to afford the entire rank of the Gunfighter's Guild. Well, my money comes by way of the American government. My commission is from President Grant himself."

A wave of surprise rippled through the attendees. But Ashley had no time for their shock. He went on.

"So let me make it painfully, brutally clear that when you step off this train, should you do anything that puts our American mission into peril, I will either personally, or by way of American authority, have you hanged or shot. And this, gunfighters, is the only—and I mean only—fucking warning you will get. How's that for clear?"

"The balls on this son of a bitch," said Combs, leaning against a corner of the car, arms crossed over his chest.

All the gunfighters laughed.

No, thought Ashley. That will not do. He stared at the hardened killer, unblinking. "You... you're Combs, right?"

Combs nodded, seeming unperturbed by the man's glare.

Ashley decided to gamble. He tucked his hands into his pockets and walked the length of the car toward one of the most dangerous gunhands living on the planet. "Number Nine in the Guild, yes?"

Combs puffed out his chest. They were equal in height, equal in unwavering eyes. "Yeah. That's right."

"You must be fast to be in the top ten..." Ashley broke his gaze to scan the surrounding gunfighters.

No cards, but he was making a wager. This was the deal.

"Faster than y—"

His hand was out of the pocket fast as a rattlesnake, without any warning, and wrapped around Combs's wrist. Combs had, by instinct, gone for his revolver, his fingers clamping around the smooth sandalwood grip. The weight of Ashley's arm pinned the gunfighter's hand in place.

That was the turn.

The river came in the form of a slender knife in Ashley's other hand, out of his pocket and whistling through the air, the terminus of the blade making a dimple just under Combs's eye.

"Faster than who, Nine?" asked Ashley.

Combs sucked in a deep breath.

"Faster than *who?*"

The gunfighter swallowed hard.

"Question for you," said Ashley. He flipped the knife over once and caught it by the handle, so that it now made a dimple in the throbbing vein in the man's throat. "You know how fast a vampire moves, Nine?"

He spoke through clenched teeth. "No."

"Well, faster than me. Which means faster than you." Ashley turned to scan them all now. "Faster than *all* of you. Make no mistake. They get this close, and you won't be the Nine, or any number. They'll unzip you, brains"—he tapped Combs on the head with the tip of the knife, then glided the blade down his shirt and belt, where he tapped metal on metal—"to balls."

Ashley turned on his heel, giving his back to the gunfighter without fear. "That's the picture, ladies and gents. That's the clearest picture I can paint for you. Do your jobs. Do what I say, when I say it, and who knows," he said, picking up his coffee cup. Just before taking a sip, he concluded, "You all might just live long enough to spend all that American money I'm going to pay you."

Reyes shoved the sulking Combs at the shoulder. Gunfighters began to laugh.

Ashley sat down opposite Sven.

Sarah shook her head, grinning wide. "Nice trick there. Getting that close."

"He'll never let you get that close again," said Sven. "None of them will."

"Getting close wasn't the point."

"Please, illuminate me then."

"You gunfighters are all the same. Just like gamblers, you love the flair of the dramatic. Love for people to see what, from a distance, you can do. It's why y'all do that stupid fucking litany before each showdown. Every one of you go through life with the absolute certainty that there are only twenty-five men and women in the world who can claim to be as *good* as you think you are. I showed you that it doesn't take a member of the Guild to get the drop on you."

"Lots of them already knew that," said Sarah.

"Combs didn't," said Ashley. "Now he does. They all do. Things go well enough for him, he'll thank me for it when this is all said and done."

"Well," said Sven, "you've played your one hand there, gambler. But hell of a hand."

"The luxury of the train ride had them loose, which was fine for then, but now," said Ashley, watching the line of tension running through each gunfighter, "now the prospect of death has been reintroduced into their minds. This is their present reality. And until this conflict with the Red Kingdom is over, this is what's going to keep them alive."

"Sure," said Sarah, rolling her eyes. "I'm sure this was all about making sure they stay alive and not about hearing yourself talk. Seeing, as you said, gamblers loving that flair of the dramatic."

Sarah Lockhart, Ashley considered, was absolutely gorgeous. Absolutely a bitch.

And, deep down, he knew she was absolutely right.

What was worse, she knew it, too.

"Where are Annie and Carson?" Sven asked her.

"If the state in which they returned to the train is any indication, either in his bunk or hers."

"Cheek to cheek?" asked the big Swede.

"And arm in arm."

Ashley watched the two of them at the expression of that sentiment. Sven looked out the window, thinking of Cornish no doubt, and Sarah fiddled with the tablecloth, remembering someone too. They both wore bittersweet smiles, the tell-tale sign of broken hearts never to mend.

He'd never say it, but he felt sorry for them. Not sorry that they had lost whatever souls had enflamed their passions—every person alive and dead had felt that. No, he was sorry that they had to watch two young people fall in love before their very eyes, with the knowledge that in this life of a Peregrine agent, a bittersweet smile would be all that was left for one of them. Life was that way. Ashley didn't know which one it would be. Maybe they'd get lucky and both die together, hand in hand on the battlefield. Or maybe, just maybe, they'd be luckier still and make it out alive together.

But in his experience, no one ever got that lucky.

The three people at the table were all living proof of that.

CHAPTER FOURTEEN

THE RED KINGDOM

A king asked John Childs his name.

John, stripped at the waist, wearing only his trousers and a pair of boots, answered.

The walls of the throne room were smooth stone, a dome shaven into the heart of the Astolats. Scarlet flames danced from iron, cage-like sconces. The ruddy light illuminated the stone throne but did not touch, perhaps could never touch, the shadow that spoke at its seat. John had seen Kristian in the dim light of the perpetual eclipse outside, but in this place, this center of his authority, the light did not so much move around him as it passed through him, the central aspect of light's nature nullified. John came to understand, very quickly, the light could not touch the shadow in this place without the shadow's consent.

That shadow had a voice.

"How come you to judge my fair city, John Childs?"

John opened his mouth. What could someone say to

such a creature? Though he could not see it, he *felt* the shadow smile.

Then, the shadow rose, allowing the fingers of light to dress him in their fiery dyes. "Please, speak freely. I know from the minds of the other cattle that you were kind in your old position, and you are considered wise and deferential. I respect the opinions of such men, for I was once a man, too."

That's impossible, John thought.

"There is much in this world that we cannot, nor will we ever, understand,"

said Kristian, clearly reading John's thoughts the moment they came into his mind. "If the passing of time has taught me anything, it is that. . ."

Are you. . . inside my mind?

"A force of habit, I'm afraid. I am, by nature, a conspiratorial creature, and so I see conspiracy in everyone around me. If you give me your word as an officer of human law, and as a man, I will draw my siphon from your thoughts. Will you be honest with me, John Childs?"

"Do not lie," came a powerful basso voice from over his shoulder, and the clacking of boots on smooth wet stone. "He will know if you do."

A tall dark figure slathered in a cape coat passed John by.

"Ah, Sigurd. Come, friend," said Kristian, and smiled. The monarch's teeth shone like wet pearl, and they were, all of them, sharp. The canines needle tipped.

Though Kristian used a monarch's title, Sigurd did not bow to him. Did not kneel. Did not do anything but approach his king and embrace him. It was such a warm gesture, such a *human* gesture.

"The American forces are. . ." Sigurd turned to look back at John, suspicion in his predatory stare.

Though John was a brave man, that gaze diminished him.

Kristian laughed. "Pay that one no mind. I'm thinking of making him my cupbearer."

The fuck is a cupbearer? John thought.

Kristian laughed.

"The American forces are rallied," continued Sigurd. "Grant knows of us now, and he understands that we are a threat. One he believes he can deal with a resurrection of his Army of the Potomac. He is drawing a measure of his strength in the form of a division of soldiers at Fort Scott, Kansas. Ten, perhaps fifteen, thousand."

"*Grant,*" said Kristian, dismissive. "He wins a single conflict against a little pretender rebellion, and now he thinks himself a champion." Kristian sat back upon his throne, again becoming shadow itself. "Tell me your thoughts, my fearsome hand."

"Send me to Washington. Give me a dozen of our eld. A hundred of our youth. And let me, with a single stroke, break a nation."

At the sound of those cold, venomous words, a sweat broke over John's brow. They would destroy not just Colorado, but the country—the very country John had fought to preserve. And at that thought, the fire of rage flared back to life from where it had been smoldering in his heart.

"My sweet Sigurd, still so young, so hot with the fire of your greener days. These are not the crusader wars, my friend, where all we had to fear was the cold bite of steel from which we could easily recover. We are faster, more powerful, yes. But the cattle are not as they once were, not with their rifles and cannons and. . . organization. Napoleon's genius has molded them into a new, more dangerous shape. Just as Philip of Macedon did, and Cincinnatus before him. How many times, my brave knight, must I teach the lesson—the lesson that my gift of long life deafens to your ear? We are ancient, and few. We worship—"

"The blood," said Sigurd, completing the mantra. "The life."

"Yes. Life itself." The shadow leaned back to look at John Childs, standing half-naked, and listening. "The cattle do not worship blood or life; their god is death, and war is their worship. Their pure, instinctual drive to dominate is what has made them this sphere's greatest surviving animal without ever becoming its greatest predator. It is what so mightily speeds their Hermes-quick ability to adapt."

"If we stamp out their leaders—"

"Sigurd," he said, the sound no greater than a whisper bearing the power of a thunderclap. "They are aware of us now. This means their governors and masters will have sought out the knowledge that, before, only a few pockets of the herd have known. The knowledge of silver and light and fire."

Fire. John let the word pass through him as easily as the light passed through the shadow on the throne.

"If Grant knows of this," the shadow continued, "it means he has fortified himself entirely. Washington, though only a few days flight on the wind of your wings, is no more available to you than Olympus to Bellerophon. And if you crush Grant, raze Washington itself, the cattle will only elect another head and find another city wherein to hide him. Whither would you go, my champion? Would you rake at the heart of their species from city to city, only to allow their great adaptation to escalate their will of survival... above us?"

The dark and mighty knight Sigurd took a step back. "Never."

"This is our position, Sigurd. We cannot have the whole world. None can. The mightiest leviathan can, to this, attest. This lightning rage you harbor isn't for Grant or for the Americans. This is about the boy. This is about what happened in Big Spring. Why you acted outside *my will.*" It was at that final word that the red fires within their iron cages shuddered, flaring white hot, then returned to their ruddy dim. "Your anger with them," said the king veiled in shadow, "your tempest for revenge over the loss of your wife—"

"Wife?" John said. The word, unlike the ones prior, John could not let go by. It had fallen out of his mind, passing over his lips, due to his inability to comprehend how these monstrosities could ever know a feeling like the one John had known for Mary Elaine.

Sigurd erupted at the sound, the cape of his coat thrown back, massive bat-like wings expanded to swallow the great stone chair and the shadow sitting upon it. "Quiet, cow."

"Sigurd..." whispered the shadow.

At the utterance of his name, Sigurd diminished. His turgid wings and shining talons heaved up and down with his deep breaths.

"Greatest of my children."

The wings relaxed entirely, receding to their hiding place. Sigurd turned back to the throne. Back to the shadow.

"Your enemies are eager. Hot blooded. They are, as they say, spoiling for a fight. They will come to Black Wells, here to the mountain. And, when they do, we will descend upon them, tooth and claw. Bloody them hip to thigh."

"I do not believe we should wait for them. We have an advantage now. Our spy has worked to bring all these pieces together in Fort Scott."

"You have one of your friends there, yes? Your young boy... Wesley?"

"A friend, yes, but not Wesley; he is too wild. He is a hacking saber thirsty for blood. No, this agent of mine is not yet one of us, but I have promised him our gift, should he prove himself when the time comes. He is working to understand how this blizzard and night remain, and he has promised me that if we grant him immortality, he will ensure the all-night forever."

"Yes," said the king, the weight of his shadow settled against the stone seat. "There is the place for assault, Sir Sigurd. The place where we can break a measure of the American strength. Destroy a whole division at Fort Scott with the ease and safety of extinguishing a candle."

"That will not be enough to break the American resolve," said Sigurd.

"One candle at a time, Sigurd. Eventually, the people of this land will run out of the fire to light them. Now," he waved a hand, "go. Take with you whatever forces you need. Destroy the division entirely. And bring me this agent of yours, that he might work among us in safety, free from distraction."

With that, Sigurd turned and exited, leaving John Childs to stand once again alone before the shadow and the scarlet fires surrounding his throne.

Kristian considered the man before him. "Mary Elaine." He said the name as if it had come from John's own lips. Careful, tender, an old wound. "She was. . ."

John winced at the sensation of Kristian's influence, crawling like a nimble spider through the cobwebs of his memories.

"She was everything to you, and I can feel that she still is. Ah," said the shadow, leaning forward to allow the scarlet lamps to illuminate his form once again. "In all my long life, I have only known at a distance a love such as this. I have felt it so many times before though—felt it in Sigurd with his sweet Abelia, like I feel it now in you. That moment birthed inside when the lightning of our will and the flame of our passions collide, twisting together in a pillar that burns consequences to ash, striking into the sands of time a bolt so hot and clear that it transforms all those many grains to a single spindle of glass."

How–how can you do this? Be inside my mind.

"How do you breathe, John Childs? Do you actively command your heart to beat? It is as simple a mystery as mystery can be. The only kind of mystery there is. I was once a man, and when I was a man no longer, I simply could. And because I can, I do. But your Mary Elaine. . . I want you to concentrate, to fall into the well of your memories and picture her. Do this for me."

John stiffened, not wanting to provide such a gift to such a creature. *No.*

Kristian's eyebrow lifted. "You are a proud man. I see that. If you do not provide that which I require, I will compel you. Our wills shall collide against one another, John. You and I know that should it come to a contest between your pride and my will—"

It will be no contest at all, John thought. But they weren't his words. Weren't his thoughts.

A deep, tremulous feeling sank into the pit of John's stomach. It was the moment he realized that there was nothing he could hide from this. . . this shadow parading as a king. A pearl of sweat fell from his brow, rolling to the thrust of his chin. It fell to the stone floor, and the softness of its sound boomed like the shot of a canon in his ears.

"Do not force to me to take," said Kristian, "that which I only wish to ask for."

John, feeling very alone and very afraid, leaned down into his memories. He brought into his mind the clearest picture of the green of the hill, the yellow of the sunrise, and the shining face of the woman who had broken his heart.

The strangest thing happened then. The image of Mary Elaine became something more, something not imagined. . . but conjured. He could feel the cool spring breeze blowing through her hair. He smelled the wildflowers. Tasted the flavor of her lips on his own. He was living inside that memory, no longer seeing it through the window of his mind but through the portals of his closed eyes.

There came a simple pressure, two points that sank deep into his neck. But he didn't mind them, because the deeper the pressure, the more vivid Mary became. And all at once she was there, holding his hand. Smiling, radiant.

Her lips parted, and in a voice that must have been a thousand miles away, she said, "Thank you, John. My cupbearer."

CHAPTER FIFTEEN

Fort Scott, Kansas

Many years ago, Judge Ellison had described the Kansas plains as only he could. "Carson," he had said, his pipe drifting this way and that with the swaying rhythm of the gelding beneath him. "The plains are like nothing you've ever dreamed. Grasses rolling out. Tall and wild and green as a cricket in summer. In autumn they glow gold with Heaven's own shine. And buffalo. . . my word, the buffalo. Horned behemoths robed in black and brown with shoulders thick as an oak is wide."

They had gone out riding for a picnic while Gilbert was off in San Antonio on a job. The Judge rode, happy as you please, smoking and swaying and storying.

"They run in the millions up there, my boy. You understand that number?"

Carson nodded, having all the confidence and not one damn clue as to what a million meant. He only knew that the word itself suggested something more than a hundred, and he had seen a hundred people all at once only a few days prior at a town festival. At the time, seeing all those cowboy hats and bonneted ladies and horses and carriages wheeling their way to the festival grounds, the hundred of them had seemed like all the people in the whole wide world.

"They start running, and the whole ground begins to shake, quaking like the devil himself is bustin' loose of Hell. Yes, sir, boss," the Judge said, winking at Carson. "You ever get yourself up to Kansas, and you'll be in for something else."

As a boy, Carson dreamed of seeing it for himself. And in his dreams, Judge Ellison was always with him, nodding with that big toothy grin shining through the mossy tangle of his black beard, the smoke of his pipe curling 'eights' in the air.

But the Judge was gone. The man would live on only in Carson's dreams.

Now, as an adult, Carson was excited to know that the first time he would see those plains, he would share that moment with Annie Miller. The grasses would not burn gold or green, not with the sun hiding its face against the cold, but there would be beauty there, he knew that. No matter what the landscape gave them, Annie would be there, and the woman herself would make pretty every visible horizon, no matter how bleak.

Peregrine agents and gunfighters climbed upon the mounts carried within the train's horse cars. None of the riders enjoyed the long time it took to unwrap the horses' legs, and the horses hated being removed from the warmth of their blankets, the train, and each other. A harsh wind bristled hide and hair on man and beast alike.

All saddled up, the impromptu cavalry of Silver Pins and what remained of the Peregrine Estate rode out from the train station of Fort Scott, crunching their way through the snowpack.

Annie and Carson, and Ashley and Sarah, rode at the point position. Their horses, big German drafters, punched a trail through frost that gave way to rolling hills of downy powder. When Sarah lifted a fist into the air and hollered, the muted thunder of their collective mounts' hooves quickly rumbled to silent stillness.

"What the hell?" asked Ashley. "The fort is still a mile or two from here. Why are we stopping?"

Sarah Lockhart shushed him, extending a gloved hand to point at the swollen, gray clouds.

Carson followed her gesture to the clouds where, in the light of the perpetual eclipse, against the steel of the cloud rack, a twisting swirl of shadows circled. The howl of the wind faded, bringing into earshot the chorus of triumphant caws.

"Vultures," said Annie.

"Well," said Ashley. "Let's go see what's for supper." He pushed forward to crest the top of the hill.

Over the hill, there came into view a white landscape desolated red. They rode down into a vast circle of churned-up snow populated with black-brown forms. Crystalized blood sparkling in the eclipse light. Countless buffaloes, their hides splayed open at their bellies to reveal purple ropes of entrails and gaping black apertures where their hearts had once resided.

"Buffalo hunters," said Ashley.

"If they were hunting for pelts then why—"

Annie cut Sarah off. "There." She pointed to a circle of covered wagons in the distance. Many of them were turned over, their wooden wheels dusted with snow.

"They were hunting all right," said Ashley. "But something else did this."

"Wolves," said Annie.

"Bullshit," said Ashley, "ain't no wolf, or any pack big enough to—"

"Not those wolves." Annie looked over at Carson. "Carson, what's wrong?"

It wasn't the word that did it, but something deep

inside Carson twisted tight. His face flushed, and his eyesight blurred with tears. Over the cawing of what must have been a thousand vultures and more, Carson began to hear a sound at the edge of his vision. No, not a sound.

"The song," said Carson.

"Carson?" asked Annie.

"It's the song of the Nine."

"Sarah," called Annie. "Something's happening to—"

Over the sound of the wind and the death music of the cawing vultures came the deafening howl of innumerable predatory throats.

In Carson's ears, the song was louder than nature and all beasts combined. The world began to spin.

The horses whinnied, steam venting from their nostrils.

"The fuck is that?" The voice of Combs busted out over the stamping remuda.

The song pounded Carson, tipping him at the shoulders. The world went dark all around him, and he fell from his saddle. He expected to hit the snowpack, to fall into it, but not *through* it.

He fell through it to the mantle of the earth. And into the dark void of space.

There, waiting for him, was the great, monstrous eye.

The dark song it sang swallowed him.

* * *

Annie heard the great beasts. The sound sent her mind rushing back to the cattle drive almost a year ago, back to Fort Stockton. The howling sent a lance of panic through her, but where others might have frozen, Annie did not hesitate. She swiveled in the saddle to look at Sarah and Ashley, and when she saw the confused looks on their faces, she knew that she was the only one who could ensure they had any chance of survival. Drawing her pistol, she turned back to Carson. His color was all gone, and his eyes were darkened with sudden fatigue. He leaned one way, then too far back the other, and plunged face first into the snow.

She screamed his name, called to Sarah for help.

This could not be happening, not now. Not at this moment, all crowded with howls ushered from throats and the hungry maws and glistening snouts that would soon smell the living flesh of horses and people. And when those monsters caught the hot scent, Annie knew their only chance would be to run.

And how could she run when the man she loved was incapable of following?

Simple. She wouldn't.

She would risk the fate of the whole world if it meant keeping Carson alive.

Every eye snapped over to her as she dismounted. Knee deep in the snow, she took Carson by the shoulders and began to lift him. Though he was not big, the weight of him seemed too much for her alone. Before she could call for help, a second pair of hands clasped on either side of hers.

"I'm here," said Sarah Lockhart.

Annie pulled and, manifesting a great strength with the help of her friend, pulled the young man from the snow.

"I've got him," said Sarah, breathing heavy. "Now, you go tell those Silver Pins how to kill those goddamn creatures before they get on top of us."

Annie nodded, then turned. Lifted her voice high into the air. "Listen up! Every eye and ear on me! Circle up at the top of the hill. These things are hard to kill, but they *can* be killed. Bullets do not penetrate their hides; aim for the eyes and the mouth!"

But no one moved, they just looked at her and Sarah

trying to help Carson up. Then they looked to Ashley Sutliff, their employer.

Ashley's turned his head to Annie, his eyes narrowing with the flurry of calculations wheeling through his mind. He drew his long rifle from its deer-hide sheath, the length of its nickel-plated barrel shining like a burning shaft of silver. "The fuck you lookin' at me for. She said circle up!"

"Annie," said Sarah, her voice low so that only Annie could hear. "I seem to recall you telling me that the only way you survived that pack in Fort Stockton was because you outran them."

Annie, desperate, looked at Carson, then back to Sarah.

A bulge formed on Sarah's jaw as she grit her teeth.

A silent understanding passed between the two women.

"Get to your horse, you're a better shot than I'll ever be," said Annie. "I've got him."

Sarah nodded, stood up, and quickly mounted her mare. The horse chopped up the snow, wheeling in a circle to face Annie once more.

"Do not let them get close to him, Sarah."

A fierce, righteous grimace cut a hard line across Sarah's face. "Never." She gave her horse a little kick and trotted through the powder to take her place at the perimeter of the circle with the gunfighters. "All right, you expensive shits," Sarah barked over the tumult. "Let's see if you're worth every red nickel this fucking gambler has promised."

The mounted men and women ringed the top of the bald hill, and through the gaps between their horses, Annie could make out the forms of the slavering, charging pack.

"Carson," said Annie, pulling him so that his shoulders lay in her lap. "Carson, wake up!"

He began to tremble. That tremble became a panicked quake. His mouth opened, wide as a snake in mid-strike, so wide that the popping of his jaw sounded like the dull, distant repeat of a rifle echoing over the plain.

"Carson!" Not knowing what to do, she shook him. Slapped him. "Wake up, goddamn it!"

"Jesus Christ," screamed one of the gunfighters.

"I always knew you were a goddamn coward, Reyes," Sven roared. Then, the big man began to laugh. "I always *knew*. Now, the rest of you, you watch and see what a real gunfighter can do."

The crunching of snow, mingled with the thunderous rumble of the approaching pack, filled the night. And over it came the voice of Sarah Lockhart. "Ready!" Then, "Not yet!"

The rumble of the pack grew closer... closer still.

Sarah, lengthening the word with a guttural strain, said, "Ready!"

"Come get some, hellhounds!" screamed Sven, laughing. Fearless.

"Fire!"

A battery of pistols, rifles, and shotguns pounded the air, ringing Annie and trembling Carson in a wreathe of smoke. There came a multitudinous shriek, the wailing of wounded beasts. So great was the accuracy of the Silver Pins that the pack of monstrosities was repulsed entirely. The circle of their defense remained sincere to its form, an unbroken ring. The howling pack twisted away as one, deterred but not defeated.

"Combs," hollered Sven, as sounds of the pack faded then began to rise again. "Did you fucking miss!" Again, he laughed.

"Comin' back around!" Ashley bellowed.

Sven roared again. "Good. Because I'm not quite done with killing today!"

Annie shook Carson. "Please."

His mouth snapped shut so hard, one of his false teeth went flying out of his mouth and into the snow. Annie felt the warmth of him receding; he was so cold that his breathing no longer steamed the air.

Was he dying?

"Ready!"

Would this be the next great cruelty in her life?

"Aim!" Sarah commanded.

No, thought Annie. She had given her heart over to this man—had staked her claim on his life—and nothing in this world could take him from her.

"Carson Watts Ptolemy, you promised me. And by God, you're going to keep your promise."

"Fire!"

Gunfire again ripped across the hill, a bevy of thunderclaps, then a loud curse and desperate whinnying of a horse. One of the massive black terrors busted through the line between two gunfighters, their rifles smoking hot against the cold, hacking wind.

"We're breached!" cried Ashley.

"Die. Die!" Sven howled, his gun barking with murderous frenzy, firing into the pack outside the circle.

Annie, seeing it come barreling through, drew her pistol smooth and quick. Waited less than a heartbeat.

She fired.

The bullet sheered a long, wet line across the creature's skull, but still it came on, mouth wide and hungry, a shining tunnel of a hundred serrated teeth. She cocked to fire again, but the beast was too fast. It smashed into her and Carson, sending them both sliding into the snow. It scooped Annie up in the crush of its massive jaws and swung its head, sending her twisting shoulder over shoulders into the snow. She rolled with her momentum, gun in hand, and fired at it again and again, but her shots failed to penetrate its thick, bristling hide. Huge and ravenous, the creature zig-zagged this way and that, impossibly quick for its size. Then it slid to a stop, drew back its wormy lips, and snarled at Annie, leaning into its forepaws.

Fingers nimble and quick, Annie broke open her pistol and began to refill the cylinder. "Sarah!" she said, hoping for help. *"Sven!"*

The creature, unknowable in its terrible aspect, lowered its massive shoulders, bringing into view someone standing behind it.

Not Sarah.

Not Sven.

"Carson?" Annie's voice a whisper.

His eyes were wide, fearsome, black as pitch. Shoulders hunched, looming behind the beast like a vulture. "I am the gate," he said, with an implacable authority.

The beast's ears shot up, eyes widening with... was it fear?

"I am the key," said Carson, stepping forward in the snow.

The beast whirled to face him.

The pitch-black pools of his eyes became slits.

The beast howled a terrifying preamble to its strike.

Carson lifted his hand, his fingers strong, outstretched. "Heel."

The creature shook violently, every hair of its hide bristling turgid, as if fighting against some unseen force.

"I am the gate," said Carson, repeating. His calm, quiet voice roiling with power. "I am the key."

Annie scrambled to her feet, watching as, impossibly, Carson's hand transformed from flesh into living shadow. The black as night hand knotted into a fist.

The beast twisted away from him, mewling in agony.

Carson slashed his hand through the air, the shadow whistling razor-sharp through the air.

The creature loosed a howl and then turned, obeying Carson's unspoken command.

Annie, without knowing why, took a step back. Where she fell to one knee in the snow.

Carson concentrated hard, his face twisting malevolent, and took a deep breath as the shadow of his hand lifted into the air. "I am the conduit, and you will *listen* to me."

The rumbling tumble of the abominable pack twisted away from the circle of Peregrine agents and gunfighters. It rushed as one collective darkness—a singular shadow across the spangling silver of the snow—beneath the light of that black star.

"We got 'em on the run!" The gunfighters and agents let out a primal bellow.

All cheered. All except for Annie and Carson, who were staring at each other. A short distance was between them. A distance that, to Annie, seemed much too wide a gulf.

And when they began to run to each other, it was Carson who ran first. His arms, no longer bearing any of the shadow inside of him, wrapped around her, then he quickly drew back to check her for injury. "Are you okay?"

"What... how did you...?" she asked.

Carson shook his head. "I-I'm not sure. Something is happening to me, Annie." He checked her again, worry on his face. "Are you sure you're okay?"

Standing in the smoke of battle, within the protective circle of twenty-seven men and women now staring at Carson, she saw in the light of that eclipse the face of the boy who had become her man. "You... you saved me," she said.

"I couldn't let—" Carson's voice broke. He took a deep breath. "I love you, Annie."

Like nothing she had ever felt before, her heart fell from a perch inside her, fell so far. Fell forever.

Directly into Carson Ptolemy.

And Carson fell with her, into a long kiss that burned away the winter cold.

CHAPTER SIXTEEN

Black Wells, Colorado

Standing before the entire population of the grand capital of the Red Kingdom, within the hidden depth of the Astolats, Sir Sigurd of Antioch addressed every brother and sister of the fang, glorified.

Wesley Burrows listened to his master's impassioned speech, eyes wet with scarlet tears. This was it. This was the moment the Red Kingdom would move Kristian's mighty claw across the breast of the American nation, and rake for the wet, throbbing heart beneath.

"Be my friends," said Sigurd. "Come with me to Fort Scott and make war with me. Not a war clandestine; those who come with me will leave their shadows behind. Let us employ famine, fang, and fire. Deliver unto them a fury unseen since the ancient nights. The nights the cattle have forgotten. The nights that only we, the immortal, can remember."

A chorus of ten thousand and near ten thousand more blood-hungry throats let loose a sound of triumph. A sound, Wesley thought, that threatened to shake to pieces the very mountain hiding that secret nation.

Wesley was the first to volunteer, and at this his master gave him an approving nod that sent his vampiric heart soaring into a realm he could have never known in human life.

Thousands of taloned hands lifted into the air, and from among the selected, Sigurd's army coalesced.

All who could fly took wing. All who could not mounted horses taken from the enslaved people of what was once Colorado. All of them ready for war.

CHAPTER SEVENTEEN

Fort Scott, Kansas

Fort Scott was a square of white-washed buildings, surrounded by timber fencing banked with ice and snow. Though Ashley prided himself on seeing the detail of things, at this particular moment he didn't give a rat shit for what the fort looked like or what it was provisioned with or what tactical advantages or disadvantages it might bear. Not a tinker's damn did he give for the patter of the long roll call of the regiments within. In time, those things would matter a great deal. But at the moment, they were not what mattered most. What did matter is what was inside those white-washed buildings. Ashley had delayed long enough, perhaps too long, and now was the time to tell the son of Gilbert Ptolemy exactly what was waiting for him inside Fort Scott.

Ashley rode up beside Carson Ptolemy, who was riding side-by-side with Annie. Carson, the fulcrum of this entire mission's possibility of success, riding next to the woman who was the fulcrum of his heart. "Annie," Ashley said, calm and polite. "I need to talk with Carson. Alone. Just a moment, please."

"Why?" asked Annie. Always asking why.

Ashley masked his face in a bluff of sincerity. "Please."

The young woman screwed up her face, that little rat-like look she had when displeased. "Fine," she said, then looked to Carson. "I'll see you inside."

She rode off, leaving the two men to fall back while the rest of the gunfighters and agents passed through the open gateway.

"What is it, Sutliff?"

Here goes nothing, Ashley thought. Then, he spoke, playing the cards he had been holding so closely to his vest when he and Carson had their chat at the poker table only a few nights ago.

"A man named Lucio is here. There are others with him, but he's the leader," he said, scanning the fort. Then, he turned and sighed, looking at Carson. "He is the head of what remains of the Society of Prometheus. He has a copy of the manuscript you described. Lucio and his people know you. Know what you are and what you did to their priest."

Ashley watched for Carson's reaction. For twenty-seven years, Ashley had gambled from one side of America to the other. He had gambled on river boats and in saloons, lost a dozen fortunes and gained them back time and time again. He had sat at tables with stone-hearted women and unreadable men. Though he was filled with an almost incalculable patience, when necessary, he was also a man who hated waiting. And when he told Carson Ptolemy that the very people who had stolen Carson's life from him, who wanted him dead, were waiting inside this very fort, that's when Ashley Sutliff witnessed the greatest poker face he would ever see.

Carson's eyes betrayed nothing. His lips didn't squirm.

Fingers didn't move. Toe didn't tap. Nothing. The young man listened and heard as if cut from stone.

He was so still that Ashley, for the first time in his life, asked the question, "How does that make you feel?"

"It doesn't make me feel anything."

"You wanna tell me what happened back there with those beasts?"

"You see what happened?"

"Sure did."

"Guess you know, then."

"Now isn't the time to be hiding things," said Ashley, trying to keep his composure, but he didn't like how short Carson was being with him. "Especially not from me. I've staked everything on you, kid. Don't forget, this goes any way but the right way, it won't be just Annie who'll be dead; it'll be all of us. The whole goddamn world."

"And that's your concern, is it," said Carson, guiding his horse so that Ashley was within arm's reach. "The whole world? Not just yourself, but everything and everyone in it?"

Ashely relaxed through the coil of tension building in his stomach. "You don't know me, Ptolemy. And make no mistake, I sure as shit ain't scared of you. If I find out that killing you will make the world right, you'll be dead before you hit the ground. Even if that means going through Sven and Sarah. Annie, too."

During his time spent gambling across the nation, Ashley had also been a Peregrine agent. He'd faced his share of werewolves, crows the size of men, and a rattlesnake big as a train car. Fear was an old friend that he'd known longer than Carson Ptolemy had been alive. But when Carson leaned close to him, that old friend fear transformed back into an unknowable enemy. Ashley didn't like the way it made him feel. Like being on the wrong side of an all-in wager.

"Threaten her again, Sutliff," Carson's voice was low and calm. Confident.

Ashley knew bluffs. This wasn't that. And it sure as hell wasn't a warning. It was a promise, only half of it given breath. Ashley knew the rest.

The wind cut through the little distance between them.

"Do your job," Ashley said. "Study the manuscript. Figure this shit out. If you can end the all-night, you'll solve near every problem we currently face: the Society, the Nine, and the kingdom. That's why you're still alive. It's why you're here."

"I know what I'm here to do, Sutliff," the young man said, colder than the ice beneath them. He gave his mount a squeeze and trotted ahead through the gap, into the fort.

Ashley let out the breath he'd been holding. It came out quavering. "I hope so, you creepy son of a bitch," he said to himself. "I sure as hell hope."

Now was the time to take in the details of the fort. Only an idiot would assume that the Red Kingdom didn't know of their existence here. They might not, but he sure as hell was going to act and plan from the premise that his enemies knew everything. That's how he'd won the Werewolf Campaign for Judge Ellison and that's how he was going to win the Vampire War.

Fort Scott was set out in the middle of the snow-blanketed plain. Brazier fires lit the fortifications well enough, but Ashley would double their number. He knew there were enough rations to feed everyone for a month. Four, if they went lean. Timber, along with all other supplies, would come regularly from the railyard by way of wagons twice a week. That supply chain was a vulnerability though. A railyard was exactly how Sigurd had gotten to Abilene unnoticed, and Ashley assumed the creature would try something similar, were he to attempt a siege.

The vast expanse of snow meant that a surprise attack would be difficult, but the soldiers' tent camp would be vulnerable, being outside the fortified walls. There were too many soldiers to fit inside the barracks, but Ashley would extend the stockade, so that even the encampment would have some kind of fortified protection. But, it was clear, right from Ashley's first view of the full encampment: If the vampires came in full thrust, this fort, even with its great number of veteran soldiers, would not withstand the attack.

That was fine. Ashley intended his people to be here only long enough to train the soldiers in vampire fighting. They had lots of silver bullets, but not so many that they could be passed out like candy. The soldiers would get one shot a piece, maybe two. The vast majority of the silver bullets would go to the gunfighters, who would prove much more dangerous with the precious commodity. Silver bayonets and fire: those were tools that the rank-and-file soldiers would be using to maximize their effect. The sun wasn't coming out any time soon, so silver and fire were the only advantages any human had against the vampire horde. And sheer numbers, perhaps, but how many vampires roamed within the borders of Colorado, he did not know. And so he planned his strategy as the inferior. In every single way, he expected to be out-gunned and out-numbered. He would not suffer to waste a single resource or overplay any advantage, should it arise in the field.

Three weeks at the fort would be all the time he required to teach the whole division the simple strategy and even simpler tactics they would employ. And because he knew he could do it in three, he decided to accomplish it in two.

He rode through the camp, taking stock of the men and women. He had seen the division off while still in Washington D.C. a few weeks prior. They knew him—knew his command was higher than their major general. There he had stared into their eyes, taking an account of their spirits. Much to his delight, all of them were spoiling for a fight after being told by their commanding officers why they had been recalled to duty. That would change, he knew. Morale was mercurial, and none of these soldiers, even though they were veterans of the Slaver's Revolt, had seen anything like what would be coming for them, or anything like what they'd be marching into.

"Sutliff," the big voice of Sven Erickson came from behind him. "Sutliff, hold up."

Ashley turned, then circled his horse to meet him.

The man's pale complexion was all flushed with heat and windburn from their travel.

"You're in charge of this whole goddamn thing, aren't you?" Sven asked.

"Of course I am."

"Then I suggest you get inside the fort and sort out the shit. A few of your soldiers just decided to make a pass at Sally Scull and, well, you can imagine how that went."

"She kill 'em?"

Sven tilted his head. "They might still be alive," he said, a grim smile on his face. "If they learned how to breathe with those new holes in their head."

"Goddamn it."

"They wouldn't listen to me. Big fight's gonna break out, and if it does, you'll lose as many soldiers as the Guild has bullets."

"Why didn't the officers step in!"

"That's the thing. They are officers. Or, well, were officers."

Ashley squeezed his mount, dashing through the camp.

Inside the fort, at the center of the square surrounded by the barracks, Ashley saw his guildfolk standing in two rows. Opposite them, a mob of soldiers in their American blues were knotted together, pointing fingers and hollering and making a whole damn mess of everything. Between the wave of blue and the silver-pinned gunslingers, one man had Sally Scull in a headlock. Twice her size, the soldier held the woman tight as a bulldog. His right hand lifted high into the air, ready to turn her face to sofkee.

Both groups drew back as his horse came between them. In one smooth motion, Ashley brought his mount to a broadside stop and slipped out of the saddle. "Turn her loose," he said.

Sally struggled, the soldier did not let go.

Ashley wasn't about to let either set of these hot-tempered peckerheads see him flustered. Ashley Sutliff didn't *get* flustered. So, he walked toward them, shoulders forward.

"Turn her loose," he repeated with the same flat intonation as before.

The big soldier, Ashley did not know his name, clamped down harder as Sally tried to peel away. "She killed Gerald and Ike, Mr. Sutliff!"

"Who the fuck are Gerald and Ike?"

The question seemed to wound the soldier. "Company B major and my captain, sir. Gerald was my best friend!"

"I'm getting angry, having to repeat myself. I said, turn her loose."

"I can't, sir. Not after what she— Quit squirmin', bitch!"

Sally Scull struggled and screamed, "I'm gonna cut yer goddamn balls off, you yankee mother fu—"

The crowd of angry soldiers and the rows of furious gunfighters broke into loud argument, yelling back and forth, hollering. And that's when Ashley Sutliff just ran out of patience for the whole goddamn thing.

He shook his head, looking at the ground in frustration. When his eyes came back up to look at the mess before him, his gun was in his hand. He placed the killing end against the soldier's head.

The soldier's eyes went wide with fear. Betrayal.

Both sides of the mass argument went quiet.

"What's your name?" asked Ashley.

"Billy," said the soldier, terrified, unable to comprehend the escalation of things. "Billy Marks. First lieutenant."

"Sorry for your loss, Billy. But, you can either keep hold of this woman and die," He said and ratchetted back the hammer of his revolver. "Or, we can all congratulate you on your promotion." He stared into Billy, piercing him with eyes that had seen tragedy and terror and pain. "Choice is yours," he said, voice chipped with ice.

The newly dubbed captain shoved Sally Scull into the dirt.

The woman cursed, gathering herself up, spitting mad as a rattler. "Come grabbing at me, drunk, like I'm some dollar whore!"

Ashley kept his eyes on Billy. "That true?"

"They was just—"

"Shut the fuck up, Captain," said Ashley. He hollered at both mobs then. "You. All of you. Get the snow out of your ears, and you listen. Any soldier or gunfighter that steps out of line from this point on gets a long drop from a short rope. And anyone too unruly for that, I will personally blow their goddamn head off." He turned in a slow circle.

No one spoke.

"You are here under my command. The whole goddamn lot of you. And it is my wish, which should carry the weight of God Almighty his own fucking self, that no one else here will lay an unkind hand unto another. I'm tired of waiting on the obedience I've been promised by President Grant and paid for with more than fair coin. My patience is all worn thin—thin as a razor blade. And I swear, the next person that lays foul of that patience will get their throat cut. Am I clear?"

The fort lay silent as a church full of guilty sinners.

"Am I *clear?!*"

The soldiers snapped to attention.

The gunfighters, all among their number, nodded.

"Good. Now clean up this goddamn mess, and fucking. . ."—Ashley shook his head again, disbelieving he had to say it to a collection of trained soldiers—*"be fucking nice!"*

CHAPTER EIGHTEEN

Somewhere on the Great Plains

Sigurd's army rushed over the plain. Where the light of the eclipse was not shadowed in the great expanse of his wings, the grassland, white and clear, rumbled and shook under the hoofbeat desolation of an army of the undying. They plowed through life, rolling from town to town, taking each man and woman and child, flesh by punctured flesh, the temperature so close to zero that the warm blood of their victims made their red, wet faces steam in the night.

Marauders, the whole of them, tilling up the otherwise placid landscape with the crescent-shod horses, violent atrocities, and spilling of blood. The estimation of their journey was taken not by the number of miles laid out between Black Wells and their destination or by how many more towns they would ravage between here and there but by how many gallons each would drink before their arrival. And it was a game for them to wonder, who would drink the most?

And so, they rode hard for Fort Scott, Kansas.

CHAPTER NINETEEN

Fort Scott, Kansas

Annie was grateful that four officers' rooms had been reserved for the remaining members of the Peregrine Estate. She had heard what life was like inside a barrack, and she knew right down to the ground that she wanted no part of that, or of the existence inside the surrounding camps. One of those barracks, the very best of them in fact, had been set aside to house the entire Gunfighter's Guild. They had eaten a simple meal, tired from the ride and the shock of battle, and now Annie and Sarah sat near the roaring hearth of the common area within the officers' quarters. Annie smoked her pipe. Sarah sipped a glass of whiskey.

"You know he's in there with a bottle," said Sarah, suspicious. Sven, though he had friends among both the agents and the guildfolk, spent most of his time locked in his room.

What Sarah suspected, Annie knew to be correct, but she kept silent. The man was doing what countless widowers had done since the beginning of loss: washing their sorrows in anything that would dull the heart's grief and the mind's want to remember.

"There was this boy," Annie said, changing the subject. "Well, he was a man. Name was Dutch."

"Big fella, right? One that saved your life in Fort Stockton?"

"Sometimes, my mind drifts and I wonder where he is. Think about how grateful I am that he was in my life, even for just that short time. Wouldn't have made it without him."

"None of us would be here without someone else," said Sarah. "All that hoopla about being independent and cutting your own way through life is just a mountain of shit that little men stand on to feel bigger than they actually are. Hell, I wouldn't be sitting with you here, sipping this fine rye, if it hadn't been for a goddamn werewolf pulling me out of the Cam River... My lord, how many years ago has it been since that moment." She rubbed her chin. "I swear, so much happens, it's hard to see the meridian between memories."

Annie rocked back, laughing. "You were going to tell me that story before Larry made us both shut up in the carriage just outside of Black Wells."

At the mention of Larry Cornish, Sarah's smile wilted to a solemn frown.

Annie smoked.

And for a time, they said nothing.

Sarah took a long, slow breath and said, "Feels strange to tell it now. Without him here."

"That's how I feel about Dutch. I want to believe he's still alive, but when I talk about him, it's like I'm talking about a ghost."

"The whole history of us is just one long ghost story, honey. Hell, I once heard an old rascal say that the Earth is just one big boneyard; it just so happens that it looks pretty in sunlight."

Annie took a long draw. "I'd give anything—well, just about anything—to see the sun again."

"Mmm, there it is."

"There's what?"

"You've got yourself a lover, and there, right there, even when he isn't in the room, you've damned the rest of us to hell and perdition if the cost of our mission requires him to fulfill it." She shook her head. "Annie, I love you like a sister, and I'm proud of you for making your feelings known to Carson. I'm happy that the two of you have each other. But. . ." Her features stiffened in the wavering firelight. "But no man and no woman are worth the whole world—not even you two. No one is. What happened to Carson in Chicago, whatever it is that he's attached to, it will lead to an unhappy terminus. Because nothing good could ever come out of that black manuscript he's tied to. Gilbert killed a man to save Carson, but Carson might have to do a lot worse to save everyone. And that means you need to be willing to give up everything as well. But, you already know that."

"No," said Annie. "I don't know that, Sarah. Neither do you."

"At the very least, you suspect it."

Annie looked away, eyes hard on the fire.

"Love," said Sarah, finishing her whiskey, "it's the worst best thing that happens to any of us."

"You're so gloomy when you drink," said Annie. "So fatal in your thinking."

Sarah shook her head, a smile on her face. "Fatal? No, you've got me figured all wrong, honey. This is me at my most romantic. Speaking of your flame, where is he?"

Annie sighed. "Sutliff called on him. Wants him to meet someone."

"Mmm. Someone. Didn't say who or why, just someone. You know," she said, then took a drink. She let out a satisfied sigh. "God love Ashley Sutliff, but sometimes I really can't stand that man."

Carson found Ashley Sutliff in the livery stable. The gambler was throwing a warming coat over his freshly brushed gelding. The horse, gleaming with a fiery sheen, leaned into the coat. Ashley adjusted it to slide over the dip of its spine and swell of croup.

"He's beautiful," said Carson, announcing himself.

"This here is Roger," Ashley said, patting the gelding's muzzle. "Seen a lot together, haven't we, you rascal."

Carson stepped close to Roger, running a hand along the coat-covered flank. "Had a friend just like him once, but with a heavy splash of white across the muzzle."

"Casualty in your war against the Society?"

Carson shook his head. "Still alive. Far as I know. But I'll never see him again. He was smart, probably found himself a rider that wouldn't put him to work chasing trains or fleeing enemies who peppered the air with pistol shot as he caught up to them."

"My brother," said Ashley. He cracked a grin, cinching the coat at Roger's throat. "Cecil was his name. One time we were tracking this man-killer that Judge Ellison put us on. Tracking him through a goddamn thicket in the Smokey Mountains, the heat on top of us like a parade of angry bulls and hellfire, those goddamn mosquitos and ticks. I remember, we lost the killer's track and bedded down for the night. The whole time, our horses were stamping and snorting. Swishing their tails loud as a sulking child having to sweep a front porch. Full of discontent. Unhappy that we'd taken them so deep in the brush as we did. Neither of us were able to sleep. Cecil, he looks over at me—I have no clue what time it was, other than closer to morning than evening—and he just kept looking at our horses. Genuinely sorry for the shitty state of their situation. And Cecil, he says, 'We ask a lot.'" Ashley looked at Carson, the whole truth of the man was in his eyes. "He was more right than he knew."

"Judge Ellison spoke very highly of your brother," said Carson. "Of the both of you."

Ashley nodded, and surprised Carson by stretching out his hand. "I haven't been fair to you."

Carson looked at the gloved hand. "I know your way, Ashley. I've seen it in lots of men over my life. Hell, been that way myself." He shook Ashley's hand. "You charge where other men shrink."

"Not you, though," said Ashley releasing the grip.

"No," said Carson. "Not me."

Ashley led Roger into a stall. "You don't trust me, Carson. And that's good. I wouldn't trust me either." He came out of the stall and closed the gate. "What happened today between the soldiers and the Guild—"

"Saw that. Were you really going to shoot Captain Marks?"

Ashley's face relaxed entirely. The coldness in his eyes told Carson the answer.

Carson nodded. "Fair enough."

"Listen kid," said Ashley. "This whole campaign hinges on you. I called you here because I want to be with you when you meet Lucio. I called on you because this fort is a powder keg and, meaning no insult, but you're a goddamn match. Folks are going to talk about what you did, how you were able to do. . . whatever the hell it was you did to that beast. They're gonna speculate about how the flesh of your hand turned into a shadow, and it's going to make them afraid of you. And when they start to be afraid of you, they'll get to talking, saying you're one of two things. You're either a problem or you're a solution. Right now, not even you know which one is right."

"But," said Carson.

"But, when you get your nose back in that black

manuscript, you're going to figure out which one it is. And when you do, I need you to trust me. I need you to tell me."

"As I recall it, not two hours ago, you were the one saying you'd blow my brains out and kill every person I love just to get the chance if it meant saving the world."

Ashley let out a long breath. "That's because, kid. . . that's because these other people, they don't know if they should be afraid of you yet. I do. You may not be able to sling a gun worth a shit anymore, but I've seen lots of terrifying things in my life, and I have never, not once, felt as scared as I did when you saw Annie in danger, and through a sheer act of will, you changed not who you are but *what* you are. And what you are is *dangerous*. With nothing more than what's inside you, you commanded a monster to do your will. That's a kind of power no man is meant to wield. It's the kind of power Sigurd and his king have over the whole lot of their brood. And it makes me wonder, Carson. What would you command those creatures to do if it meant saving the people you love. . . or yourself?"

Carson's anger boiled up in his chest. "I would never—"

"You already did."

The words shot through Carson, sending a cold serpent down his spine.

Ashley put a reassuring hand on his shoulder. "You're asking a lot of me to trust you, and I'm asking a lot of you to trust me. But, like Cecil said. . ."

"I hear you," said Carson.

"So, cut my words from earlier out of your mind and hear these: No matter what happens or what you turn out to be, no matter what is required, I'll give every measure to make sure that your friends, who were once my friends, and that woman you love, who has no love for me"—

they both chuckled at that—"I will protect them, Carson." His smile had slanted serious again. "I will keep them safe. You have my word. Not my word as a gambler, but my word as a Peregrine. My word as a brother. As a man."

"I want to believe that. I really do, Ashley."

"Talk is cheap. But, when the time comes to prove it, when the moment arrives, you'll see what kind of man I am."

The two men walked across the parade yard toward a two-story barrack set opposite the others. It was like the other barracks with a second story ringed by a balustraded parapet. At its center, the parapet was split by a black staircase leading to the main doors on the second floor. At the top of the stairs, near the door, a woman stood. All covered in black buffalo hide with a gun belt cinching her at the waist. A hood hid her hair. Her mouth and nose were covered with what might have been a beaver-pelt scarf. Only her eyes could be seen. They were liquid brown pools shining darkly below the pale flesh of her forehead.

"Sutliff," the woman said, her voice almost as low as a man's.

Ashley did not respond as they ascended the steps toward the woman, their boots thumping up the snow dusted stairs.

Upon Ashley and Carson's approach, the woman stepped in front of the door, blocking their path.

"He's busy," she said.

Ashley reached for the doorknob. "Not too busy for this."

She drew the gun without any measure of quickness or fear of what it could do, holding it next to her thigh. "Why is it with you, Sutliff, I'm always having to repeat myself."

"It ain't because I'm hard of hearing, I can tell you that. I told you I'd deliver the man, and here he is." Ashley indicated Carson with a nod. "Lily, say hello to Carson Watts Ptolemy."

The sound of the woman pulling back the hammer of her revolver beat his salutation.

"I should kill you right here, Ptolemy."

Carson saw anger in the woman's eyes, a widening gyre of rage.

Ashley rocked back on his heels, feigning surprise at Carson. "Old flame of yours?"

"I have never met this woman," said Carson.

"No," said Lily, her low voice lowering further. "My name is Lily Rose. You killed my father."

"Jesus Christ," said Ashley, shaking his head as if put out with frustration. "What is it with you people and killing each other's goddamn families."

Lily stepped around him to stand eye to eye with Carson. Her breath misted in the air between them. "What right did you have?"

Carson met her gaze, then pulled at the fingers of his glove until it slid off his hand. The cold wind snapped its fangs into the misshapen redness of his swollen fingers, chilling him to the marrow. He reached those cold fingers into his mouth and pulled his false teeth out. The saliva frosted between his fingers. He drew his lips back to show her the blackened gums. "Every right," he said, the words sloppy in his mouth.

Lily's eyes tensed, then quickly relaxed. "He do that to you?"

Carson slid his teeth back into his mouth. "You all did it. Him, the gunhands that worked the Society, and all those fuckers we left for dead in Chicago. The Society's purpose killed my first father, and your people trying to unlock that purpose killed my second. So, as I see it, I'm still owed."

"If you wanna square things up now, cripple, I'm more than happy to—"

"Oh, shitfire, woman," said Ashley, yanking her back by the shoulder. "The whole world's common theme is the death of fathers. Besides, you know who this man is. Know what he is. And, honestly, I thought you all would bow down and start worshiping, him being the key and gate or whatever the hell he is. But, hey, I know fuck all about your weird doom-cult. We're going inside." Ashley threw up a hand in exasperation. "Shoot us if you want, but I'm not standing in this goddamn snow arguing. Rather take a bullet in the fuckin' skull."

Lily Rose didn't shoot them. She let them step into the common room of the barrack and shut the door.

And when that door was closed, both the woman and the cold evaporated as factors on Carson's mind. The scope of his vision took in the common area, the half-dozen people sitting around the table, even the shadow of the figure at the head seat. Carson saw them all, and yet saw none of them. He did not see the table, the people, the man, or even the fire. Did not hear their voices go quiet at his and Ashley's entry. Did not hear the man at the head seat welcome them inside. He did not see or hear these things because of what was on the table before them.

It wasn't a copy of the Black Manuscript.

It was *the* Black Manuscript.

The same one he had read from during his captivity in Chicago. He knew because he could feel it. From within its dark and oily-slick cover and the folds of its hidden pages, Carson began to hear the song. The dark, primal melody he had experienced in the High Priest's study. The terrible enslaving song the Nine desired to be heard in every human ear unto every corner of the Earth for all time.

Carson's heart beat hard and heavy in his chest, the pull of the manuscript bearing down on him with crushing power. He had seized that power only hours ago when Annie had been in danger, but that capability was lost to him now, as if it had been someone else taking the power of shadow and madness so masterfully in their hand. Now, at this precise moment, Carson was nine years old again, his father's lunatic eyes flashing. Above them, the sacrificial knife flashed hotter, ready to end his life. Breathing became difficult for him, coming in short staccato, almost hiccupping sounds.

"For all these long months," came a voice over the song, "we believed that you had somehow overtaken our High Priest. Outwitted him by guile or cunning."

The members of the Society of Prometheus looked on. The man at the head of the table took a single sheet of paper and slid it over the top of the closed book.

The song was silenced.

The man strained, pushing himself up to his full height. "Imagine my great discontent and disappointment at this, Sutliff. You promised me more than this. . . this wretch who trembles at only the sight of so great an object."

"Carson," said Ashley, concerned.

"How did you silence the manuscript?" Carson asked. The man came into detail now that Carson could focus on him. He was old, wizened. Eyes sunk deep into sockets overshadowed by a pronounced, wrinkled brow. Thick lips pulled back to reveal a cavern of a mouth populated with only a few crooked teeth.

"I am Lucio Gandolfi. I am the chief scholar of the Society of Prometheus, a collection of the faithful that you have all but burned to the ground with your abdication of destiny and privilege."

"How?" asked Carson again.

Lucio seemed to tire at the question. "I have read the manuscript, understand its language, but I am only a man. Reading these pages has only illuminated me with the mechanics of the book's alchemy and none of its secrets. The symbol writ on the page, now set upon the cover, acts like a bowl placed over a great undying flame." The man wheezed a scoff. "You have no idea what is within these pages, do you, boy? You read the words but have no conception of their meaning."

Carson didn't speak even though he knew it would tell them everything.

"You have the sight and the will to keep it from annihilating you outright, but"—the man wheezed again, this time a laugh—"you have the intelligence of a haystack."

The men and women on his left and right all laughed too.

Lucio's mouth opened with surprise, a jagged cave of teeth revealed again. "O–Oh my goodness. You don't know."

Carson grit his teeth.

"You haven't come here to enlighten us as Sutliff promised," Lucio continued. "You're here because you don't understand... anything."

"And you're going to help him learn," said Ashley, his voice calm and cold. "And if I sense, or get the smallest indication, that you're doing anything but that, Gandolfi, I'll put you back on that hangman's gallows where I found you."

"You really think death frightens me?" asked Lucio, mocking. "Frightens any of us?"

"Not one bit. But I do know that you cult types can't stand the idea of missing out on whatever apocalypse you're hoping for."

Lucio's face twisted grim.

"You know our deal. You teach him, I let you go. We stave off the end of the world and maybe, one day, you get to try again."

Carson slashed his eyes over to Ashley, furious that he had made such a deal.

But then, chewing it over, he realized that if Ashley had just allowed this man to die, the knowledge of how to set the world right would have died with him. And so, he relaxed, letting the tension slide out of him.

"Yes," Lucio said. "Yes. I know our deal."

"Good." Ashley looked over at Carson. "How do you want to play this, kid?"

Carson considered for a moment. "Everyone out. Everyone but Lucio."

Ashley shook his head. "The two of you alone? I don't like it."

"We aren't going to be alone," said Carson. "Get Sarah over here. She's all the protection I need."

"Couldn't agree more," said Ashley. "Now, all of you other peckerheads come with me."

One of the men placed a delicate hand over his heart, fearful. "Why? Where are we going?"

Ashley winked at Carson. "Why, out into the parade yard with the rest of the soldiers."

"I'm no soldier."

"Well, then you'll want to pay extra close attention to Sven Erickson when he starts teaching you dandy fucks how to fight a vampire."

CHAPTER TWENTY

The Parade Yard, Fort Scott, Kansas

Annie stood next to Sven as the patter of the long roll summoned to rank the captains of each company. The captains of every company stood next to each other, talking, but their chatter died and they snapped to attention when Ashley Sutliff strode next to Annie. Tripods pregnant with fire illuminated the yard enough for Annie to see the fatigue pulling on Ashley's face. He was like a finely tailored suit that began to show age with each passing day, fraying at the edges, depth of color fading. It wasn't just the miles or the roughness of this campaign, she knew. He had fought for Judge Ellison for years. He'd lost a brother at some point in the Peregrine's service. And, though the gambler had tried to hide his weariness along their journey, there was no hiding it here in the tripod light.

"You'd be proud of your man," Ashley said to her, staring at the line of captains. There was a sad smile on his face. "I know you're worried about him." He gave her a knowing glance. "Don't be. I'm not."

Annie smiled too. Not because she believed him, but because that was the moment she figured out Ashley Sutliff's tell. It was the tone. The ribbon-width thinness between cocksure and confident. They looked very much the same, almost identical, but spending enough time with him had revealed what was counterfeit from what was genuine. Part of her wished she hadn't finally seen it, because in doing so, she saw that he was lying.

He *was* worried about Carson.

And her worry swelled to an incomprehensible magnitude. "I'm not worried one bit," she said.

He winked at her, a compact that without a word said, *Let's share this lie, because it feels better than the truth inside us.*

Annie laughed, her shoulders hopping slightly, at her second realization about Ashley Sutliff. The gambler was all-in on what might become the final hand of his life. There was a whisper of the very best of humanity in his tired eyes. In his weary smile.

That's when she realized something about herself—something she hadn't thought possible. She liked Ashley Sutliff. And impossibly, in that moment, she wanted to call him a friend, to share this little secret with him.

"Everything you sons and daughters of bitches know about fighting a war is wrong," he shouted to the line of captains. "If you choose to fight the vampires the way you fought those rebel slaving bastards or the glorious army of Abraham's republic, you'll be dead before you fire a second shot. Do you get me, sweethearts?"

Well, so much for warm sentiments, thought Annie. There would be time for that later. Right now, there was only this. The training that would hopefully lead to victory in Colorado, and to Sigurd burned to ash by her own hand. That anger inside her, younger than a year, burned with the aged heat of ancestral revenge.

Ashley walked down the line, his boots crunching in the snow. "The first two lines of your companies will be provided with two shots of silver before each engagement."

The captains began to look at each other, confusion on their faces.

"Two shots?" said Captain Marks. "For just two lines? That ain't going to be enough to cut down a company."

"Captain Marks, so glad to see you again, and thank you for proving my point. Vampires don't attack in companies. They aren't an army. They're ambush predators. Far as we know, they don't even use guns. Lead does nothing to hurt them; they take a bullet and keep on coming. Silver, though, silver burns them to ash. And as you may or may not know, Captain Marks, silver is a precious and rare commodity. More precious to us than you are to your own mother."

Annie was surprised when the company collectively laughed at the insult. Ashley Sutliff knew the language of these soldiers.

"Because the vampire attacks as a predator does, you will train your companies to ball up in a hedgehog formation the moment the second line fires their first shot. Bayonets outthrust to handle what will be an onslaught of pressure on all sides. And make sure to let every swinging dick and frozen honey pot know, if they allow that—if the formation is breached by even one of our enemy—the company risks total annihilation."

"I still think we ought to get more than two shots, Mr. Sutliff," said Marks. "I've seen all those crates of special ammunition you brought with you. There's plenty there for us to do what needs to be done."

Ashley stopped, barked a cuss, then stomped over to stand before Marks. "Got your side arm there, do yah, *Captain*."

"Yes, sir."

"Ms. Miller, how far would you say that big ole haystack over my shoulder is? What? Thirty yards?"

Annie didn't hesitate, knowing his reasoning. "Give or take a few, sure."

"See it, Captain? The one with the wooden post sticking out the top?"

"Sir. Yes, sir."

Ashley turned aside, taking in a quick breath. "Fire!"

The big captain turned his head, confused. "But—"

"Your enemy is now five yards away! Fire, goddamn it!"

He wasn't the sharpest man, that much was clear, but the veteran of the Slaver's Revolt drew his revolver smoothly, aimed and fired. The bullet slapped the ground a yard before the stack, spraying the snow into the air.

"Congratulations, Captain Marks, you're dead. And so is the rest of your company." Ashley patted the man on the shoulder mockingly. "Oh, and to answer your question as to why I'm not giving your company the majority of the silver shot?" He looked back over his shoulder and said, "Sven."

Sven's draw was so quick and smooth that Annie felt the wind of the movement before she saw him turn, even before she heard the whip-crack of the gunshot. The lead bullet splintered the bark, spraying wood shavings high into the air.

Sven cocked. Fired again.

Where the first bullet had blown the layer of bark away, the second struck so closely in the same spot that a fissure split the top of the wooden post. The thunder of the revolver's repeat rolled on even after Sven had spun the revolver and holstered it.

Ashley tilted his head to look at the captain. "Any more questions?"

Marks glowered.

"Make no mistake, Captain, you and your brave company are vital pieces to our battleplan, but your companies exist as a mobile stockade that will keep our gunfighters safe."

"So," said one of the women, "we're just a wall here to keep the vampires off the sharpshooters."

"Close," said Ashley. "You'll *appear* as a wall, but when those vampires try to leap over you and get to the Guild, we're going to contract our lines, and you're going to chew them to pieces with those bayonets. So, don't think of yourself as a wall, Captain, think of yourself as a millstone. The vampires are the grist."

She smiled at that metaphor, taking it to heart. "We'll grind 'em to dust."

Ashley and Sven worked with the captains for several more hours.

Annie listened and watched, though from time to time she would find her attention wandering to the Dragoon Barracks where Carson, protected by Sarah Lockhart, was diving into the Black Manuscript again—returning to that damnable book and its goddamn language that he'd so plainly said he wished to be done with. She thought herself silly for it, but she concentrated all of her hope toward those barracks, all the hope that a human heart can reserve within the greatness of its tiny expanse. She hoped that within those pages of madness and terror, cold and plague, Carson would find a way to free himself and unfetter their world from that of the Nine.

The captains, all of them modeling a company, practiced the maneuvers and calculated the paces and speed required to achieve both the protective shell and the contraction that would crush any breaching forces. Sven modeled the gunfighters, explaining the spacing required for the twenty-five members of the Guild to have optimal firing lines.

All in all, Annie was impressed. Even Captain Marks's ego had fallen away when given a clear plan and the methods required to achieve it. It was a good plan, too.

Ashley gave the company captains a few words about bravery and trusting the strategy, before he sent them away to begin training their soldiers. As Ashley spoke, Sven strode over to Annie.

"This plan is going to work," said Annie.

Sven smiled grimly. "No plan survives contact with the enemy. It'll work if the situation stays within the circumference of our best hopes. But, in my experience, that doesn't happen often."

She didn't like his tone or his lack of confidence. "You make it sound like we've already lost."

The big gunfighter lifted a single hand into the air, gesturing at the world itself. "Look around and tell me we haven't."

"I don't—"

"Annie, stop. You've got these ideas in your head about what's going to happen, but it never, ever goes like we think it will. Make no mistake, when we send the full thrust of ourselves against the Red Kingdom, the snow will steam hot and red. There are thousands of them living in that mountain. *Thousands*. They have advantages... abilities that defy our understanding. And the oldest of them? They've probably seen battle a hundred times more than the most seasoned of our soldiers. They have no fear of injury, but they do have an unwavering dedication to the command of their king."

"These soldiers know what we're fighting for. They're brave too."

"Bravery counts in battle; tactics count more. I think the world of you, Annie—admire you, even. You've seen the worst of what Sigurd and a few of his brood can do and you survived because the doorway served as a choke point between you and them. But you haven't seen them out in the open acting as one compelled force of catastrophe. Neither have I," he said. "No one has."

"Sven's right," said Ashley, crunching his way over to

them. "And, to be frank, none of this will matter if your man doesn't figure out how to end the eclipse."

"Then, why?" Annie balled her fists tight within the warmth of her coat pockets. "Why are we doin' this!"

They both looked at her with vacant stares, as if confused by her outburst.

"Why are we going to fight in a war if we can't win it?"

"Because this is the direction set before us, Annie," said Ashley. "The only direction that can lead to an ever-brightening future."

Annie knew the words. The Judge's words that he had spoken so many times during her time in Abilene while pointing at the falcon weather vane set atop the Peregrine Estate house.

"This is what it means to be a Peregrine," said Ashley, giving her that hard gambler's stare of his. "In many ways, this is what it means to be a human, alive and free on the Earth. We bind all our love and rage and fear and joy around our hearts, and we face what's coming. That was what Judge Ellison knew best. We may well lose, Annie. We may lose everything, or win it all. The final turn of the only hand humanity has ever been dealt. Our strength is in each other. I know that the Red Kingdom is stronger than us, but, I also believe that, time and time again, you put humans against the rest of the whole world, and we'll find a way to win the day."

Annie's eyes blurred with angry tears. "But these people," she said. "They're going to die because of us."

Sven placed a hand on Annie's shoulder, its great size light as a feather on her. "Cattle die, kinsmen die, the self must also die, but I know one thing which never dies: the reputation of each dead man. And if they die, Annie, if it be against the Red Kingdom, it will be unto a glorious purpose. A firebrand that'll scorch a blackened scar on the annuls of time. And that scar will be our final marker. A worthy marker. One that says that while we failed, our final death song will echo in the ears of our enemies for eternity. The vampires took the whole of Colorado into slavery, and if it means dying to try and end that pestilential bondage, I will ride happy into that darkness, hoping that at my end, I will see my husband again."

"Unless," said Ashley, looking over to the Dragoon Barracks.

"Yeah," said Sven. "Unless."

"Carson." The collection of Annie's hopes was all wrapped up in that name.

"The weight is on him," said Ashley. "But if anyone was born and raised for the moment, by God it's him."

"He'll need you tonight more than ever," said Sven to Annie.

Annie's eyes fell to her boots. "I believe in him."

"I know," said Ashley. "We all do."

* * *

"What do you believe in, Mr. Ptolemy?" asked Lucio, leaning forward, arms folded over one another to support his weight.

Carson turned to look at the fire. "Why?"

"Beliefs are the genesis point of prejudices. Your prejudices against the Black Manuscript and against even us, the Society, will hamper your understanding of our language within this book."

"It isn't your language," said Carson. "It's the Nine's. I might not know the language itself, but I know where it comes from. Know its intent."

Lucio leaned closer. "It is *our* language, boy. The Nine wrote it, yes. Delivered it, certainly. But centuries of scholarship and study have made us equal masters of it." The old man tapped a fingertip on the paper sheet covering the manuscript, where upon the sheet was scrawled a strange symbol in red ink. Then, Lucio pressed his finger's weight on it and slid the sheet from the black cover.

As before, Carson began to hear the rolling drumbeat of the song, as if it came boiling out of the uncovered manuscript.

Lucio, grinning maliciously, quickly slid the sheet back over the cover.

Again, the song died.

"You've seen the manuscript, vaguely made out the letters. Tell me, have you seen this letter within its pages?"

Carson looked at the strange symbol upon the sheet, considered it. "No."

"That's because one of our people crafted it, long ago. In our historical texts, it is written that early on, conduits that interacted with the manuscript would commit suicide long before they could enter the ritual that unlocks the gate of distance between our world and the place of the Nine. And so, a scholar greater than I found a way to not only *write* in the book's language but to *create* words in that language. Words that have *effect*. Power, Mr. Ptolemy. Do you know how many conduits have stepped the Earth before you? Can you even imagine within that thick skull of yours the number of duos that have lived and died without ever knowing they were the gate and the key to return to natural order?"

"So, you can write words that have power over that fuckin' book?" Sarah Lockhart spoke from across the room.

Lucio growled. *"No.* I said one of us could. He gave us the runes to use, but he never shared how to *make* them."

"Imagine that," Sarah said, picking her teeth with a sliver of cedar. She had her boots up on the table, balancing her chair on two legs, reclining. "Imagine a secret Society member keeping secret knowledge secret so they can have power over the others. I swear, all you cults are the same."

"But," said Carson, "you're saying there is a way to use the language against its creator?"

Lucio slowly clapped his hands together. "Congratulations. You've just managed to discover the basic power of all false religions, Mr. Ptolemy." His voice dripped with sarcasm. "It's a wonder you didn't unlock the manuscript upon its first reading."

Carson curled his fingers so tightly into fists that his fingernails clawed the table. He spoke through gritted teeth. "I am so tired of this arrogant elitism you and your people have. You have this belief that the whole world isn't worthy of existing for itself, for its own sake, and that people don't matter. That there is some law and order to the universe that we've somehow gotten away from."

Lucio smiled. "The truth is painful for those still outside what the Society knows to be true. Your life, your beliefs—whatever they are, Mr. Ptolemy—they falter in the dark light of the Nine. You've seen them."

"I have."

"And what makes you truly angry is that you blindly believe in a god of love that you cannot and will not ever see, and yet you have seen the gods who are real. And you hate that they are real and yours is not. This is what Ezra, your real father, knew. This is why he betrayed us. And betrayed you."

"My father went insane because of your Society and this damn book. And in the end, he tried to destroy it."

"Yes," said Lucio, his old wrinkles whitening with expansion. "And in an effort to destroy us, he used the language of the manuscript to *make* his son a conduit."

Carson's heart suddenly felt very heavy, its beat very, very slow.

"Only now do you understand. Your father killed one of the conduits, and when that power went to find another, he used the language of the manuscript to drive it into you." Lucio laughed. "The Nine didn't select you to be a conduit, Mr. Ptolemy. Your father did."

"I—"

The years came roaring through him. The memories flashing like veins of lightning through his mind. He saw Ezra's face, smiling. Remembered the feeling of the man's strong slender arms around his shoulders. The scent of his hair. The warmth of every fatherly kiss placed on his brow. He heard in his ears, even in his heart, Ezra's words, "I love you, son." All of those bittersweet memories: meals, stories, lessons, and the early years of fatherly love that make that soul-deep impression into the firmament of the son himself. That bedrock of fidelity Carson had held on to for so long spider-webbed with the betrayal of the attempted sacrifice was utterly broken in that moment. The fissure became a gulf. A gulf that stretched wide as the gap between Heaven and Earth. So wide that not even love itself could span its distance.

"Carson," said Sarah, leaning forward so fast her chair legs slapped against the floor. "Carson, take a breath."

"Oh," said Lucio, his smile widening. "He didn't know."

"Shut up!" Sarah barked. "Carson. Carson!"

He couldn't breathe. Couldn't understand why someone would choose his own son when anyone else, any living person, could have received this curse and destroyed the Nine's claim on the world.

"Your father betrayed the Society, Mr. Ptolemy, but make no mistake: he betrayed you first. And he betrayed you the worst."

Carson's eyes snapped up to look at Lucio Gandolfi.

The smile died on the old man's lips. Eyes widened with horror at what he saw.

"This is what I hate the most about you," said Carson, his voice sounding nothing like him. "The happiness you get from the suffering of others."

"No," recoiled Lucio. "What—"

"You. All of you. You want to see." Carson felt the roiling shadow within him manifest itself. He lashed out with a hand made of shadow, cuffing the old man's wrist.

Lucio screamed in pain as the shadow seared through his sleeve and the flesh below.

Sarah shouted, "Carson!"

"You want to see, Lucio?" said Carson, using his other hand to slap away the paper sheet covering the manuscript. Then, he lifted his hand high into the air above the book.

Lucio's eyes widened further, terror seizing the old man by the throat. "Stop!"

"Let me show you!" Carson slapped his hand down onto the manuscript.

There came the sound like the tearing of a great sheet, and Carson fell through the surety of reality into the dark, glimmering void. Fettered by the young man's grip, Lucio was pulled through the invisible aperture through which they fell.

The song of the Nine crushed all sound.

And there, no longer just an eye, was the full, unrestrained sight of a living titan deity.

Lucio screamed. Louder and louder. At the seeing, the old man's eyes seared, losing all their color. He clutched his ears, the fingers flooded through with scarlet. His skin blistered against the cold vacuum, peeling his lips back so that every crooked yellow tooth in his head flashed the white of hoarfrost, then shattered.

Lucio shriveled and tried to turn away from that indescribable monstrosity that only a conduit might look upon, but Carson twisted his fingers into the gray whisps of his hair, so that the man's bleeding, ruined eyes would gaze upon one of the Nine the man had for his whole life worshiped.

"I am the gate. I am the key, Lucio. I have seen. And

now you see! This is your god. And I give to you that which you want for the world."

Lucio's hollow eyes spilled over with wet crimson pearls. His screams became mumbles of abject insanity.

Then, with the power of the conduit, Carson let go of the manuscript and brought them rushing back to the table. Back into the Dragoon Barracks. Back into reality.

Carson let Lucio go.

The old man, weeping bloody tears, opened his quavering mouth and keened a sound older than language. The sound of the animal that humankind had forgotten it had once been. And what humanity had forgotten, only the Nine and wailing Lucio now remembered.

It was then that wailing Lucio stood up, terrified eyes looking for some place to hide himself from his revelation. And he found it. Tears streamed down his face, tears that glowed like molten silver in the hearth's firelight. Into the hearth Lucio ran, and, for need of grievous injury to undo the pain Carson Ptolemy had put upon him, he rammed his head into the yellow flames, right into the red heart of the fire. Insane and wild, he beat his head against the black iron fireplace grate.

"Oh god!" Sarah bellowed.

Hands suddenly began to fall on the door leading outside. The voice of Lily Rose demanded entry.

Lucio screamed as the sickening crunch of his skull smashing against the iron filled the room, along with the stench of immolated flesh and hair. With one final scream, he brought his face down onto the upthrust section of the grate, where he plunged the slender spike of iron through his eye.

Lucio Gandolfi, greatest scholar of his age, ended his suffering. And his life.

And while Lily Rose smashed her hands upon the locked door, Lucio's body began to burn.

"Carson, what did you do?" said Sarah, looking at him in a way he had never seen before.

Carson, simmering with rage, said nothing.

"Lucio!" Lily called. "Lucio, are you alright?!"

Sarah looked at Carson. Within her eyes shining in the firelight, Carson saw something: a change. As if in an instant he had been one thing to her, and only a choice later something else entirely.

"Sarah?"

"Stay there," she said. "Don't you—don't you say anything!" Her hand went to her pistol. "Ms. Rose, your man Lucio is dead," she called out.

"What? You let me in this goddamn door, and I mean right now, before I start shooting, goddamn it!"

"You start shooting, and I'll blow your head clean off. There was. . . something happened with the book." Sarah was so flustered she went to pull her gun and almost sent it flying out of her hand.

Carson had never seen her like this.

"I'm. . . I'm gonna let you in. But you come in with your hands on a gun, and I'll end you. It was a fucking. . . it was an accident."

Sarah opened the door, gun in hand. She pointed it at Lily, who bolted into the room.

"Lucio!"

Her voice sounded so distraught, Carson thought. So young.

"What in the hell did you. . ." She tugged at the old man's legs, trying to pull him out of the fire. If the grate hadn't been bolted down, she might have yanked the whole fire into the common room. The old man's head slid clean off the iron spike, his face a ruin of blackened skin and boiled blood.

She threw herself onto the dead man's chest, trying to beat out the fire that was burning the clothes that remained. "No. No, no! What did you do?" She turned back to look at Carson. "You goddamn monster! What did you do?"

Carson stared at her. Though she seemed so far away, her pain was right on top of him. The weight of it. The pain and the anger.

But he found little empathy for the tragedy playing out before him. Though a part of him wanted to explain himself, even to apologize, that section of his heart felt very small, smaller than it ever had been. The other part of him was the one who answered Lily's question.

"He wanted to see the world you've all being striving for," he said. "I showed him." Then he stood up and began to walk out of the Dragoon Barracks. "The rest he did to himself."

CHAPTER TWENTY-ONE

Fort Hayes, Kansas

The fort lay upon the plain, golden fires burning within, where voices and music rolled over the midnight landscape. Stars burned bright and clear. A roiling wave of black clouds, swollen with frozen rain and hail, hid the snow, stars, all. All except the fort and its ring of light.

Sigurd's army approached, unfazed by darkness. A hundred vampires and more crawled, spider-quiet, ready to strike. Wesley Burrows, his brood of three following close behind him, came to rest just outside the ring of light blooming from the fort's flaming braziers.

Town after town they had slaughtered. Blood stained their clothes, crusted their hair, dried black under their long, sharp nails. Fort Hayes could have been the same: encircled, rushed, and destroyed without injury, the brood laughing in red delight. Carmilla would have enjoyed that the most. She had been with them, for a time, but Wesley hadn't seen her in days.

Wesley had heard she was something else entirely.

Wesley had heard from others that she was Kristian's consort. Others went so far as to call her the secret queen of the Red Kingdom. Before he had been killed by those damn great wolves, Roland had told Wesley that she was from a far-off place that was so old time had forgotten its name, and that only Kristian was older than she. One thing was shared among all of the storytellers: Carmilla was very old and very, very powerful. She delighted in cruelty, never making a brood for herself as Sigurd did. She would turn men and women from time to time at the king's command, but she never cared for them. Never kept them close as Wesley's master did.

Sigurd deigned that the fort would be used as training for those who had never made war in the vampire way. It had been more than a century since the last red crusade. Among them, only Sigurd had served in what was referred to as the War of the Dozen Moons: a year-long conflict between the Red Kingdom and the Lunar Sodality of Saint Catherine.

It had been the war for the Astolats. A war for survival and home. And a war won at a great cost. The Red Kingdom had suffered tremendous losses, but ultimately Sigurd, Carmilla, Roland, and other elders, even King Kristian himself, drove the Catholic she-wolves into utter annihilation. But that was then, and this war would be different.

This war would be a battle not for a mountain but for a kingdom. Sigurd's war. Kristian's kingdom. And if the eclipse remained, Wesley believed the kingdom would flood over the whole goddamn world. A world where he and his people would rule the herd in an unending night that would run red for the rest of time.

All that happened would happen all at once.

Wesley heard the booming gale of Sigurd's wing, high above. Watched as his master—the father to his immortality, the reckoner of his revenge—beat the air to rise and rise and rise. The vampire knight whipped his black wings a final time, reached the apex of his flight, then turned over, light and nimble as a feather on the wind. He spun wing over wing, becoming a silhouette against the eclipse visible within a gap of thunderheads. There, Sigurd seemed to float, unshackled from gravity, a specter glowing radiant as Lucifer in starlight. He tipped forward, building speed, and plunged headlong to the fiery heart of the fort.

A man screamed. He shouted panicked words, but Wesley didn't care what they were; the only thing that mattered was what would come next.

Sigurd's mass, winged and terrible, burst into white mist. The vaporous gale billowed through the interior of the entire fort and, like the great clouds overhead hiding all light from the stars and the moon, extinguished tripod and brazier, torch and candle.

A black curtain fell over the world, but Wesley could still see everything. He could hear, even from hundreds of yards away, the thousand thundering hearts of the men and women and children inside the American fortress, the wails of fear as they were cast into the second to last darkness they would ever see.

The vampire horde that had waited so patiently for their master's signal rushed the fort. Wesley, wanting to prove himself as Sigurd's most trusted soldier and diligent friend, outpaced them all at the front. He leaped the timber stockade effortlessly. On the other side, soldiers stood confused, clutching their rifles and pistols like cattle seized with inaction in a mountain fog.

Wesley ran past one soldier, tearing out his throat with a single slash. The wet pulpy mass was in Wesley's mouth before the man even knew he was dead. Then, he was behind three soldiers, the woman in the middle shouting for someone to tell them what was happening.

Wesley answered her question with a word. "Conquest."

They twisted around to face the sound of his voice, but he was no longer there. Now he was beside them. He lifted the woman in the air, grabbing her by the shoulder and the navy fabric of her breeches. She cried out, a sound that became an animal's death bark when he brought her down with all his strength onto his knee. The force broke the woman's spine and split her flesh and uniform open at the waist. Her blood sprayed hot and glorious into the air.

Wesley was disappointed that her fellow soldiers could not see how it steamed and streaked wildly, but there was a joy to be found in seeing their eyes widen as her blood sprayed across their faces. How stupid they looked. How afraid and confused.

Wesley had been that way once, but never again.

One of the soldiers turned and fired into the dark, screaming. Wesley snatched the pistol and the hand holding it, twisting both free from the man's arm. More ignorant wails. More blood. Wesley drank them all in rancorous delight. His own brood, formerly the Culliver Gang, were stalking shadows slashing and reaving, drinking their fill.

They all drank, slakeless in thirst.

All except for Sigurd, who came swirling back into bodily form, demanding that his army bring forth all surviving human cattle.

Wesley and the rest found them huddled in barracks and in stables, hiding in privies, praying to impotent Christ in their church.

The little chapel where the music had been coming from. It must be a Sunday morning, but Wesley could only guess, for he no longer cared to keep the time. He had no need of it.

There were at least two hundred of them. And each and every one, none spared for age or gender, color or social class, Carmilla had put under the power of her domination. Wesley marveled at her power—at her dark beauty that ensnared so many with seemingly so little effort.

And it was in that chapel that Sigurd brought the whole sum of his force together. Amid the quiet of that desolated tabernacle, Sigurd instructed every vampire, as he had instructed Wesley, to transform these cattle. To drain them slowly, and then, when death was close, to give them a small portion of vampiric blood. A large measure of blood would make them a part of the brood, but this small measure would transform them not into equals but into ghouls. Blood slaves.

Wesley was confused at this. Hadn't Sigurd chided him, even threatened him with death for doing the same thing? Certainly, there must have been a greater lesson the young vampire had failed to learn by his master's teaching. He loathed that he could not discern the difference between what had been Sigurd's triumph and Wesley's great mistake. And so, Wesley partook. Easily taking the lives of the immobile men, women, and children, swelling the vampiric ranks.

When Fort Hayes was conquered and every heart stilled and every mind subdued, Wesley went to Sigurd.

Bravely, he asked his master the difference between what he had done and the actions his master now took.

Sigurd looked upon Wesley with. . . was it pity? Was it rebuke?

"One day you will understand the difference between our blood as a gift and our blood as a curse."

He then threw out his great wings again and took to the sky, leading them to the next town so that the newly changed cattle could make themselves strong. Strong enough to fulfill Sigurd's requirement.

Strong enough to win the war.

CHAPTER TWENTY-TWO

The Red Kingdom

John Childs was his name, but that was no longer who he was.

He was now the cupbearer of a king. The vessel from which Kristian drew power and strength and red shuddering pleasure.

Sometimes, if enough time passed between the king's meals, the cupbearer would remember his own name. And then he would remember his anger. But each time he was called to the king's throne, he knelt, cowed in willful obedience. Kristian would reach inside the cupbearer, find another memory, and bring it forth to the cupbearer's mind. Then, he would drink.

The cupbearer knew what the king was doing. He was taking more than the cupbearer's life and blood; he was drinking the memories—drinking all that the man had been, stealing away all the sweet, all the bitter. Everything.

There was nothing the cupbearer wanted more now, not even Marie Elaine, than to run from this place. Far, far away into the mountain or, blessed Lord, back to his little home where the Cam River came spilling out of the mountain, running clear and clean, a purple current of charging waters when the sun set.

And sitting in his little stone room atop his stone bed: a question.

Though he was alone, he spoke it aloud: "Will I ever see the sun again?"

He got up, tears falling down his face, though he made no sound of crying. He did not like to cry in front of the king. Not because Kristian despised tears but because when John cried it drove the vampire to the height of his appetite. Kristian never commanded John to cry though, never asked him to sorrow. This was not out of some kind of largess, John knew; it was because Kristian was patient. The waiting was what magnified the taste of grief. And this time, as John mindlessly went to the king's throne, the tears fell more heavily than they ever had before.

At the sight of John's entry, Kristian inhaled deep and slow and hungry.

At the sight of Kristian, John once again became the cupbearer.

CHAPTER TWENTY-THREE

OFFICERS' BARRACKS, FORT SCOTT, KANSAS

Annie Miller didn't understand. "Carson did what?"

Sarah Lockhart sat at the common table in the dining room, head down, drinking whiskey. She hadn't even bothered to take her hat off. Annie had never seen Sarah rattled. Never. Not during gunfights or arguments, never not once. But now, the woman was more than shaken. She was terrified.

"Annie, it was the craziest goddamn thing I've ever seen. His skin became blacker than shadow. Hell, blacker than the night sky. And when he slapped his hand down on Lucio, the two of them shot straight up in their chairs. I started hollering at them, tellin' Carson to let him loose, but he didn't. He just kept that hand on him. And then Lucio started screaming..."

Annie shook her head. Sat down next to Sarah, still listening.

"Screaming and wailing," said Sarah, lifting a bottle to refill her whiskey glass. "Bawling in a way I've never seen a man bawl." The bottle's mouth, shaking in her hand, struck the whiskey glass. The rat-a-tat-tat of the bottle on the glass shattered the woman's resolve.

Annie Miller slumped in astonishment. Sarah Lockhart wasn't just rattled; she was crying, her shoulders trembling, chest rising and falling. This woman—this strong, unbreakable woman—was spending every effort to keep the tears inside. But the tears came, spilling over her dark cheeks, pooling at the round pudge of her chin. "A-And then Lucio got up, and he threw himself into the fireplace, Annie. And when the fire wouldn't kill him fast as he wanted to die, he—my God." She drank her whiskey hard and fast then blew out a long, harrowing breath. "He smashed his face into the fireplace and... *Carson,* he's just watching him. Unmoving. I mean still as a goddamn statue, unphased by Lucio's suicide playing out right in fucking front of us."

Seeing Sarah so upset made tears come to Annie's eyes too. "He killed himself?"

"No— I mean, yes. Goddamn I don't know. He smashed his own damn brains out, but it was Carson who did it to him, Annie. Carson said that he showed Lucio what the son of a bitch wanted to see. And I know all those Society bastards deserve anything and everything they have coming to them, it was... it was just the sight..." She regained a measure of her composure. "The sight of him destroying himself... my god." Fresh tears fell. "My god, Annie."

Annie placed a hand on Sarah's back and rubbed softly. She wanted to comfort her but didn't know what to say. "I don't understand the world anymore," were the words that came out of her. "It seems like everything gets meaner and darker and colder every day. It's making us like it. I hate it, Sarah. I hate the Society for doing it to us."

Sarah looked at her. Those big hazelnut eyes clear as stones resting within a summer stream. "I know you love him, Annie. I love him, too. We all do. But whatever the Society did to him, whatever that goddamn orb cut out of him, it filled him back up with part of itself. I'm. . ." She reached around to take Annie's hand into her own. "I'm not sure the Carson we rescued was the same Carson we went to save, sweetheart."

A sudden dread filled Annie's heart, a thunderous emotion that erupted suddenly like a rainless lightning storm come upon a sleeper in the night. She suddenly felt the world was all too big and all too distant to know, like nothing she knew could be trusted. Sarah couldn't be saying what Annie thought she was hearing. "What do you mean?" she asked.

She rubbed Annie's palm with her thumb. "What happened in the Dragoon Barracks, Annie, no one forced him to do that. He *chose* to expose Lucio to. . . whatever it was that he shattered him with. We all love a man who may no longer be a safe companion to us. . . and you are most in danger as you are closest to him."

Annie slid her hand out of Sarah's tender grip. "No."

"Annie, now, wait—"

"No. I won't, Sarah. Whatever Lucio got, he deserved. You said it yourself. In Chicago, you made it clear that these people are a plague on the world and that you'd burn them all down if you could."

"I did."

"I'll talk to Carson," said Annie. "Where are the others?"

Sarah took a deep breath, as if collecting her thoughts. "Ashley's with the Society folk, trying to keep them from storming this building. Carson just killed their last remaining figurehead. Who knows what Ashley is having to tell them."

"Sven?"

"Training the companies, or off somewhere with a bottle. Who knows these days."

"Carson in his room?"

"Yeah. Please just be careful." And then, sweet as a forlorn sister, she kissed Annie on the cheek. "Please."

Annie wrapped her arms around Sarah, hugging her. "We can trust Carson. He's still the man we all believe him to be," she said. "I'll talk with him about what he did to Lucio. Why he did it. We'll figure this out."

Sarah nodded, but there was no confidence in it.

Annie headed upstairs toward the primary bedroom. She went slowly, the stairs groaning as loud as the frozen surface of the Mississippi River in Baton Rouge, where she had waited, heart in her throat, for Carson to come through the front door of that hotel. That felt like years ago to her now. Her mind raced with questions, unsure of what she should say first.

She pushed on the heavy wooden door. It swung open to reveal Carson sitting on the bed, his back to her as he stared into the blazing fire in the hearth. He looked more shadow than man, the firelight blistering away almost every detail.

The slumped silhouette turned its head. "Annie?"

She stopped, then started forward again, shutting the door behind her, letting her love for Carson cast out all her fear. "Are you all right?" She went around the bed and looked at him, the fire's light illuminating his face.

His eyes stared into the red hot coals, burning bright and clear as dewy grass beneath a spring sun. When he didn't answer, she asked again.

A line of tension ran through his jaw, bulging. "I killed Lucio."

"I know."

"First person I've killed since I attacked the Baroness's train." He let out a deep sigh, considering. He laced his fingers together, staring deep into the coals. "Back when Gilbert was alive, we were sitting in front of a fire—not like this one, a campfire— I had just taken a life for the first time. It changed me. Changed me in a way I couldn't understand. He tried to explain that feeling. That feeling I felt then. The same feeling I'm feeling now."

Annie placed a hand on his leg. Careful in every way. "What did Gilbert say?"

"He said that every time we take a life, it takes a little piece of us with it. He was right, Annie. And I'm getting to the point where I don't know how much of me is left." He turned to her, those spring grass eyes dying to pools of black without the light of the hearth. "I don't want to do this anymore."

"Do what?"

"I don't want to hurt people anymore. I don't want to be the conduit. I don't want to fight in this war or to kill or to see everything I've been asked to witness. All I want is to be who I am." He placed a hand over hers. "I just want to be myself: A man in love with you."

She didn't hesitate. "I love you too, Carson."

It was the first time she had said it, the first time she had given herself over to it entirely, let the words fly out into the world. The moment they touched reality, she knew she would never stop saying it. Not to this man.

And it was at that moment that she finally understood the tremendous grief her mother must have felt at the loss of her husband. Annie suddenly became afraid, even though Carson was right there, his fingers laced together with hers, the fire burning before and between them. Carson was there, and still she felt the heart-shaking realization that though they had one another now, they could not have each other forever. No one could. The realization only made her grip his hand tighter.

"So much of me wants to be someone else," he said, and his eyes shied away, the words weighing heavily on him. "But all I can feel right now is how lucky I am to be here with you. Be this *for* you."

"I love you," she said again, because it felt right, and it

felt true. More true than anything she had ever said up to that moment.

Carson took a deep breath.

Then, another.

"What you did to Lucio—"

"I know," he said. "It was a mistake."

Annie let those words mill around in her mind. Was it truly an error on Carson's part to give Lucio all that he had wanted, all the darkness he wanted to see, all the cold he'd wanted to fall over the rest of the living world. "I don't know what to do with all this either," she said. "The longer I'm alive, the less I understand about why what's happening is happening. I only know that everything feels wrong. Everything except for you. And Sven and Sarah, and. . ." She laughed. "Even that son of a gun Ashley Sutliff."

Carson laughed, too. "I know. He's something else. I can't stand that he was outside the door that morning after. . . our night together."

Annie smiled, blushing.

"I know how you feel," he continued. "Everything about you feels right to me too. And, honestly, Annie, sometimes I don't know what to do. . . what to do with all this love I have for you. All this love inside me."

Annie didn't have answers for lots of questions. Didn't know what to do about the world other than fight for it. But she knew the answer to this one, and she told him straight away. "Share it with me," she said, a hand sweeping up to rest on his face. "Make it a gift to me. A gift we'll share for the rest of our lives, Carson."

It was sudden: the change. Where one moment their conversation had been filled with fear, shame, horror, and uncertainty, now there came over them a fire, flaring brighter and hotter than the one before them in the hearth. The world was tossed aside. The only thing that existed in the entire universe was the fire, the room, and the two thundering hearts inside.

Their lips collided. Fingers glided between gaps, sliding cloth from flesh, until nothing remained but two vessels giving themselves away. Giving and giving, each vessel emptied of itself, filled with the love of the other. It was their second intimacy. The first, virginal. The second, transformational.

She pushed on the heavy wooden door. It swung open to reveal Carson sitting on the bed, his back to her as he stared into the blazing fire in the hearth. He looked more shadow than man, the firelight blistering away almost every detail.

The slumped silhouette turned its head. "Annie?"

Carson finally spoke, breaking the long span of moments that had been filled with only their paired breathing and contented smiles. "I'm going to find a way, Annie." His eyes were closed.

She combed her fingers through his hair. "I believe you."

He turned, opened his eyes, and looked at her.

In his face she saw all that comprised him. The fear and the will to face that fear. The wounds and the weariness he would forever have to bear. And a fragile power strong enough to destroy the man and the whole world with him.

"I believe in you," she said, sliding her palm to his cheek.

His lips pressed together hard, he nodded. Believing.

Carson kissed her again, then rose and with the great meticulous patience his hands now required, he began to dress himself.

"Where are you going?" asked Annie.

He turned, looking back at her. A quiet strength was in his voice and the fire of his eyes blazed once again. "To keep my promise."

CHAPTER TWENTY-FOUR

DRAGOON BARRACKS, FORT SCOTT, KANSAS

It was one big goddamn mess. The door hung open, snow blowing in. Lily Rose was up in Ashley's face, her spittle freezing to his skin with every wet bellow. The other members of the Society of Prometheus had crowded around the charred corpse of Lucio Gandolfi, some wailing, others mourning silently, all of them crying.

Sven stood next to Ashley, drinking lazily from his bottle like a man half-amused and equally bored. He gestured with the bottle at one of the Society members, who was trying to lift the body now. "Believe that head's gonna come off if you try to move—"

The blackened skull snapped loose from the spine, rolling into the knees of a wailing woman. She shrieked, drew back. But then, grief fell over her and she lovingly took the skull into her hands.

Sven sucked wind through his teeth. "Well, that's no good."

"You fucking liar," Lily said, and Ashley wasn't sure how much more he was willing to stomach. "You promised us safety! Gave your goddamn word that nothing would happen to us. Especially to *him!* I *told* Lucio not to trust the word of a goddamn gambler, and now he's dead. The greatest living master and scholar of our order. Dead."

"Listen, Lily. . ."

"No." She jabbed a stiff finger into his breastbone. "You listen—"

Ashley calmly reached up and encircled her finger, still pressed into his chest. He thought about snapping it off but decided against further enflaming the fires of conflict. "Take your goddamn hand off me. I had nothing to do with this. Shitfire, woman, y'all are the ones who were supposed to know how to handle Carson. He's your fucking dark messiah or whatever. He just showed Lucio what only the conduit could see. It's not my fault that Lucio lost his mind."

"And his head," said Sven, taking another drink.

Lily balled her fists, leveled her rage at him. "Shut the fuck up, gunfighter, or I'll—"

"You'll what," asked Sven, all the levity out of his voice. Ready. Willing.

"We're leaving," said Lily, changing course quickly. "We're taking the manuscript. Going back to someplace safe."

"You can go. . ." The voice came from behind Ashley. "But that book stays here."

He turned to see Carson standing in the open doorway. He was wearing a heavy coat and dusted with powder from the snowy gale blowing powder behind him.

"You." Lily's voice filled with rage.

Ashley caught, in his peripheral vision, that the woman was going for her gun. He started to react, to reach out and slap the gun away, but before he could even lift his hand Sven's revolver barrel was extended over Ashley's shoulder, pointed at Lily's head.

"Sven," said Carson.

The word saved Lily's life.

Ashley, though he was in absolute awe of Sven's quickness, set his face in the imperturbable mask that had won a thousand poker hands over the course of his life. He looked back at Lily. "The book stays. And anyone that stays with it, choosing to help us, will be warm and fed. Or you can take your people and risk walking from here to town in that." He nodded to the blowing storm outside. "And we both know, Ms. Rose, that if the blizzard doesn't kill you, it'll be those giant wolves you adore or the goddamn vampires."

Lily looked at the storm, then at Carson, then back to Ashley. "You're leaving us with nothing."

"I'm leaving you with your lives. Which is more than your goddamn Society deserves."

"There's a reckoning coming for you," said Lily, venom in her tone. "All of you. The world will be set right. The Nine will have their due. The whole sum of it."

Her words seared the air, burning silence into the crowd.

"Get them out of here," said Carson. "I need time with the manuscript. Alone."

"Still think you can figure all this out without Mr. Crispy over here?" asked Ashley.

Sven let out a grim laugh.

"He can't," Lily barked. "He doesn't even know what he's reading!"

"And I suppose you'll read it for him?" he asked her.

"I know more than you think, Sutliff."

"You can do it by yourself?" Ashley asked Carson.

"Yes," he said. The word was firm. Confident.

Ashley nodded, then smiled at Lily. "There you have it. You and yours pack your shit. I'm moving you to one of the other barracks."

Lily burrowed a hole into Ashley with her stare. "This isn't over."

"No, not yet. But he's gonna see to that. Now, go on, get. Like I said."

The Society members gathered their things, along with Lucio's remains, which they reverently wrapped in a tent canvas, and tramped out the door, a defeated people. Ashley had Sven escort them, partly to keep them from causing any trouble but mostly so he could get a palaver with Carson.

When the door closed behind them, Ashley sat down. He took off his hat and ran his fingers through his hair, as if that would help the pounding headache that had come on him.

"Well." Ashley let the word hang.

Carson wordlessly picked up a sheet of paper off the ground and laid it over the top of the book. A strange symbol had been drawn onto the sheet.

Ashley shook his head, wanting to give its mystery none of his attention. "Jesus, kid. How the hell are we supposed to figure this thing out without Lucio?"

"Ever let your anger get the best of you?" Carson asked.

"Once or twice."

"There you have it."

"Your mistake may have cost us our best last chance to stop—"

"It didn't," said Carson, sitting down opposite him. "It won't."

Ashley tried to rub the headache away by pinching his nose, massaging his eyes. "Awful confident of you."

"Lucio already gave me everything I needed from him."

"Oh, well, that's reassuring. I'll just go let the others know that you've solved the puzzle that threatens to kill the human race."

"I'm not bluffing, Ashley."

He looked up, studied the young man's face. He was telling the truth. Least, he thought he was. "You're serious."

"I am."

"Want to let me in on your secret?"

"This whole time, I've been reading the manuscript, letting it affect me. Change me." He turned his gaze on the sheet-covered book. "And not once did I consider that the book was written in a language that Ezra taught me to read. Lucio was right: I could read it, but I didn't wholly understand it. I know the letters and the words but not their meaning. But it never occurred to me, not until Lucio mentioned the idea, that maybe it was time for me to stop reading from the Black Manuscript. It's time for me to start *writing* in the manuscript."

Ashley shook his head, the headache getting worse. "I don't understand."

"I'm the key, and I'm the gate. I hold within me part of the power that wrote this goddamn book. Other writers have come and gone before me, written in its pages, derived rituals that caused this whole mess. Well, what if I wrote a ritual that *undid* those things. What if I used the power of the conduit to close off the channel forever?"

Ashley didn't like the sound of that. "Sounds like a powerful ritual. And if I know anything about anything, kid, it's that powerful rituals... they have a high price."

Carson stared back at him, unflinching.

In that moment, Ashley came to see the steel passed down from Gilbert Ptolemy's eyes in those of his adopted son. "What do you need from me?"

"Time."

Ashley had to laugh. "Anything that I can *actually* provide? This war has a fuse, kid. A short one to begin with, even shorter now. And if what Sven tells me is right, those goddamn vampires aren't going to wait on us to come to them."

"All the time you can then."

Ashley shook his head, considering. "You've got seven

days before we move out. After that, you'll have to do your work on the march to Black Wells."

"I'll do my best."

"Be careful," said Ashley, rising. "But hurry, every chance you get."

* * *

Outside the Dragoon Barracks, the howling wind blew hard and mean, whipping the tufts of yellowed grass peeking out of the snow. Ashley took out his flask, took a sip. The whiskey warmed his throat. Then his belly. Just outside the stockade, all was quiet. Fires burned brightly. He could see the lookouts from their towers, their braziers burning like flames atop timber candles.

He needed to talk to Sarah about what to do with the Prometheans, and to Sven to see if anything else could be done to ensure great success for the gunfighters. He also needed to discuss drilling schedules with the officers and send a telegram back to Washington to request more trains to transport all the companies. They certainly wouldn't try to ride or march the entire seven hundred miles from Kansas to Black Wells. Not in the winter cold, out in the goddamn open.

He wondered if he should tell Sarah and Sven and Annie that there would be no supply chain built to support them. About that, Grant had been quite clear; this was an all-or-nothing attempt to take Colorado from the Red Kingdom, and the whole damn country would lose their minds if they knew that a division had been raised to face such a conflict. That's why the papers had been flooded with government writers to talk about the blizzard and the long, unending night as a kind of astronomical anomaly. The religious masses accepted it as God's punishment for slavery and Southern insurrection and the war that had split the country at the heart. The government had given all it was going to give. General Sherman and his whole rank and file of blustering, fat-ass officers had made that clear too. They wouldn't risk the whole country's sanity for the Colorado Territory.

No, it would fall to Ashley Sutliff to see the war won. The most quiet war in the history of the world, he thought. Secret wars—they had been his whole life.

And he was just about goddamn well done fighting them.

The shrieking wind died, leaving quicker than it came. His head was now pounding so hard he could feel the blood thundering in his temples. The right side of his vision was getting blurry, and a bright spot blotted out the far most edge of his eyesight entirely.

"Ashley," came Sarah Lockhart's familiar voice. "Why are you just standing there in the cold?"

He turned to see Sarah standing near one of the flaming tripods between the Dragoon Barracks and Officers' Barracks. She was wearing a long, heavy coat, her dark hands extended over the tripod, a hat pulled low. "Come over. Get the chill off your bones."

He sighed, his breath visible in the cold, clean night. He walked down the steps, boots shattering the smooth slate of snow. "Been wanting to talk with you 'bout a couple of things," he said. "But what on earth are you doing out here?" Sarah was, at times, a solitary person, so it didn't surprise him too much to find her here away from the others.

"You know me," was all she said, her voice flat. She must have still been shaken after what she had seen Lucio do to himself.

"Well, let's go inside. Get a drink. I want to talk to you about the Society folk. I've ordered them over into that barrack over there for now. You've dealt with them before; what should we do with them?"

"You're the one in charge," she replied. "What do you think we should do?"

Ashley went and stood next to her, trying to ignore the throbbing ache inside his skull. "Well, we can't kill all of them, that's for sure."

Sarah laughed, her voice muffled behind a scarf Ashley could barely see beneath the hat. "No. We certainly can't do that. They're too important. Especially Lucio. The others are expendable though."

The hair on Ashley's neck bristled. His heartbeat began to drum deep and heavy in his chest. "Right," he said. The wheels in his mind were turning, but the pounding inside his skull made it hard to comprehend. It was like a huge hand had wrapped around his brain and was squeezing so hard that blood might come rushing out of his ears.

"Oh," said Sarah. It was a long, sad sound. "I see it now. It took me a moment to find it. He's already dead."

Ashley's mind wasn't just in pain it was. . . somehow receding. Pulling himself away from. . . himself.

When she turned to look at him, he saw a woman's eyes, but not the hazelnut eyes of Sarah Lockhart. They were burning eyes of blue, the color of a falling star. "Ashley," she said, though he did not know this woman and could not understand how she knew his name. "Ashley Sutliff."

"Who," said Ashley.

"Who," the woman said, the word sounding like an owl's haunting call.

Ashley went for his gun. Maybe he could move fast enough, faster than he ever had before, and blow this woman's goddamn head off before she had a chance to—

But Ashley didn't move a muscle. Couldn't twitch a finger. Not while the woman's eyes were on him.

Carmilla.

The voice came not from her lips but from inside Ashley's head.

She stepped close to him, sliding her arm around his elbow, like they were two lovers about to go on a long, romantic stroll. "I am Carmilla, Ashley," she said. Her voice smooth as satin, warm and welcome as a summer day. "I feel your struggle. Your want to call out. To scream. And you will, Ashley Sutliff, in time you and all the soldiers here will scream. Scream for me. And those screams I will take back to my king as a victory song. My brother Sigurd is coming, his will directed for revenge against your friend inside that building," she said, lifting her lips to slide across Ashley's earlobe. "You should come with me, I think. Come with me to take Carson Ptolemy to my brother. A gift."

Ashley opened his mouth to let out a warning scream.

"Yes," said Carmilla. "Give it to me."

The vampire moved faster than Ashley could have believed, locking her mouth over his. His scream flew not into the air but into Carmilla's mouth. Down her throat. Her sharp teeth pierced his lips, and they kissed. There was no pain. Only terror. And the muffled scream Ashley did not even recognize as his own.

She swallowed him. Blood, mind, and will. The pleasure of the pain seared Ashley's brain, melting away the throbbing pain of his headache. She was so much stronger than he was, but she didn't need any measure of that power to keep him close. He was hers. Blood ran over her lips, over her snaking tongue that licked the roof his mouth and glided over his teeth.

When she pulled away, as quickly as she had descended, she shattered Ashley. Without realizing what he was doing, he took her slender waist, his big hands wrapping almost all the way around her, and mindlessly cowed his head to kiss her again.

With a single finger pressed against the dimple of his lips, Carmilla held his want at a distance.

"Good," she said. Her long, black tongue snaked out of

her mouth, savoring the slick, wet redness upon her supple lips. "Oh, you have a fire in you Ashley Sutliff. I think I'll keep you."

And that was all Ashley wanted in that moment. He didn't care about the war or the people, or about Carson or that pinch-faced bitch he loved. Sven and Sarah and the whole goddamn world could burn up, and he wouldn't give a damn. What he wanted was Carmilla. Her, and nothing else, even if it cost everyone every goddamn thing.

"Let us go to Carson. Together," she said. "Go to the door. Knock. Use his trust to bring us inside. There, we will take him and that manuscript that has such possibilities for us, Ashley. Will you? Pretty please, will you?"

Ashley didn't answer. He moved.

Arm in arm, they walked up the steps to the second floor of the Dragoon Barracks. All the way Ashley smiled at the taste of his own warm blood in his mouth. There was something that made it sweet as honey to the taste. He rolled the flavor around in his mouth like the savoring of a fine whiskey.

He knocked on Carson's door, as he had been told.

No answer came.

"Call to him, Ashley," said Carmilla.

"Carson, it's me. Got something I want to talk to you about." His voice sounded strange. Far away. Dreamy.

Again, no answer.

The vampire reached up and ran the smooth side of her talon-like nail, black and long and sharp, against Ashley's cheek. "Open the door. I will handle the rest." The words were so soft, an impossible tenderness in their finality.

Ashley opened the door.

Carson was sitting there, the fire roaring behind him. His face was slack as a death mask, his eyes rolled back so far they were all milky white. His hands were moving though, fingers gliding over one of the pages of the manuscript. And from his throat came a low moaning sound. *No,* thought Ashley. He wasn't moaning; he was humming. Humming a low tune that when Ashley heard it, it immediately soured the taste of Carmilla's honey-flavor in his mouth. All he could taste now was the iron of his blood. His heart began to race.

Though Carson's voice did not raise in its volume, the song coming from his throat intensified, growing in power. Ashley began to shake, and the ice that had frosted over his eyebrows began to melt. The droplets ran down the slope of his eyes to mix with the tears he hadn't even realized he was crying.

"What..." Carmilla let loose of Ashley. "What is this?"

The vampire's power over him diminished, and suddenly, his mind was his again. And with it came the red roar of alarm and action. He had filled his revolver with silver bullets when they arrived at the fort, never knowing when the vampires would make their assault. And now, free of Carmilla's grasp, he was going to blow her goddamn head off, making her the first vampire casualty of the war.

He went for his gun, smooth and quicker than ever before.

Carmilla was fast though. So fast that one moment Ashley had his fingers around the grip of his gun and the next the world was flashing white hot and he was across the room. Something long and jagged was sticking up out of his pant leg, and the ankle below was turned all the way around, his foot facing the wrong way.

He wanted to go for his gun, but his hands shot instinctively to the sudden swelling rush filling up his leg like a balloon. Then, the pressure relaxed, and his pant leg started to soak through, dark and wet. He looked up to see Carmilla, calm and cool and forever-free of caution, approaching Carson.

Ashley opened his mouth and took a breath to scream Carson's name, but Carmilla's sapphire eyes snapped their potency back on him. The churning fire in those eyes took hold of Ashley again, and a battle unfolded between the will of the vampire and Carson's terrible tune.

"Quiet, little bull," she said.

Ashley obeyed, letting out the air in a shuddering exhalation. Everything relaxed: his mind, his hands, and the shattered leg they held.

"Carson," said Carmilla, her voice sweet and satin-soft.

He watched impotently as the woman approached Carson. As her attention fell upon the young man, his hands suddenly stopped flowing over the manuscript.

Carmilla smiled, her lips peeling away to reveal their red, shimmering wetness. "That's it. There you are. Look upon me, Carson."

Carson's head lifted, turning his eyes to look up into the bright, burning pools of blue fire within the midnight darkness of her skin.

Part of Ashley, some acreage of his mind that had fallen into lunacy, felt a deep pain of jealousy that Carson was so close to Carmilla, deeply gazing into eyes Ashley wanted only for himself. Forever.

"Who are you?" asked Carson.

"Why, I am the object of the rest of your life's affection, sweet child." She blinked those big blue eyes, and Ashley was on fire for her. The heat of his want for this divine creature of dark grace and beauty sundered his heart. To hear her give Carson a term of endearment drove him to the brink of madness, the craze of his desire so hot that all at once he thought to pull his pistol and shoot the young man dead where he sat.

If not for his damn leg and the pain, Ashley would have marched over to Carson and given the young pup a beating, whipped his ass until the man's brains were splattered all over the table; and in his mind it was happening. His fists falling over and over. He would have taken out his knife and carved out the hot, red heart and handed it to Carmilla without her ever asking. Handed it to her, dripping, to become Carmilla's champion and singular lover.

Carmilla leaned down, slowly, looking over Carson's shoulder back at Ashley. Her sweet, smooth cheek caressed Carson's, and she smiled, draping her arms around the skinny neck of that son of a bitch.

"Please," begged Ashley. "Please, no. Please, not him. Not anyone else. I'll do anything, dear Carmilla."

"Oh." She stretched out the word, breathy. "I just want a taste. A taste and nothing more."

Ashley was powerless to stop her in that moment. Or in any moment that would ever come again, so long as those eyes were upon him.

"Carmilla," said Carson, and the little bastard's voice was thin. Flat. "Where is Sigurd of Antioch?"

"Why, only a few days ride from here, but do not worry, sweet child. Though he is coming for you, I will take you to him. The both of you. We'll all go together. One long red party where we'll all dance around the smoldering fires his army will make of this fortress."

And that sounded like absolute heaven to Ashley. His jealousy would have to subside. He resigned himself to that quickly, knowing that if sharing Carmilla with Carson was the only way to have her, he would live that life happily, for as long as she would gift it to him.

"Before we go, I'll have my kiss," she said. And with that her eyes went wide and furious, the flames within roaring, burning so hot that Ashley moaned in unashamed ecstasy. The mouth filled with those needle-sharp fangs widened as she rocked back like a gorgeous snake ready to strike.

But she never came forward.

Pain lanced through Ashley's leg. And all the burning lust, which had melted the ice of his will and turned it to water, flared out, leaving a cold empty space where it had once been.

Ashley's vision suddenly focused on a glittering blade of silver between the vampire's fangs. A single, powerful thrust that pierced Carmilla's chin and drove itself up into her skull.

The creature's burning blue eyes shrank to black pinpricks. Her smooth, dark skin shriveled to leather, which blackened and flaked like charred paper. And then, what had once been the most beautiful thing Ashley Sutliff had ever seen, fell to the floor with a heavy thud, stiff as a board.

Carson grunted, yanking the knife free of the creature's face. He placed the edge to her throat and sawed back and forth. Blood, black and thick, smelling like a thousand graves broken open, filled the air. His other hand twisted fingers through the black hair gone gray as ash, and with a steady, vicious jerking motion, he pulled the vampire's head free.

And all at once, the pain streaking through Ashley's leg shot up his thigh, sending his stomach churning and heart hammering. Sweat poured down his face. "What. . ." he managed, then bit down so hard he felt a hunk of his tongue fall into his cheek.

Carson tossed the head away and hurried to Ashley.

"That was a vampire," said Carson, as he rolled up Ashley's pant leg to assess the severity of the break. "And to quote Gilbert, 'I don't know about you, but I sure as shit could use a drink.'"

Ashley opened his eyes.

Carson Ptolemy was grinning.

Grinning like a man who had just learned a very valuable secret.

CHAPTER TWENTY-FIVE

The Red Kingdom

The cupbearer would never forget the night that it happened: the night a red king wept upon a black throne within the scarlet-lighted city of his mountain-shrouded kingdom. Laying within the shadow of his bed, a hollow section carved into the stone, the memory of the man John Childs had once been rolled over and over in his mind. He had been dreaming before it happened. Dreaming of the night before, when King Kristian had taken him to stand at the massive overlook that jutted out like half a tea saucer perched over the lip of a great table, hovering above the whole expanse of the stone city. Within the mountain, the overlook was the topmost point of the vampire world. Kristian told him of how he'd stood here and watched the passing of decade upon decade, watching over his people and the herd that sustained them.

The cupbearer looked out onto the great city, red lamps shining bright and clear, their flames kissing the beads of condensation that dripped from bony stalactites like so many bloody spears. The water twisted around the stoney spindles, spiraling into pink ribbons that fell a long, long way into big natural cisterns smoothed out over thousands and thousands of years. The human cattle trod among narrow, wending paths, carrying buckets for drinking and washing and cooking. All of them worked, none of them spoke. It was not allowed. Once a human cow or bull passed under the archway into the Red Kingdom, they came under Kristian's rule. His law.

"That is the problem with your people," said Kristian, overlooking the jewel of his accomplishment. "Once they start talking, they begin to conspire. Conspiracy sharpens to conflict. Conflict to the shedding of blood. And unlike your people, John, to us, the blood is precious."

The more the cupbearer listened the more he agreed.

Afterall, what had the cupbearer's life been before this grand creature had shown him the true meaning of being a vessel—what it meant to be the life which sustained his immortality. Had any man or woman before known such a purpose? Such an honor.

Life before the Slaver's Revolt had been hard. The war had made it even harder.

"We should have been better to one another with the world that we made," said the cupbearer. "You'll show us a better way."

The cupbearer did not know if this was true; he only knew that saying it would make the king smile. And when he smiled, something climbed to the height of the topmost overlook in the cupbearer's heart, approving.

"I will," said Kristian.

The memories of the cupbearer's life before were almost all gone. The king had taken them. All of them: grief and pain and sorrow, loss and even the fear of death. None of them remained. What remained was purpose and the desire to serve such a monarch.

"Are you thirsty, my king?"

Kristian took the cupbearer by the hand, guiding him away from the overlook. "I am," he said. The king drew him close, curling a slender, delicate hand around his neck. And though the vessel was taller than he who would drink, he felt small and safe in the vampire king's soft, strong embrace.

And as he had so many times before in such a short span, the king drank.

John Childs gave gratefully. He gave his blood and memories. All his worldly cares. His hopes and dreams. He gave so much that he couldn't remember the name of the girl who had broken his heart, and he gave it all away freely.

All of this, the cupbearer had been dreaming upon. Thinking over. Relishing.

It was the howling scream, a rending thunder of a wail that shot down the stone corridor leading to the throne room, that shot John up from his bed. The lamps that lighted the path flared red to blue, blue to white, burning to the height of their heat. It sent him running as fast as he could, which, as it turned out, wasn't fast at all. All he felt was tired. Fatigued. All worn through from Kristian's unrelenting thirst. His back ached from sleeping on the hard cave bed, and the bones in his hips and legs felt as cold as the stone flying beneath the raw skin of his bare feet.

He rushed into the throne room only to find it as dark as the spaces between the stars in the night sky. For anyone else, the darkness would have filled them with fear, sent them running in whatever direction would carry them away from that impenetrable shroud, but John felt no fear. He had been in this place so many times before that he knew how many footfalls were required to reach the throne from which all this darkness emanated. And so, he rushed headlong into the darkness until he found its center, and the invisible form of his king. Throwing himself before the king's feet, the cupbearer wrapped his arms around the monarch's legs.

"What happened?" the cupbearer asked.

"Carmilla's shadow. . ." Kristian's voice was low, filled with grief. "It's gone."

"Gone?"

"The portion of myself that I gave to her, I can no longer feel it. My daughter. . . my eldest daughter is gone."

Those words filled John with grief. He had no love for Carmilla whatsoever, but to hear his king speak with such pain in his voice filled John with anguish. He began to weep so profoundly that his tears fell onto his hands, which still cupped Kristian's feet.

"Those. . . *animals* have stolen her from us, John. I do not know how or where, only that they have."

"Damn them," John's voice a harsh whisper. "Damn them to Hell. You should have gone yourself. Listened to Sigurd, my king. Crossed this continent and burned to ash this nation and all the rabid vermin populating it."

"They are vermin, aren't they, John."

"*Yes*. All of them. Childish and ignorant. They cannot understand you or the ways of your people."

Kristian sighed, and with that exhalation he seemed to blow the scarlet fires back to life, setting aglow the throne and the wide cavern whence it sat.

John looked up into the king's eyes. They shone like molten gold, burning indomitable. The cupbearer's grief fell away at the sight, his great love for Kristian raging hot as the eyes upon him.

"You have given me so much, John. And now your interior is coarse and dry. Veined with fissures. You have little left to offer me, and I have so, so much to offer you. Your poor mind is sunken, your heart ossified white and hard, yearning for something more. You are still one of the herd, John, but you no longer think like them. Your thoughts are like ours, like my own. I saw this potential in you the first moment we met—saw that you could be one of us, that you could be my friend and my cupbearer. And now I come to you with an offer of more. Of life immortal, John Childs. If I offered my wrist to you, dripping with deathless power, would you take it?"

The cupbearer's mouth was so dry, so parched, that his tongue felt thick and sticky against the roof of his mouth. He felt the raw skin of his lips peeling away as they slid against each other in hungry anticipation.

"I–"

"Oh, he hesitates, though I bid him come."

It was the word 'bid' that sent the cupbearer down, down into the parched fissures residing within what remained of the man. Within the caliche-hard desert of his heart, one that had once blossomed with wildflower passion and the rolling greenery of life's sweet promise— of one day finding fulfillment and happiness and love— John Childs remembered what Kristian had done to the mother and her child. He saw it so vividly, as if it were happening right there before him all over again. The king —whom he had given the whole sum of his soul over to, though he could not understand how it had happened— this glorious, terrible creature had made a bawling baby girl a club, and its screaming mother the object of the club's destruction.

All of the savagery, all the horror, flooded up from a wellspring inside him. It was deeper than any ocean, more powerful than any thirst. It did not come slowly but came in a rush, pouring over and out of a cupbearer, who, in that instant, remembered more than his name. He remembered himself. The whole of himself. His want for justice. The vow he had made to protect the people of Black Wells. To be their sheriff. To wear a Silver Star until his duty claimed his life or the stars above him burned out.

And with that rediscovery of self, John looked upon King Kristian. And with all his strength and will and soul, the man who would never again serve as cupbearer or servant to a red devil of any kind achieved what perhaps no mortal man had ever achieved before. He drew the needle of Kristian's invisible influence out of his mind, letting loose a bellowing cry that, to John, seemed to shake the very foundation of the mountain jail these red slavers called a kingdom. Without thought of injury or fear, he threw himself at Kristian, striking him in the face, about the ears. He rained down blows with a human strength so magnified that it would have felled Goliath without the use of stone and sling.

The vampire took the waylay, his head twisting left, then right. And blood, there was blood streaming down his lips. Yes. This was it. John had found the great strength of ancient myth. He would batter this blood demon until the very fires of Hell came to consume him.

As John's fury began to slow, he felt pain running through his hands. He drew back, looked at them.

All his fingers were bent wrongly, misshapen. Lacerated to the bone.

"Oh, John," said Kristian, running a finger across the crimson wet splotches upon his fair skin. He examined the blood, let it drip from the sharp talon shimmering black and red within the scarlet lamps. "I would have made you like Carmilla. Like Sigurd. But I was wrong about you. How could one so weak ever be made strong?"

John's heart raced. When he tried to ball up his fists again, he felt the wounds about his hands widen, coursing lightning pain from fingertip to elbow. But John Childs was a veteran soldier, the goddamn sheriff of Black Wells, and no matter what it cost—

One moment Kristian was on his throne, the next he was less than arm's length away. The vampire's face was all John could see, and he could only see it out of his left eye. John's legs shot turgid. All he could hear was the sound of his breathing sucking violently and rapidly through his teeth. He felt something, a pressure squirming like the barbs of a convulsing centipede inside his skull. John began to scream. The squirming pressure looped around his nasal bone, and then, he was blind.

"What a disappointment you are," said King Kristian. "What a friend you would have made."

It was the strangest sensation that came next, the swift, downward tug that tore his face and jaw from the rest of his skull. He fell forward, coming to rest against Kristian's warm embrace.

"Shh," hushed Kristian.

As blood fountained from his ruptured skull, clutched in the dark embrace of that vampire monarch, John Childs died both terrified and unconquered.

CHAPTER TWENTY-SIX

Fort Scott, Kansas

Annie, standing opposite Carson and Sven and Sarah from across the medical table, looked on in angry disbelief at what she was seeing. Watching the angry, pain-filled tears streaming down Ashley Sutliff's face as he grabbed the field doctor by the collar.

Though greatly maimed, he pulled the scrawny, bifocaled man close and spoke through gritted teeth. "Set the goddamn bone and let's be fuckin' done with it. I've got shit to do and no time for this."

To the field doctor's credit, he simply pried Ashley's bloody fingers from his shirt, now stained with swirling fingerprints like embroidered rose petals upon the cloth. "Mr. Sutliff, sir, you're not hearing me. Listen. There is no setting this bone. It's shattered all the way through. The skin is the only tether keeping your leg on, and that's split open here at the shin."

Ashley lay back, his breathing swift and sharp. Sweat poured off his face in slender rivulets.

Annie placed a hand on his pale brow to try and help him relax. His flesh was cool to the touch. "Breathe, Ashley. Try to relax." She shot her eyes up at the doctor, questioning.

The skinny man swallowed hard. Shook his head. Then, he ripped open the lower section of Ashley's pants, revealing the split curtain of flesh and the bloody, jagged bone peeking out from its hiding place. He wrapped a section of cloth around Ashley's thigh, knotting it so tight that Ashley's back bowed off the table where he lay.

"Fuck you, sawbones!" hollered Ashley.

Annie looked away, and her gaze fell upon Carson, who stood just behind the doctor looking tired and every shade of furious.

"Fine," Ashley swore, resigned. "Cut the goddamn thing off. I'm not going to die of blood rot."

"It will be very painful, even after the laudanum takes effect."

"There's nothing you can do?" Annie asked the question that Ashley hadn't bothered with.

"Seen it a hundred times during the war, ma'am. This break is bad as a cannonball shot. Shin and ankle are beyond any procedure of medicine. Maybe a miracle could do it. Seen lots of men survive this. Never once seen the divine intervene."

"Aw, it ain't her fuckin' leg to bother about," said Ashley, looking up at the doctor. "Get yer shit and be quick about it."

"I'll return as quickly as I can," the doctor said, then pushed his way past Carson and Sven, then Sarah. The woman looked on, tears running down her tired face.

"Goddamn it," said Ashley pushing himself up to rest his weight on his elbows. He shook his head, looking at the mangled, bloody rags of his pants and the twisted limb that would never again carry his weight. He sucked his tongue over his teeth, frustrated. "Goddamn it all."

"I'm sorry," said Carson.

Ashley was having none of it. "No. Don't you say it, Ptolemy. Don't you goddamn say it to me. You will not be sorry for me. I will not abide it. Not a single shred of pity from the likes of any of you. It's a leg. Hell, I've seen lots of one-legged men stand taller than any two-legged bastard. Now all of you, you listen to me... Sven, you keep working with the captains and the companies. I want them swift and organized, you hear? Repeating shot and into formation quicker than a cloud of starlings."

"I will," the big man said, hat in his hands, gazing upon Ashley as if attending the man's funeral.

"Wipe that goddamn look off your faces," said Ashley, then exhaled so sharply the wind whistled between his teeth. "Carmilla let it slip. And it's as bad as I thought it might get. Sigurd has himself an army, and they're coming for us. They know where we are, and more than likely they'll know something happened to that bitch when she doesn't come reporting back. So, we're going to assume that they know we know they're coming for us. Sarah, I need you to work those gunslingers. I want their belts filled with pistols, their pistols filled with silver shot. If they're gonna die, I want it to be with all those pistols smoking hot and empty. Prepare for the worst, like Sven is doing with the companies."

Sarah nodded solemnly.

Ashley reached over, his cool hand encircling Annie's wrist. He pulled her around to the side of the table to look upon her. "And you," he said. "You're gonna lead." His voice was flat, brooking no argument.

"Me?"

"Goddamn right you. And don't pretend like it ain't what you want. Hell, if it hadn't been for me getting Grant's backing and showing up in New Orleans, it would have been you and the Guild up here, trying to do what we're doing all by yourself. Only now you've got more to work with. This goddamn doctor is going to cut off my leg, and who the hell knows if I'll catch rot or die outright from losing this much blood."

"Don't say that," said Annie, finally feeling within herself a love for this previously unlovable man. "You're going to be fine."

"Goddamn it, Annie. You're not getting the point. This ain't about me or if I'm gonna be fine. I'm not the hinge on which swings our hope for success. Sigurd and his people are days away—*two* at the most. Two days ain't near enough of the time I thought we needed.

"When the battle starts, we'll need someone unshakable. Someone who sees things clear, someone to stay calm in the face of all of it. And I have never seen a cooler, more stable mind than I did the other day when those wolves got after us. Sven needs to be with the Guild, and Sarah needs to be protecting Carson, just in case he ain't figured things out by the time they get here. Because he *is* a hinge on which we depend." He squeezed her wrist. "But so are you, Annie. You've lived through how many moments like this? Yellow Hill. Fort Stockton. The Peregrine Estate. How many massacres have you outlived? Not because you've seen a hundred battles or studied war, but because when the whole world sped-up lightning quick, you managed to ride it out and survive. And that's why you'll listen to Sven during the battle planning and then, when the lightning comes for us all, you're gonna be the voice that'll see us through the storm."

"Why would they listen to me?" asked Annie. She felt so small in that moment, overwhelmed.

Ashley's eyes rolled, and he laughed. "Because I'll be goddamned if you haven't made every other person in this room listen to you when the time of reckoning came to account. All you have to do, Annie Miller, is just be who we all know you to be."

"He's right, sister," said Sarah Lockhart.

"I've never seen a cooler hand," said Sven. "They'll listen to you."

"Why me?" asked Annie.

"Because it is impossible to refuse you," said Carson. "Impossible not to believe in you when you speak."

A powerful anguish came over Annie, gazing into the eyes of her friends and her lover. Had anyone ever known such love and dread at the same time?

"You aren't going to do it alone, Annie," said Ashley, letting out a big breath. "Lots of people think they can. Think they could rise up, alone to make a triumph unto themselves. But that's all horseshit. We're not going to survive this battle *because* of you; we're going to survive it *with* you. My meaning is this: we don't need you to be everything. We just need you to be you. All of yourself that you can bring to bear."

Annie's heartbeat slowed.

Silent for a long time, she stared at them. Then she decided.

"Sven," she said, looking up at the big man. At that look, the man's face steeled hard and determined. "Get the Guild together. I want to talk with them. All of them."

"Now?" he asked.

"Right now. Officers' Barracks."

The big man moved out the door without another word.

"Sarah, get the captains up. Get those drummers rolling. Every soldier is to be battle ready from this moment forward."

"Goddamn right," said Sarah.

The slender doctor came pushing in the door as Sarah left. He carried a large black bag.

"What do you need me to do?" asked Carson, eager to help.

Annie clasped Ashley's hand, gripping it tight. "You're gonna come over here and hold Ashley's other hand, because what he's about to go through, we're not going to allow him to go through it alone."

Carson did as he was told.

"Are you ready, Mr. Sutliff," asked the doctor, removing a series of sharp, angular tools from his bag.

Ashley looked to Carson, then to Annie.

He looked up at the doctor, impatience masking his face. "Well, hell yes, look at me, sawbones. Don't I fuckin' look ready?"

* * *

Annie came out of the Dragoon Barracks wiping the sweat and blood from her hands onto one of the doctor's rags. Carson, walking beside her, took the rag when she handed it to him.

Carson stopped. "You go do what you've got to do with the Guild," he said.

"Where are you going?"

"I've been thinking about it. The Society members are a problem. Been my problem almost as long as I've been alive. I'm going to go solve that problem."

"You aren't going to. . ."

"No."

"Okay. I trust you."

"And I believe in you," he said, and then he walked away into the deepening cold and the long-standing night, heading toward the burning lamplight set within the windows of the barrack across the parade yard.

Annie watched him for a moment, the details of his form slowly ebbing to become more and more like the night into which he traveled. She turned, letting all her love and fear for the man slide out of the captain seat of her heart. What took its place were her thoughts of what was to come. What was required. She thought of Yellow Hill. Thought of Sigurd.

She stamped toward the Officers' Barracks with nothing but venom in her blood and hate in her heart.

Every numbered member of the Gunfighter's Guild was in the big dining room. Eight, including Sally Scull, Reyes, and Combs, sat at the long table, the rest of them stood huddled near the hearth. The murmur of their conversation faded to silence when Annie shut the door.

"Swede here says you're in charge, girlie," said Combs. His droopy eyes clouded over with the smoke rising from the cigar pinched between his teeth. "Got something you wanna say to us."

Annie ignored him. She went to the far end of the table, so that she stood before all of them. "I'm in charge now, it's true. Sutliff, for now, is out of the game. The great game. Our enemies are coming for us. They'll be here in two days, maybe one. They are stronger and faster and killers all. And more than likely, when they arrive in their full strength, many of the soldiers outside will turn and run. I've seen it myself—I've run from it myself—and when you see it, you'll know that no amount of money was ever worth what's coming." She paused. Considered all the anger inside her. Measured it alongside all that had happened. Weighed it against everything that was at stake in this moment. "But there is no more running."

Annie sighed but didn't allow herself any more hesitation than that. "Sven, take off your pin. Put it on the table." She knew what she was asking in asking for this.

They all laughed, shaking their heads at the ludicrousness of such a request.

"Like hell," said Sally Scull.

The laughter stopped when Sven, without a word, opened his coat, removed the pin, and tossed the silver onto the table, where it clattered and slid to a stop before Annie.

She picked it up. "Larry Cornish was my friend," she began.

The invocation of his name set all the smiles into grim lines. Sven's mouth twisted as he clenched his jaw.

"In trying to help me understand the Guild, he once told me that, more than anything, all of you wanted nothing more than these pins. To wear a symbol that identified you as the fastest, the most fearsome. The best."

Annie held the pin up between her thumb and forefinger so that its silver burned in the rays of the hearth's firelight. "The pin, Larry told me, was made of silver. He also told me that each of you had a kind of competitive sickness, a desire as pure as the metal, to wear that final pin. The pin with the single, straightest number there is: the One. All of you want it. You've killed to get it. Earned the curve of your numbers in blood. This is your way."

She set the pin back on the table. "I should say, this *was* your way." She leaned her fists into the table, setting her weight upon them. "What's coming for us, and coming for us very soon, doesn't care about the number on those pins. They don't care what you are, who you are, or how fast you can draw. They don't care about your competition or that you're the quickest goddamn gunfighters the world has, or will, ever see. They only see you as a minor obstacle on a path to utter conquest. I am certain they have heard of you. Who hasn't? But though they know your association and of your game, they do not know you. They do not know your names, or the numbers on the pins you wear.

"But I do. Larry taught me your ways. Sven, too. And in learning it, I have come to understand it. And in understanding it, I have come to *hate* it. Hate it as Judge Hezekiah Ellison hated it. I hate that violence and the blood you aggrandize with old words of challenge. I hate the killing and the want for more that has made each of you who you are. I hate your ways because of what they have cost me: a friend. And they cost my friend Sven Erickson," she said, leveling her eyes upon Sven, "the great love of his life."

The chairs beneath the eight sitting at the table groaned as they shifted to look at the big Swede, who worked so hard to keep the tears out of his eyes.

"You are sitting in this room because of your ways. And because Ashley Sutliff has purchased your lives and your guns for our collective purpose. But I am here to tell you that your ways, the ways you glory in and the words you use for challenge, they will be nothing if we fail. And so, I am asking each of you to forget about the money and the pins and the competition.

"I am Annie Joy Miller, leader of the Peregrine Estate, and the way of the Peregrine Estate is not for profit or fame or pins. Our way is perseverance. To do whatever life and circumstance require, so that the world continues to spin. We rage and battle against creatures greater than any singular gun, greater than any army we could hope to amass. Our way is toward the sunrise of an ever-brightening future."

Annie stood erect, bringing her shoulders up to their full height. "I'm offering you not to be one among twenty-five, but to be the feathers on the wings of the Peregrine Estate. *My* twenty-five feathers. The world doesn't need a number-one best gunfighter; it needs all her best gunfighters to act as one. As guildfolk, you were only ever a number to each other. I offer you, as my agents, something more. Something that money can't buy and that a number could never give you."

Combs spoke up. "That being?"

"Immortality, Mr. Combs," she said. "Not a number etched onto a pin but a name etched on the whole span of time. The names of those who helped humanity see the sun again." Annie watched them, her eyes scanning the room.

Combs wrinkled his brow, considering.

But it was Reyes who moved, slapping his pin onto the table, his dark eyes leaning hard on Annie in acceptance.

Another pin hit the table. Sally Scull's.

Then another, and another.

Until, piled upon the table's surface, were twenty-four other pins, the numbers etched into their silver faces no longer bearing any of their former meaning.

Annie nodded and once again looked to Sven. "Sven, get these agents all the pistols and silver bullets they can carry. We've got a sunrise to see."

* * *

Carson took his time getting to the barracks where the last remaining members of the Society of Prometheus resided.

What do you say to the people who have hurt you the most, he wondered. To those who were happy to have taken your everything: two fathers and the whole singular prospect of who you wanted to be.

He did not know. All he knew was that when the Society came to mind, his anger began to boil, and his head would shake side to side. His jaw, which constantly ached, would clench. Fingers, once strong and fast and nimble, would ball painfully into fists whose bones would shatter with ease were he to try to use them. It was a strange sensation that, to feel the weakness in himself. Feel the absoluteness of infirmity in a time that should have been the prime of his strength. And again, the rage came over him. With each step closer to the barracks, the deeper grew the hot, wild want to do to them what he had done to Lucio.

Wasn't that what they deserved?

Wouldn't that be fair? To take all their everything as they had taken his?

Gilbert's words echoed in his mind: *'Neither death nor*

grace have any bit of fairness to them. That is one of the hardest of life's truths, son.'

Carson stopped suddenly, the wind cutting hard against him. He understood, now, what his father had truly been saying.

Life in its unfairness was fair to all. The choice to offer grace or death existed outside of that unfairness. And that choice did more than describe a person. It defined them.

People like Jeremiah Hart, the Baroness, Walther Rose, the High Priest, even Doctor Clara Van Horn, they had all seen the world as it was, and they had chosen death for it. And so they worked to bring about the Nine as a way of 'remaking' the world as it once had been. But what they could not understand, what Carson now understood, was that though the Nine had once ruled, something had overcome their power. Banished them. The Society wanted their return, which meant the Nine had once been exiled. The manacles of cold and terror, slaughter and death, had been thrown off. If they had been defeated once, then, Carson now fully believed, their power could be stopped again.

This was what he would tell the Society members, including Lily Rose, that would help them see the way. The truth. That would be the grace he would provide them.

He was the conduit. The gate and the key. Who else would be able to help them see this new and different way.

Carson ascended the steps leading up into the barracks. The wind howled, snow already beginning to powder the gray slush smeared about the staircase. Before he knocked, he looked up to the silver circle of the perpetual eclipse. The black star loomed, a titan in the sky.

Carson defied it with his gaze, and now he would do it again with his words.

He didn't knock; he just pushed open the door, ready to show the people who had taken everything from him the grace Gilbert had taught him.

The door swung open, revealing the common area where all the furniture had been pulled to the edges of the room. And there, silhouetted against a roaring fire, lay figures of various human shape, unmoving.

He swallowed hard. He stepped inside, and his foot slid on something. He looked down to see a short, broad smear of blood beneath his boot.

As if not wanting to rouse the bodies from eternal sleep, Carson closed the door softly.

They had been set in a clear, defined pattern that he did not understand, but the blood sign drawn upon the wood was one Carson knew all too well. It was the glyph that Lucio had drawn upon the sheet of paper. The ancient sign that the Society and Lucio had used to control the manuscript's power. The sign represented a word they could use but never understand. A sign whose meaning had been lost among the annals of time.

Among the bodies, Carson found Lily Rose. The fingers and palm of her right hand were smeared in blood. She had been the crafter of the blood sign. And, being the last of them alive, she had taken her own life with the gun that lay a few feet from her hand.

All of the rage and fury that had flown to hope fell upon Carson again. He could not understand these people. Would never understand them.

And then despair fell over him, because he realized that they would have never understood him or his message. Life had unfairly born them into—or driven them into—a cult that they would never escape; even their deaths belonged to it.

Pity in his heart, Carson moved toward the fire, where he saw an envelope. He went over and opened it.

It contained a message made up of three sentences, a proclamation: *'We will not be subject to any human masters. We go now to our Nine, who will soon come unto you. We choose our own way.'*

Carson stood there, looking at all that remained of the Society of Prometheus, all of them dead at his feet. His and Gilbert's ultimate goal complete.

He didn't feel any sense of accomplishment or triumph.

All he felt was emptiness.

CHAPTER TWENTY-SEVEN

THE PLAINS OF KANSAS

With a dozen cities razed, Sigurd's horde swelled to three times greater in number than whence it had left the capital of the Red Kingdom. The two hundred ghouls, mindless blood-thirsty husks, were guided by the dark, irrepressible power of Wesley's master. The massive gap of land that lay between Sigurd's army and Fort Scott, once seven hundred miles long, was now less than five sliver-thin miles. All the space between had been traversed, leaving behind a trail of red. The longest wound slashed into the geography of humankind in the history of the vampire.

A cut so deep it would leave a scar on the world.

Sigurd, stoic in his leadership, was worshiped by ghoul and vampire alike. When the army was not putting cattle to death by the thousands, it charged through the night like a swarm of locusts, chewing and gnawing and drinking from the broken-open ribcages of the weak, their hearts still pumping, steaming hot in the air—the bloody spoils of conquest. Sigurd's conquest.

When they drew close to Fort Scott, Sigurd descended from the sky to stand at the center of his people.

Wesley shouldered toward him, passing through the bloodstained, tatterdemalion press of vampires and ghouls, to stand tall and proud beside the one that had made him first among the rest. The ghouls rumbled, licking their hungry mouths, the thirst already on them again. They were nothing more than cannon fodder, Wesley knew. They would be sent first into the fray.

"They are a part of my revenge," Sigurd had told him only the night before. "This fort is not like the other, Wesley. They know our weaknesses. I am certain that they have rifles and pistols filled with silver. Knives forged from it."

"This is why you cursed them with our gift," said Wesley. "They strike, the cattle respond. Then, we will swoop in for the kill."

Sigurd grinned. "You are beginning to understand, my friend."

Wesley beamed.

"They have a battle plan, a counter for our rush. The humans know nothing of our numbers, but they know we are stronger, faster. They expect a lightning raid. We will give them this instead. The two hundred will take their toll, perhaps overwhelm them entirely."

"But you don't think they will," said Wesley.

"No. And even if they do, the ghouls are mindless. They will kill and drink indiscriminately, and that I cannot allow. My friend Lucio, the agent who will help us ensure that the long night lasts, he and his friends must be allowed to live. Them and the object of my personal vengeance."

"That son of a bitch Ptolemy."

"And for you, the girl who came so close to ending your life. Annie Miller."

Wesley snarled at the name.

Sigurd placed a hand on his shoulder and, father-like, looked him in the eyes with those big, cougar-like orbs of his. "Learn from my mistake, my friend. When you see your quarry, do not revel in the revenge as you did with Culliver. She is cattle, but dangerous, as all the Peregrine agents are. When you lay eyes on her, you must be quick. Decisive."

"How do you know she is there, master?"

Sigurd's lip curled into a sneer. "Ashley Sutliff leads Grant's army. Sutliff was one of the Judge's agents, and those agents have a way of roosting together. There will be other agents there too, I suspect, but make no mistake, those little birds Miller and Ptolemy nest together. It is how they respond to our strength, to swarm a predator greater than any one of them could ever be."

Wesley looked at his master, not through his eyes but through the dark gift Sigurd had given him. Never had he seen Sigurd roiling with a greater strength than now. The vampire pulsed with a dark radiance as fearsome and clear as the swirl of silver-white light of the great object held in perpetual eclipse overhead. Wesley had only ever seen Kristian emanate with such glory, such power. The recent blood of a hundred, and the old blood of thousands more, coursed through his ancient veins, and Wesley saw in Sigurd, in that moment, the centuries of power all stored up unto this one glorious purpose.

A purpose only five miles away.

For a second, perhaps even less, Wesley Burrows feared the one who had made him. He was grateful that it was those within the fort, and not Wesley himself, who was the target of Sigurd's revenge. To be called Sigurd's friend was everything. To be his trusted agent, greater still.

"You will lead, Wesley," said Sigurd, his voice soft, kind. "You know my purpose and my will. The others will listen to you, because they know you are mine. As I am the most fearsome hand of Kristian's kingdom, so now you will prove yourself to be such a hand. You are ready."

"I am," said Wesley.

"The time is upon us. Now," said Sigurd, unfurling his dark wings, "let us show these wretches the tolling of the time. The final hour of human primacy. The first clock-strike of our ascension."

PART THREE

Amid the Vastness of All Else

"All my life, I have never seen such wonder of stonework nor grandeur of territorial outlay. Nor have I ever known such terror or despair than those days I lay so quiet, hidden and perched above a city teeming with enslaved humans and the creatures who, even in the streets, drank from their necks. And in my heart, I felt a great swell of fear such as I shall never know again; should there ever come a day that these creatures design to rule the world, no living king or army could ever overtake them."

– Ennio Malocello, *Il Regno di Luce Scarlatta*

CHAPTER TWENTY-EIGHT

THE BATTLE OF FORT SCOTT, KANSAS

Carson and Annie stood before the fire, face-to-face, hands interlaced in the little space between them. "They never would have listened to me," he said, his voice quiet.

"No. But that choice was made for them a long time ago. The only thing that matters now is that you have the manuscript, and that means we have a chance to set things right. And in the end, that's all any of us can hope for. That chance to see the sun rise on a new day."

Carson squeezed her hands. "You sound more and more like Judge Ellison every day, you know that?"

"He would have loved to hear you say that."

Carson laughed. "No one more than him." He fixed his eyes on her. "I am very proud of you, Annie. There's no one better to lead. Sutliff understands that. Speaking of, how is he?"

"All hopped up on whatever that doctor gave him. He drifts in and out. Doc says the wound is clean, but it's still early. He's not out of danger."

Carson laughed at that, too. "When was the last time anyone was out of danger?"

Annie shied away. "I know you're just doing that thing you do to try and normalize all this, but I'm scared, Carson. More afraid than I've ever been."

"You're strong. And you have us."

A soft knock came at the door.

"Who is it?" said Annie, frustration in her voice.

"Someone who doesn't want to walk in and see the two of you rooting around like hogs in slop," Sven's voice boomed through the door.

At that, Annie did laugh.

"It's unlocked," said Carson.

The door opened to reveal the gunfighter. He was holding something in his big hands. He stepped inside. "Captains took to your speech real well," he said to Annie, approaching. "Every man and woman's blood is up and spoiling for a fight. We've brought as many soldiers as possible within the walls of the fort, the rest are sleeping in their battle dress for when the bugles rouse them."

"Cannoniers?"

"Filled with silver, enough for two salvos, maybe three. Your twenty-five are also armed and positioned, ready to take to the center of the companies within the fort when the time comes."

"And the strikers?" asked Annie.

"Strikers?" Carson asked.

"See, that one even I wouldn't have thought of," said Sven. "You wanna tell him?"

Annie nodded. "When Sigurd attacked us at the Peregrine Estate, he came in the form of some kind of smoke, blew in through the room and cast us into darkness. If they can all do that, it stands to reason that they'd try to do the same here. Their night vision is vastly superior. The strikers are positioned inside the barrack houses, ready to re-light every fire within our interior defenses should they come at us that way."

"Canny as ever," said Sven, now so close that Carson could smell the whiskey on his breath. "We've got our own folks that have night vision as good as it gets. One of them being newly promoted Captain Marks. Kid's got sand and bluster to match. Says he can spot a snake in the grass at half a mile. So, I've put him in one of the watch towers. So, when a bunch of vampires come swooping in, I'm sure he'll see their shadows on the snow."

"Good. And we'll need to be more than canny," said Annie. "We'll need all the luck the world has left in it."

"How goes the effort on your end, kid?" Sven asked Carson.

"Sarah tell you what happened to the Society members?"

"Yeah." A look of disdain fell over his face. "Fuck 'em. What about the book?"

"I've got a notion as to what I need to do, still chewing over the idea."

"Well, that's less than reassuring, but I believe you'll figure it out. If you don't, and you've got to get back to simpler means, I've got this for you." He lifted his hand to reveal what he was holding. It was a pistol.

Gilbert Ptolemy's pistol.

"Oh, Sven," said Annie. "Tell me you didn't. . ."

"I assure you I did nothing you would not approve of. Combs gave it up of his own free-will. Damndest thing I've ever seen. He didn't say he was sorry for what he did, just that it belonged to you. And that son of a bitch is too damn proud to give it to you himself."

Carson looked at the revolver. The heirloom.

He took it. It felt so heavy in his hands, heavy with the weight of loss and want and its considerable mass. He ran a finger over the cylinder, tracing the long dimple to the trigger guard. Then he handed it back to Sven. "Tell Combs

I'll take it back when all this is over. It's useless in my hands, dangerous in his."

"Well, I stand corrected," said Sven. *"That* is the damndest thing I've ever seen. You're sure?"

"Never more so."

"I—" Sven began.

A battery of horns shattered the black, midnight serenity outside. All three of them perked up, listening.

Sven nodded.

Carson looked to Annie.

She changed.

Her beautiful face, the face he had dreamed about for so many years, shifted. The soft, lean features he had come to love more than any other hardened into her *other* face. Not the face of his lover or the creature who so completely owned his heart but the face of a woman who has grown tired of losing. Tired of running. Tired of being on the defensive.

Annie's eyes swung to meet his. In those eyes, Carson saw the power and the rage, the will and the hunger for Sigurd's head.

The bugles blew again, and with them this time came the howling chatter of captains crying out for soldiers to make ready for war.

Annie flicked her killer's gaze over to Sven, her most trusted agent. She said one word: "Sven."

"They'll be ready," Sven replied. He turned and pounded out of the room, the heavy footfalls booming through the barrack. Even from outside, Carson and Annie could hear him call out to the twenty-four others, who, like him, were the most dangerous men and women time had ever known.

He cried, "Feathers of the Peregrine Wing, Silver Pins of Annie Miller, collect yourselves and your guns. I don't know about you, but I'm ready to turn this goddamn parade ground into a fucking vampire graveyard."

A great cheer broke over the bugling horns and the patter of the long roll calling the division into conflict.

"I'd better get to Sarah," said Carson, turning to pick up the Black Manuscript from the bed. "Finally figure out my place in all this."

Annie snatched him by the elbow. With all her desire and hope and fear burning within, she curled an arm around his neck and yanked him into a deep kiss. There was such strength in that embrace. A hunger that an eternity of eternities spent in that kiss could never satisfy. When they drew away from each other, Annie pierced his heart with those big eyes of hers. The hearth behind her, flaring red and yellow, turned her auburn hair into twists of ruby set on fire.

"That is not the last goddamn time we will do that, do you understand me?" she said.

"I do," said Carson.

"We're going to win today. And the next day. And we may lose a time or two, but not you and not me. You stay alive Carson Ptolemy. Stay alive, and I'll make you the happiest fucking husband that has ever taken a wife."

Carson smiled, his mind a void that only wanted to be filled with more of her.

"You promised," she said. "Now, I am, too. This is my promise to you."

"I believe you," he said.

"No matter what happens," said Annie, as she passed him by and grabbed her gun belt off the bedpost. "You stay in the barrack and figure out that book." The anger was roiling off her, the audacity of complete certainty in success. She buckled the gun belt, slapping the leather tongue through the brass loop. "And Carson," she said, looking up at him one final time before rushing out to meet the greatest calling upon her life. "You're the gate. You're the key. And I love you, no matter what that ends up meaning."

Carson felt the hunger of love, the fear of loss, and the thunder of his own heartbeat as Annie Miller pushed out the door, ready to strike down the creatures that had taken everything from her.

Everything but him.

* * *

In that last moment, as Annie Miller gazed upon the man she was going to make her husband, to see him gaze back was the only thing in the whole wide world that could have made her hesitate. And she did.

But only for a moment.

Her blood was up, and she descended the stairs. Standing before the roaring hearth, Sarah Lockhart was throwing on her coat, cold vengeance in those wide hazelnut eyes. Annie went to her, threw her arms around her, and kissed her cheek.

When she pulled back to give her best friend a command, Sarah spoke first. "I won't let it happen, little sister."

Annie grit her teeth, her eyes welling with tears. "Or to you."

"My life is my own. Ain't a motherfucker been born yet that had the sand enough to take it from me. Go. They need you."

Annie nodded and headed for the front door. She paused before opening it. Outside, the bugles were booming, feet were churning a storm, and the captains were loosing words of courage upon their brave companies. She closed her eyes. She took a deep breath.

"All right, Sigurd," she said as if leaning her lips into the vampire's ear. "Let's see just how fucking fearsome your ferocious order is."

She swung the barrack door open, where before her lay the parade yard. Soldiers set within row and rank in their navy uniforms stood in staggered lines upon the snow, a checkerboard of blue and white. Within the square of companies, with their silver bayonets affixed to their shadowed rifles like so many silver candles burning against the torchlight, stood the twenty-five Feathers of the Peregrine Estate. All the gunfighters were grim-faced, pistols jutting from belts and holsters or clutched in hands, and ready for action. Their breath billowed hot and white in the night.

There came over Annie a great sense of pride, and a feeling of finality. The rare human epiphany of finally understanding your place in the world you have been born into.

She slammed the door shut behind her. And, lifting her voice higher and clearer than ever before, she cried out, "Captains!"

At first the clamor of the army was too great for her to overpower. But she cried the word again, loud and booming.

The captains turned, hearing her, and so bellowed an order. With that, all fell silent, turning to look upon Annie Miller, a woman younger than twenty, who stood above them supreme.

"An army great and terrible comes rushing at us now. They've slaughtered and reaved our people. And they've enslaved the people of the Colorado Territory. They took the life of my mother and my friends." She paused. "But I say, no more. They will take not another inch. Not another single innocent life. Their leader is Sigurd of Antioch—terror itself to behold, but a terror that bleeds. A terror that can die."

A great cheer rose up from the rank of soldiers.

"He claims to have lived a hundred lifetimes," she said, voice ringing. "But in a hundred lifetimes, he's never seen us. Never known the wrath of a people who will suffer his terror no more. And so, if I don't get the chance to kill him myself, if it's one of you, you make sure to let that bloody bastard know. Let all of them know that when they tried to take Fort Scott, it was the beginning of the end of them."

Voices cried out. Bugles howled. And every American within earshot of Annie Miller believed.

With that, she stomped down the steps toward the center of the formation to stand next to Sven.

The big man was smiling, sliding his pistol along his sleeve. The cylinder rolled where it clicked and clicked and clicked again. "Pretty good speech," he said. "Thought maybe you were going to call down a legion of angels or some shit. Got your gun, got your voice. You ready to pop enough of these bastards to take the want of battle out of them?"

"Want of battle? I don't want to steal their will, Sven. For me, this isn't even about killing Sigurd anymore. Or about revenge." Annie took a breath, then, filled with absolute certainty, she said, "What I'm saying is, that if it all came down to burning the whole Red Kingdom—hell, maybe the whole world—to ash just to keep Carson Ptolemy here with me for the rest of my life, then Sigurd doesn't need to worry about me finding him on the battlefield. He should be worried about me finding a match."

* * *

Silent as a plague descending upon a city, Wesley Burrows and his brood-folk, under the shadow of Sigurd's wing, gazed upon their prey. The fort was well within sight, and much to Sigurd's displeasure did they see the roaring fires surrounding the stockade and outer defenses, where stood rank and file better than half a division of American soldiers. Wesley had never seen such a sight.

So keen had his vision become that, even from this distance and even in the blackest night, Wesley could see the tendrils of smoke wafting off the whipping flames of the torches. And so, he reached out his ear, letting his powerful hearing focus itself on the companies who were blind to the vampiric horde less than a mile from them.

There, upon the snowy plain soon to become a field of slaughter, he heard the gale and rush of the human cattle breathing. He focused further, so as to hear the greater-than-ten-thousand collective beat of the soldier's hearts. All of them thundering. Further still, Wesley leaned the power of his ear to hear the rapturous sound of blood pumping through their veins. The sound was intoxicating. He let his mind drift, imagining all the bodies, every single one, piled upon each other taller than the fortress itself. He envisioned raking his claws from the topmost flesh down to the earth, so that every body was torn open at once, and, like a dam bursting, the white plain would flood with an ocean of blood. Wesley, now a dark predator like his master, gazed upon the fort's forces not as opponents but as a feast.

Sigurd stood next to Wesley, thrumming with power. And then, with silent expression of his dominant will, the master of the vampiric army sent the mass of two hundred ghouls out from him.

The ghouls fanned out, their hurrying feet crunching through the snow so softly no mortal would hear them before it was too late. But Wesley could hear them, all of them, their racing steps as clear to him as a pack of snow fissuring before the cataclysmic rush of an avalanche.

Wesley felt a strange kind of displeasure, worrying that the ghouls would rend most of the human soldiers before he would gain the chance to make his own charge. But Sigurd had promised Wesley his revenge on Annie Miller. And Sigurd always kept his promises.

And at that moment, there came a blowing of a bugle. A warning bellowing from one of the towers.

Impossible, thought Wesley. How had they been spotted?

And just as the first bugle cut the quiet of the night, its

sound beginning to fade, another and then another joined the rolling cry that shot every human to attention. Each and every heart, all of their thousands, suddenly began to race with the lightning rush at the preamble of battle.

"Impressive." A frustrated word, but it was all Sigurd said before his massive wings unfurled.

The wind from those wings slashed into the snow, cutting deep trenches that blew up into little, white hills. Those hills blew apart like dandelion tops when Sigurd flapped his wings once, twice, and shot skyward. Once again, he flew high. And higher still. He twisted, rolling into a dive. The eclipse light caught the whipping spurs upon his wing, and they shone like two falling stars tumbling through the canopy of space.

Sigurd of Antioch, with the power of his will over the ghouls and the near limitless power of the stolen blood rushing through his veins, was both the commander and the vanguard. This was the way of old kings, to fly headlong into battle, fearsome. Fearless.

A choir of human commanders, now spotting the onward rush of the ghouls, rallied their forces. "Companies ready!"

With the veteran timing of hundreds of years of making war, Sigurd, a wraith tearing through the night, swooped low over the ghouls and suddenly expanded into a tempest cloud that flooded the outer stockade, perfectly and completely snuffing out tripods and braziers. Mist as thick as cannon smoke choked out the ring of light surrounding Fort Scott, just as it had at Fort Key. But unlike in the attack on Key, there came no panicked sound from within the roiling cloud.

Wesley narrowed his eyes, gazing hard upon the ghouls now rushing into Sigurd's cloud. Many of them rushed on four legs, loping like hungry cats, others rushed on two, claws raised high in the air to rend and slash and tear.

The field grew quiet suddenly.

A single, powerful command shattered the silence. "Fire!"

A flash of yellow light flared through the mist, and blossoms of blue-silver fire suddenly illuminated Sigurd's cloud. A torrential wave of gunfire rolled over the plain, pounding the air.

Fear, that sensation which Wesley had forgotten entirely, lanced into him for the first time in half a year. Then somehow, through the anguish of his master, Wesley felt the rending mental slash of a quarter of Sigurd's ghouls bursting to ash and smoke. The whole horde surrounding Wesley, one-hundred strong of his kin, let out a collective moan of disbelief.

Over the tumult came another order from the human line, and a second volley striped the cold, white mist of Sigurd's power with yellow lances of rifle shot. Again, the horde howled. Half of the ghouls were silenced, never again to hunt or thirst, never again to do their master's will.

The horror, not Sigurd, was the master of the horde now. And they wailed, when golden roiling flowers of fire bloomed into the outer field, bringing back to life the whipping flames and the light of the tripods and braziers. Sigurd's great cloud flashed as if struck by lightning. Wesley bellowed in distress at the sight. Sigurd, wounded, swirled away, recoiling from the newly ignited fires and transforming from thunderhead to vaporous retreating serpent. They could feel their master's pain, the horde, but none of them more than Wesley, the greatest of Sigurd's friends. And it was Wesley who suddenly sprang forth from the horde as fast as his dark power could carry him.

A blur upon the snow, Wesley ran, his form little more than a slash of shadow to the keenest human eye. All the while, looking up toward Sigurd, far away, who rose higher and higher, trying to get out of range from the flurry of rifles.

The vampire master came fully into his physical form, trying to flap wings that no longer shone in the eclipse light but were smoking, all sundered with gaping holes glowing red and yellow and gold, as if jeweled in embers.

And from the great height, unable to fly further, Sir Sigurd of Antioch fell—a smoking meteor that crashed into the snow, unmoving.

Two of the companies saw this and at the immediate command of their captains charged the fallen vampire knight, their bayonets flaring white hot in the light of the resurrected fires within the stockade.

"That's him," one of the captain's cried. "Their commander!"

And they ran in the hundreds, set between Wesley and the mighty fallen Sigurd, who still lay motionless in the snow.

"No!" Wesley, girdled in power and ferocity, reached the mountain top of the dark strength Sigurd had granted him. Wesley became the night itself, a red-black blur of slashing claws, a force incomprehensible to the navy-clad soldiers he waded into. From the company's rear, he reaved and slashed, shattered limb upon limb, tore open throats. Spattered in blood and viscera, he put upon the human army an oppression of vampiric desolation. All the while swearing by blood and darkness that his work here would live on in every human survivor, passed down through generations, conjuring nightmares among the cattle until the end of time.

"Sigurd," Wesley screamed, ripping a rifle from the hands of a soldier, whirling it, and thrusting it so hard into the man that it pierced him and the two men running alongside him, driving all three to the ground. Wesley threw himself into the air, and suddenly, without knowing how, his body became mist—a smaller but no less able cloud of terror than that of his master. Sweeping through the companies, shifting from mist to physical form, then to mist again, his slashing talons made fountains of soldiers' throats, so many, so quickly, that he found himself making war in a rain shower of blood.

The final soldier stood between servant and master, a white-bearded man twice Wesley's age, stood over Sigurd, bayonet poised for the killing stroke that would mark the greatest tragedy of this new vampiric age.

"This is for Annie Miller," said the man. "Now, go to Hell you goddamn—"

Wesley's fist went through the back of the man's skull and burst out through his mouth. The man's yellow teeth scattered upon the scarlet-soaked snow. Wesley yanked his hand free of the gore-soaked aperture. Heaving, breathless with blood thirst and rage and fear for Sigurd's life, Wesley loosed a primal sound that harkened back to an ancient time he himself would never know but now claimed as his own heritage.

There he lay, the greatest of them, his flesh charred over, all of his great, dark beauty ruined by fire, his torso sheared open by soldier's bayonets.

Lying helpless in the snow, Sigurd moaned.

While the battle raged on behind him, Wesley gave the fullness of his attention to Sigurd. More than his champion, more than his friend, Sigurd was his vampiric father, more precious to him than even King Kristian.

"Sigurd, please," he cried, though he could not vocalize all that he wanted in that moment.

"Wesley," said Sigurd, but the word came out all wrong. The vampire's fangs were chipped and shattered, no longer bearing any of their pearly shine. He opened his eyes wide. The luminous green eyes that had transfixed and dominated how many thousands in Sigurd's long and magnificent life were now empty of color, ablated of their power.

Wesley curled his arms around his master's shoulders, pulling him close. "Come," he said. "There is blood. You must drink."

But rather than attempt to rise, Sigurd seemed to relax. "Wesley, my friend. Dearest Wesley."

"Please," said Wesley, feeling tears of blood begin to fall from his eyes. "Sigurd, please. I will help you."

"Debt," said Sigurd, his voice flinty and frail.

Wesley did not understand. "Debt?"

"Now," said Sigurd, straining. "Now is your time to pay your debt to me."

Wesley would have done anything in that moment. He would rush over, crush the stockade himself, and bring unto Sigurd as many human throats as were required to bring his master back to the fullness of his potency. And this was what he turned to do.

But Sigurd took him by the shoulder, turning Wesley to face him again.

"He that dies," said Sigurd, his fingers burying themselves deep into Wesley's pale flesh, so deep that his talons pierced his shoulder blade and burst through Wesley's chest.

Wesley opened his mouth to scream, but the wind was stolen from him as Sigurd's jagged teeth buried themselves into his neck.

The pain flared Wesley's vision white.

Wesley watched Sigurd, his master and friend, draw back after his deep, sating drink. The charred skin was white and beautiful again. The teeth sharp as beveled razors. And the eyes, glowing green and hot with the power that had, at their first meeting, terrified Wesley into Sigurd's embrace.

Wesley fell over onto his back, landing in the cold embrace of the snow beneath him.

Sigurd stood up and gazed down at him, green eyes burning in the dark brighter than any sunrise Wesley had seen in his life. At least, in the life he'd had before that night in Prescott, Arizona, when the master had first saved the servant. Transformed him.

Sir Sigurd of Antioch, fully revived from Wesley's vampiric blood, unfurled his great wings once again like a great demon of some ancient myth. Sigurd soared away toward his revenge.

Snow blew over Wesley's face, and just before he died for the second time in his life, he found himself looking up into the sky, staring at the silver band of eclipse light burning a circle into the night.

* * *

At the center of Fort Scott, the forward gate broke open. A messenger from the front, a short, ruddy woman twice Annie's age galloped on her mount through the opening then through a gap between the companies, toward Annie at the center of the parade ground. A command was given from the watch tower, and the gate shut.

Sliding off her horse in dismount, the messenger breathed heavy, ready to report. Blood matted her blonde hair. The horse beside her chuffed steam, lathered in sweat. "We've repelled their first wave," she said. "Several companies were descending upon Sigurd as I came to you, ma'am. Just as Sven said, he came upon us like a cloud, and when we flared those braziers to light, it cooked that son of a bitch something good."

"But they didn't kill him?" asked Sven.

"Not as of yet." The messenger smiled at Sven. "But he weren't in no condition to fight, sir. Not after what we hit him with. He soared high into the air and then smashed down maybe a hundred yards from the frontline. Our companies have balled up, and we've decimated those that rushed us. First volleys set them alight." She turned to

Annie, her big smile somehow growing. "Damndest thing I've ever seen."

Annie nodded, then commanded. "Report back to the captains that I want Sigurd's head brought to me the moment it's cut from his shoulders."

"Gladly, ma'am." And with that the messenger threw a leg over her mount, cried out, and the horse sprang away.

"You don't look too happy at the news," said Sven as the gate swung open for the messenger riding back into the thick of the conflict.

"Something's wrong," she said.

Above them, from the topmost defenses of the fort, someone bellowed, "We've got 'em on the run!"

A cannoneer issued a sharp command, and the twelve-pound Napoleon guns, all in one accord, boomed like God's own hammer falling upon the anvil of the world. The cannons rocked back on their wooden wheels, belching swirls of twisting smoke into the night. Through the closing gape of the gate, Annie watched the cannons assail the retreating vampires with a volley of silver grapeshot, cutting a swath of them to ribbons just before their bodies ignited bright as gunpowder set to match.

"They've never faced an army before. Maybe Sigurd was overconfident," said Sven.

"You don't believe that," said Annie.

Sven nodded gravely. "I do not."

And just as the gate was about to fully pinch itself closed, Annie heard a bugle cry out, then another, and another.

Sven's eyes shot wide, a harrowing revelation masked his face. "No!"

"What is it?"

"That's the signal to charge. They're going to pursue the retreat." Sven turned and bellowed to the gate captain, "Sound the stay! Do not let them get out of formation!"

"Why would they charge?" asked Annie, panicked and confused. "You told them to stay in formation!"

From beyond the wall there came a rallying cry and the sound of thousands of soldiers charging deeper into the field, far outside the protective firelight and out of the hedgehog formation that had protected them.

It dawned on Annie then. "It's Sigurd," she said. "He's controlling the commanders." The vampire knight had some ability to control the actions of those who fell under his shadow, just as he had done that night in the Peregrine Estate. Both Sven and Carson had said that it was unlikely that Sigurd's power could control them in the thousands, but if he focused on the captains alone...

She twisted around to speak to the gate captain. "Open the gate!"

"Goddamn it, girl, what do you think you're doing?" Sven asked, grabbing her by the shoulder, his big paw twisting the leather of her cavalry coat into his grip.

"We have to help them!" Annie tried to tear away from him, but the man was too strong. His grip too fierce.

"No! That's the mistake he wants you to make. You roll us out of these fortifications, and it wouldn't matter if you had a hundred of the best gunfighters, Annie."

"Let go of me!"

"Listen!" he cried. "Think! How do you think you and Orrin survived that attack on the Peregrine Estate? It was the goddamn door that made a choke point."

He was right.

Goddamn him for being right, she thought.

"Captain," said Sven, "You keep that gate shut."

"Oh my God!" the gate captain cried at what he saw transpiring over the fortifications.

"What is it?" Annie yelled, though it came out almost like a scream.

"They're... *they're...* *It's a slaught*—"

Before the man could finish, a winged shadow

screamed over him, lashing out with talons shining in the eclipse light. They pierced the captain's skull, streaking with such speed that he went sliding heels first against the fortified wall. When his back collided with the timber, his head was ripped from his body like a cork sabered from a champagne bottle, and blood sprayed from his neck.

The companies within the inner fort cowed, their knees buckling as blood rained down on them.

"Die, you son of a bitch!" cried Sven. And, standing taller than any among them, he fired round after round toward the winged terror. But all his shots sailed without purchase as the vampire passed over the southern wall faster than Sven could score a hit. Sigurd was gone.

Annie drew her pistols, ready.

The fortifications went quiet. All the soldiers were rattled, and twenty-four of the Peregrine Feathers had not fired. "He's here," bellowed Sven. "Stand up and fight!"

"What the *hell* was that?" said Combs, his voice trembling.

"Your goddamn end if you don't fill your hands, Combs!"

The soldiers stood again, but Annie could see the fear in their eyes. Their rifles shook in their tremulous grips.

The sound of a storm upon the plain rolled toward the fortress. Then, suddenly, over the top of the gate came the leaping horde of vampires, a hundred or more.

"Ah, shit," cried Combs. "Ah, *shit*."

Sven boomed. "Fuck the shooting, companies! Form up! Gunfighters, let it fly!"

The companies rushed to form an outer barrier of silver bayonets, and between their slender gaps every agent, old and new, of the Peregrine Estate drew back their hammers and sent volley after volley into the oncoming rush of wild, wide-eyed vampires. But the vampires were more than fast; they were agile and cunning. They came, rolling like a wave onto the upper wall, slashing through cannoneers and soldiers. Men and women screamed in fear, howling in death.

Annie aimed at a vampire who had grabbed a soldier by his coat, her lips drawn back, fangs bared like a striking snake. Before the vampire could claim the soldier's life, Annie's bullet took her just above the eye. Her head snapped back, flesh and hair seared in blue-white flames, crumbling to ash.

The feathered wing of the Peregrine Estate shot round after round, pounding the open air in a deafening salvo. Sven roared. Combs found his courage. Reyes, next to him, wheeled his gun around. "They're behind us!" The gun bucked in his hand.

* * *

There was fire and smoke and slaughter outside the room where Carson Ptolemy sat, reading through the pages of the Black Manuscript, the damnable book that had seemingly guided the swaying river of his life. And now here the book lay before him once again, still openly hiding its greatest secrets. Carson turned the pages, reading the insane ramblings and rituals of the conduits and prophets of the Nine who had come before.

"You're the gate. You're the key. And I love you, no matter what that ends up meaning."

Annie's words crowded over him now. He didn't deserve her or her love, but still he clung to it. And to the hope that outside, where the battle raged, she and the rest of their friends would prevail against Sigurd.

Hope.

A life without it was no way of living, Gilbert had said, years ago.

"I wish you were here," said Carson to the empty room, addressing the man that had saved his life so many times.

His fingertips, wet with sweat, began to tremble. "I don't know what to do. I don't know how. . ."

And then there came the song, the dark, rolling hymn that, as it had so many times before, began to dominate all sound. The song that had played over the entire play of his life.

The song of the Nine.

Carson placed his hand upon the leaflet bearing the symbol Lucio had revealed. With one hand on the sheet and the other on the Black Manuscript, the song began to fade. He turned the pages one after the other, until finally he came to an empty page.

Carson took his hand off the symbol sheet and picked up a fountain pen he had taken from the officers' supplies. He made a choice to stop denying what had happened to him. To stop denying what he was.

Carson took a deep breath.

Then another.

Then, once more.

His fingers clutched the pen with what strength he could muster. In the light of the hearth and under the shadow of the Nine's dark song, he began to write. Not as the twice orphaned child or the victim of circumstance or prisoner of his own choices, but as the conduit. The letters that flowed from the pen swooped and swirled, revealing the secret words hidden away from the eyes of humanity for so long but not hidden from those who had cowed before the Nine. And not from him.

He wrote in the Nine's symbols. Manifesting in ink words that cannot, and should never be, spoken from human lips, for they were words born only for calamity, destruction, and pain. And it was in that moment, writing upon pages older than Carson could ever guess or understand, he wrote a ritual that used the old letters to create new words. Expressions the Nine never intended to touch the pages of their annihilating document. The ritual would be simple. It would not center itself on the spilling of blood and it would only require one artifact for its activation. And what would bring that ritual its full power was a single, spoken word, a term that the Nine had no tongue for. A single admirable word that encapsulated everything Carson wanted the world to have and everything his own heart desired.

And when he wrote this new word, in the old language of that deplorable manuscript, the song of the Nine suddenly ceased.

The writing had taken him into a trance of sorts, his eyes fully focused on the swirling ink drafting upon the page. But when the last symbol was writ, he saw that from fingertip to elbow, elbow to shoulder, running all over him was not his own flesh but the smoking shadow. The power of the conduit that he had first seen in Chicago with the High Priest now robed him. The shadow power strengthened his hands, swelled his senses so that he could feel within himself every tiny skirmish of the battle outside. More still, he could feel the great object in the sky that had for so long cast the world into cold and blocked the light of the sun. It was a power that might have been something grand and wonderful in a time before, something beyond description. But the darkness had taken it, and never again would it rise.

The others were warring outside. Killing with fearless tenacity. Shooting and slashing, maiming and dying gloriously for Red Kingdom or the American nation. For them, the Vampire War was still roaring in its first conflict.

But for Carson Ptolemy, the conduit, who had written a new secret in the old, old manuscript, the war was already coming to its end.

* * *

One vampire, insane with bravery, bounded up into a great leap that took him over the protective wall of silver bayonets surrounding the Peregrine Feathers. He landed light as a cat before Sally Scull and, with a sweeping strike, slashed the woman across the throat. Streaks of scarlet sprayed Reyes in the eyes, blinding him.

Sally threw a hand over her throat, trying to catch the blood rushing down flesh and buffalo coat. Her mouth opened wide to breathe or wail with injury, achieving neither.

The vampire smiled.

Annie screamed.

Sven roared.

But Sally, her hands unfailing, eyes narrowing, pressed her revolver into the vampire's chin. And before her killer knew what was happening, Sally Scull ended his life with the final shot she would ever fire. Bullet blew open the back of his head, he burst into ash, which dusted over Sally like black snowflakes tossed in the winter wind. The woman fell to her knees, dying among ash and snow and blood.

Reyes and Combs threw their backs against one another, firing quick and accurate like two brothers set against the ranks of hell's own gates broken open before them.

Something blurred in front of Annie's vision—something large and powerful and fast. A cold grip, black and terrible as the grave, coiled around her throat, shaking her so violently that she lost her grip on both pistols. She threw her hands around the wrist holding her tight as a vise, and when her eyes opened, she found herself looking into the pale green luminosity of Sigurd of Antioch.

"No!" Sven cried.

Sigurd, swift as death itself, backhanded the big Swede so hard that the man went flying, twisting shoulder over shoulder. He slammed into three other gunfighters, taking them out at the knees.

Annie tried to call for help, but the vampire knight's grasp choked the words from her.

Sigurd flared his wings and whipped them forward, sending a blast of air so powerful that it threw whole companies into the ground, breaking open the defensive shell. Claws and fangs of wrath fell upon them, peeling open their soft, tender flesh. Blood and screams and terror filled the walls of Fort Scott.

The Feathers of the Peregrine Estate whirled their pistols and fired and fired, but they were overtaken. As if destined to share a fate, both Reyes and Combs fired their final shots at the same time, their guns smoking hot and empty in the night. Completely surrounded, they looked over to see Annie in Sigurd's grip. Together, they pulled out their silver-bladed knives. With fury in their eyes, they rushed at Sigurd with all the rage and desperation the human heart may bring to bear.

In the face of that fury, Sigurd laughed. They came at him screaming. His eyes pulsed once, then again.

The two gunfighters came to a sudden stop. Their arms fell to their sides, their oppressed gazes trembling within their skulls.

Sigurd spoke. "Kill each other."

And without pause, the two men pivoted into combat stances. With tears in his eyes and a knife in his hand, each man buried his blade into the other. Pumping furiously, blood painting scarlet the snow beneath their battle, their blades sank deep.

Annie tried to kick away, to pry the grip from her throat, but the effort was useless.

"Look, cow," said Sigurd, amused. "See how easy it is."

It was Reyes who came out on top, finally burying his long knife deep into Combs's chest. Combs went slack, eyes rolled up, dying at the hands of his friend.

"Good," said Sigurd. "Now, finish it."

Yanking free his knife from fallen Combs, Reyes began to scream, fighting for all he was worth against the power put upon him. Both hands squeezed tight around the knife's hilt, then he drove the blade into his own throat. He fell to his knees and tipped forward to lean his weight against Combs's body. And though he breathed for a short time, he did not move.

Sigurd turned and put his eyes on her.

"Annie Miller." The vampire's voice was smooth as satin, the intonation unhurried.

Inside her mind, Annie's rage and fear, all her pain and want for revenge, were nothing against the strength of the vampire knight.

"Your army is broken. Your fort seized," he said, gesturing at the desolation surrounding them. "There are thousands of us, and look what I have done with only three hundred. Is this all the war you cattle have to offer?"

"My—" a muffled voice came from somewhere unseen. "My name—"

"Look, Annie," said Sigurd, turning. "One of your birds is still cawing."

A pile of corpses shifted, as if they might all come rising to their feet, but among them, only one rose.

It was Sven.

His face was shorn open in a long curve, temple to chin. His blood, streaming from that wound, flowed darkly from shoulder to fingertip. A mighty winter gale caught his long, black coat, snapping it in the wind. "My name is Sven Erickson," he said.

Sigurd laughed.

Those among the vampire's brood laughed too.

"As the One," he said, swaying with exhaustion. Casting his baleful eyes at the vampire, he seemed to find his strength in his legs. And then in his voice. ". . .I approach you, Sigurd of Antioch, you and your murdering, slaving kin, within the rules of my association, and I challenge you, all of you and your kind, to a contest of the gun."

The brood, triumphantly standing near their master, laughed again. Their long teeth sparkled in the eclipse light.

"Will no one rid me of these pestilential birds?" Sigurd said, more annoyed than afraid.

Annie watched, incapable of moving to help her friend. "Sven," she cried, the word escaping her throat seized by Sigurd's grip.

"Put the girl down, you goddamn coward," said Sven, tears and blood mingling together to fall down the riven flesh of his cheek. "Face *me*."

Three vampires moved suddenly to do the will of their master. They were so fast—faster than Annie could believe.

Sven was faster still.

The draw was smooth and slick, quicker than anyone there had ever seen a mortal man achieve before. The shots cut the night air rapid succession, assaulting the air as one mighty thunderclap. Three silver bullets flew. Three vampires erupted, smoking to ash.

Then his gun was pointed at Sigurd. He pulled the trigger.

Click.

Sven looked at his gun as if betrayed, chest heaving.

Enflamed with rage, Sigurd tossed Annie away. She flew through the air, and a duo of vampires caught her easily.

"Sven Erickson," said Sigurd. "I know the name." He rushed forth, the wind billowing up behind him in his wake, and in one fluid motion of impossible alacrity, he pierced Sven at the shoulder, his long talons driving out of the gunfighter's back.

Annie screamed.

Sven's eyes shot wide, though he made no noise of injury.

"I am Sir Sigurd of Antioch. You have plagued my people for too long. Now, you will plague us no more." He lifted his other hand, talons glimmering.

"Abelia," the word echoed over the parade yard.

The word stalled Sigurd's hand.

Every eye turned to see the slender figure stepping out from the barracks, out onto the snow.

The vampire knight turned. He drew his lips back and snarled, not with power but with rage.

There, standing tall and unafraid, was Carson Ptolemy.

"Carson, no!" Annie cried, trying to pry herself free of her captors.

"*You.*" The word a profanity. "You will *not* say her name." Sigurd threw Sven away as if the giant man weighed nothing.

Carson looked at the vampires clutching Annie, his green eyes burning in the torchlight. "Let her go."

To her amazement, the grip of the two vampires went slack, and they quickly stepped away from her.

Sigurd snapped his gaze to the obeying vampires. "What are you doing!"

The vampires unmoving, stared at their master. . . no, Annie saw. At their *former* master.

Carson, his tone cold and calm, set a command upon Sigurd. "Surrender."

Sigurd, his dark rage pouring off him, unfurled his mighty wings and howled. "Surrender? Who are you to command me!"

Carson walked forward, and when he did, the vampire brood opened themselves so that he could pass by. "I am the gate. And I am the key. I have heard the words of the Nine, and I tell you now that I have written a new word—a word I have yet to say. If you surrender now, you and the people of your kingdom may yet live to hear it for yourselves."

Sigurd shook his head as Carson approached.

"This is my requirement, Sigurd. And if you do not meet it, I will compel you. As you have compelled so many others over your long life."

Annie saw, for the first time, for perhaps the only time she or anyone else would ever see it, fear in Sigurd's gaze. Fear and more. There was doubt in those ancient, terrible eyes.

Sigurd barked to his brood. "Kill him!"

None of the vampires moved.

"Your will is great, Sigurd," said Carson, walking slowly toward the vampire knight. "But to me—to the power of the Nine—it is less than nothing."

Sigurd's eyes flared, and the power of their smoldering luminosity pulsed like a predator's fury catching the light of a full moon.

And that is when Annie realized what was happening: although Sigurd was—impossibly—afraid, it wasn't his fear that kept him in place. He wasn't waiting to act. The dominating, winged terror of the Red Kingdom, its most fearsome hand and ageless champion, was himself dominated.

"Kneel," said Carson.

Sigurd, though straining, obeyed. "How?"

"There are things greater than you. Greater than even your red king, Sigurd. Things that, when seen, drive the sane mad. Rend the heart. Boil the blood to steam. Turn soul to ash. I have seen them, Sigurd. I have seen the darkness through which they wheel. Seen their cold palaces, cut from black, seamless stones, each abode greater than the tallest Earth-born mountain. And running up these impossible walls are rivers. White streams wider and longer than the Mississippi, each one climbing the stone like frosted ivy, so bright they hurt the eyes. And from those nine terrible palaces, there is a song that echoes within the infinite hall of space, though there are no walls to catch its sound. And the cold. . ."

At the word 'cold', Annie watched a tremor run through Carson's shoulders.

"Even we, all of us struggling to survive this oppression of a six-month winter, have not the faintest understanding of what true cold is. Not with ten thousand winters, could any of us, human or vampire, conceive of what will fall upon us if we do not close the gate. Close it now. Close it forever."

Carson had never described any of this to Annie. Though she did not understand why, the more he spoke of the things he had seen within the Black Manuscript, the more her tears fell, only to freeze upon her cheeks.

"My father is dead, Sigurd. Gone forever. While living, he told me that every person deserves a chance to make a choice, no matter the previous choices they have made: a choice to choose what is best. Not for themselves, but for everyone. For the people they have called enemy." His eyes bored into Sigurd's. "For those they call friends." He flicked his eyes over to Sven, who was struggling to rise. Then he looked to Annie. "And for those whom they love more than their own life."

Sigurd's teeth flashed angry. "And is this my time to choose, *Ptolemy?*"

Carson shook his head. "No. This is me telling you that *I* am choosing. You've killed, maimed, and razed, and you live only as an agent of annihilation. You killed Judge Ellison, Professor Robert Bass, and my love's mother and her best friend. You killed how many alone in Abilene? How many before that? How many lives have you taken? How many have you made victim, feast, or slave? How many, fearsome Sigurd?"

"All that I have done," said Sigurd, "was for the survival of my people!"

"I know," said Carson. "I have also lived this way."

Suddenly, Carson fell to his knees, so that he and the vampire were eye to eye. "I am *sorry*. I am sorry for killing Abelia, your wife."

At her name, Sigurd turned suddenly away, unable to meet Carson's gaze. The vampire took a deep breath.

"And so, in this moment, it is *my* choice to do what I am doing now." Carson stood up. He turned to look at Annie.

The man she loved seemed so strong and yet so frail at the same time. There was deep sadness masking his face, and the perilous fall of regret in his eyes.

Then, he looked back to the kneeling vampire. "Rise, Sir Sigurd. Go back to your red king in the mountain. Tell him that you came to Fort Scott looking for war, and what you bring back to him is an offer of peace."

Sigurd sprang to his feet, Carson's dominance no longer upon him. "He will never—"

"He will," said Carson, looking somberly into the vampire's fierce countenance. "He will because you, all of you here, will convince him. He will release his hold over the Colorado Territory. He will recede back into the Astolats. And when I arrive there with my friends, we will write a compromise that none before us has ever been brave enough to compose."

Sigurd leaned forward, bloody tears streaming down his face, fangs drawn up in fury. Then, without word, the vampire whipped his wings and climbed high into the air. His brood turned, shrinking away from the fort and those fallen within it, to follow their master.

There were no cheers. No grand cries of victory. There was only the wounded, the dying, and the dead.

Only the desolation of shattered Fort Scott all around them.

CHAPTER TWENTY-NINE

ABOARD *THE JUDGE*, EN ROUTE TO BLACK WELLS, COLORADO

Thousands lay dead on the field of battle, thousands more within the fort. Of the American division given to Ashley Sutliff by President Grant, which had numbered twelve thousand and more, fewer than a hundred now lived. Too many dead to bury them.

Annie Miller went to Ashley, who lay upon his hospital bed. She had not known what to do next, and so she went to him to both check on him and gain his advice. Sven and Sarah stood outside. Carson and Annie had embraced for a short time, but after what had happened, there were few words between them. The battle had taken all their strength, all the words from their lips, too. The aftermath of violence, Carson had called it.

Annie stood over the sleeping gambler. She roused him gently. His eyes, normally keen and calculating, opened to reveal themselves dreamy, heavy-lidded. His skin pimpled with the sweat of fever. The doctor who had treated him had not been seen since the battle's end.

"I figure seeing you here means we won, huh?"

Annie nodded. Worry filled her heart, and it must have been in her eyes, too.

"I ain't dying," said Ashley. "So you can wipe that look off your face. I've grown impatient with lots of things in my life, girlie. Living ain't one of them. The wound is running red and there is no stink of rot. Reckon my body is just taking its toll on me to heal, which I figure is fair, considering all I've done to take my toll on it."

Annie laughed.

"Now," he said. "Tell me what happened."

Annie told it all. Tried to tell it plainly, though that was difficult with all that had happened.

The tension in Ashley's neck seemed to relax, his head falling back into his damp pillow. "So, the kid did it," he said. "Had my doubts, but he made a believer out of me." He placed a hand over hers. "So did you, Annie. You did fine work. Judge Ellison. . . and your mother. I know they would both be proud. I know I am."

Annie shook her head. "We would have lost if. . ."

"Stop," he said.

Annie screwed up her face. She had come to care for this man, but cutting her off would never be allowed. "No," she said. "This is the reality. Had it not been for Carson, we would, all of us, have died. I failed to hold the fort. It's my fault that all those soldiers will never go home again." And it wasn't just the weight of this massacre that she felt but all the massacres that dotted the map of her life. Yellow Hill. Fort Stockton. Abilene. Chicago. All of those places gone, all of them destroyed.

"And how did Carson find his way?"

Annie wrinkled her brow, confused. "Through learning how to read the Black Manuscript?"

"No, Annie. You wonderful, stubborn creature. It was *you*."

A weight that had been dangling from her chest was

suddenly snipped loose. It fell past her heart, grazed her soul, and then fell out of her being entirely.

"I don't know much about love, but I do know people," said Ashley. "I've seen the want to win and the fear of losing in every person, Annie. Seen it at card tables, saloons, and in the eyes of every human being I have met on this wonderful, harrowing trail we call life. And I have never, ever seen more want to win or more fear of losing someone than I did between you and Carson. I knew, from the moment the two of you came together, that, ultimately, if Carson was going to succeed, you would be the reason for it. You saved his life in Chicago because you were his friend. And he saved all of our lives here because you loved him in a way no parent or friend ever could. If our survival has been balanced on the edge of a knife, Carson might be the blade, sugar, but I'll be damned if you weren't the hilt holding it steady."

Annie smiled, trying to hold back tears.

"Now, you take our friends, and you go with Carson to Colorado. I can't travel, and I've seen enough of those goddamn bloodsuckers and this strange darkness to last me a hundred vampire lifetimes. And when the time comes to make terms with them, to make that compromise, it needs to be you that does it."

"Me? Why?"

"Carson can dominate them now, and that means they'll be afraid of him. And any compromise made out of fear may last for a time, but it can't last for all time. The terms have to be agreed to based upon mutual understanding, mutual respect, and," he said, rubbing his tired eyes, "mutual fear. We are making this compromise because of the Nine, because of the Black Manuscript. The Nine are the ones that we—humankind and vampires—should be afraid of. Have Carson show them that." He chuckled to himself. "Well, I mean, don't have him show them like he showed Lucio. But he can make them understand the fear we should all have. Now, go on. I'm so damn tired you're starting to look beautiful."

Annie laughed.

Ashley grinned, turning to look toward the ceiling. "Yes, ma'am. I am exhausted. I think. . . when I'm done with this place, I'll head up Canada. Take Sven with me. Doesn't sound like he's up to traveling with you. Maybe see if we can find Julius and that family of his. Maybe take our time getting there, play a little poker on the way. Won't have anything to fear, seeing as I'll have the world's fastest gunfighter traveling with me."

"I hope I see you again, Ashley."

The gambler's grin widened to a smile. "I'll make you a deal. You and Carson build yourself a little cabin in Black Wells, one with a view of that valley and the mountain, and I'll come visit. But if you go back to Texas, I swear to all that's real and holy, you'll never see my one-legged ass again."

Annie wrapped her arms around him. Squeezed him tightly.

"Goodbye, Ashley. For now."

"Only for a piece," he said. "Only for a time."

* * *

Carson rode alongside Annie, heading toward the train station in the city proper of Fort Scott. Sarah rode just ahead of them. The wind was so cold that it seared the uncovered patches of flesh about his eyes. They traveled on together, little to be said, but Carson looked at Annie often, her long eyelashes frosted white, making her blue eyes glitter like jewels even in the cloudless light of the eclipse.

As they neared the train, Sarah Lockhart made a few jokes about how much she hated the idea of going back to Black Wells, mentioning again how a werewolf had once saved her from drowning in the Cam River. But, she said, it was too cold to tell the whole story.

They boarded *The Judge*. Stocked up with coal, the train began to knife its way along the rail, wheels churning, whistle blowing. A long trail of steam and smoke trailed behind them.

On that first night, they did all they could to forget the road that had brought them there and the road upon which they were headed. They drank and ate well: whiskey and wine, and steaks and potatoes and carrots smothered in rich brown gravy. When they retired to their sleeping cars, Sarah went in one direction, Carson and Annie went the other.

Annie and Carson made love, sweet and slow, kissing and holding each other so tightly that all their many cares and all the heartbreaks of their lives left them for a time. When they were through, they remained holding each other, arm in arm.

"How did you do it," Annie asked him, finally bringing the burning question to the surface.

Carson didn't know how to describe it or what to say, so he took a long time gathering his thoughts.

Before he could answer, she said, "The word you said you made, the new word in their language, what does it do?"

He looked at her, gazing deeply into her eyes. "It relinquishes the power of the conduit. Sends it back to the place I told you about. If that power isn't here, it can't pass on to another. Without two conduits, the Nine will be gated from us... forever, I hope."

Annie's eyes widened. "And what will that do to you?"

"I won't know until I speak the word."

She swallowed hard, squishing her eyes shut. And she pulled him close, burying her face in his chest.

"I need to ask you to do something for me, Annie," he

said, placing his chin to rest within the curls of her auburn hair.

"Anything," she said.

"I need you to make the peace between us and the Red Kingdom."

"Ashley said that, too."

Carson nodded. "He's right to think it. If there is anyone who can show how greatly we can forgive, it's you. If I go in and simply dominate their king, it will feel to them like a shackle of threat. It will be us treating them as they have treated us. And the moment I don't have the ability to dominate them, they will rebel, and all of this damnable fighting will just continue when we can no longer enforce that threat."

"I know," she said.

"Can you do that for me, Annie? If you can't, I will understand."

A long time passed between them. Their bare chests breathing against one another.

"I will."

"I know," said Carson. "You can do anything."

"Because I'm so stubborn?"

"No," he said, breathing in her scent. "Because you're the strongest person I have ever met."

"I'm still scared, Carson."

"I know," he said. "I am, too."

CHAPTER THIRTY

THE ASTOLAT MOUNTAIN RANGE, COLORADO

The *Judge* burned over the track, cutting a black line through the abysmal cold blanketing the entirety of both Kansas and Colorado. They reloaded with coal in Denver, where they found no sign of vampires or the Red Kingdom. Only people bustled through the streets—free people.

"Guessing your words to Sigurd had their intended effect," said Sarah Lockhart.

"Maybe," was all Carson said.

They punched through the rest of the journey as far as they could, until they had to offload and take a carriage into the Astolat Mountain range, which so darkly hid within its crescent shape the sweeping valley, the black satin waters of the Cam River, and the city of Black Wells.

The gaiety that had filled Denver was nowhere to be found in this city. Most of the people stayed indoors. Carson saw in their eyes the heart-rending trauma that he himself had known at the hands of the Society of Prometheus.

"They're broken," he said.

"No, they've just been unchained," said Sarah, a fierce understanding in her words. "And now they don't know what to do with this world made for them, because their oppressors are still among us, hiding in the mountain."

Carson nodded.

"They're feeling what my people felt in this country for near a century. Perhaps, when we're done, I can help them do something about it."

They slept in the same hotel that Sven had been staying in during his time in Black Wells. Annie and Carson stayed in the same room where Sven and Larry Cornish had so sweetly expressed their love for one another.

When they awoke, they took their time together, taking a meal in the same dining room where Annie and the Peregrine Estate had decided to go to Chicago to rescue Carson.

During breakfast, Annie, whose nerves were giving her stomach fits, excused herself to the powder room.

While Annie was gone, Carson tried to tell Sarah how appreciative he was for all she had done, and for all she had meant to Gilbert Ptolemy.

She waved the sentiment away. "Hell, handsome. Loving your pa was the easiest goddamn thing I've ever done. I miss him every day. I know you do, too."

Carson nodded.

"I've decided something, and I've already told Annie," said Sarah. "I can't forgive those pale-skinned bastards for all they've done. For all they've taken. If I get up in that mountain with that red king of theirs, I will, without question, blow his goddamn head off. I am and always will be a stick of dynamite when it comes to them. And you don't take dynamite into a room filled with fire."

Carson slid his hand across the table, placing his over hers.

She took his hand and squeezed. And she smiled that

big knowing grin of hers. Without him having to say it, she replied, "I know, kid. Me too."

* * *

Annie and Carson bought two horses from the stableman in Black Wells. Carson's horse was a gelding of bright blonde, tall and proud with his big sandy tail swishing against the wind and the snow. Annie's was a big brown mare who took to the woman quick as you please.

"Gotta name her," said Carson. "She's gone her whole life without you. Now that she has you, she's got to have a name to go along with it."

Annie patted the mare's nose. "Maple. I think. Cause she's sweet, aren't you, girl?"

The mare chuffed, bumping lightly against her.

"You ready?" asked Carson.

Annie slid atop Maple. Then she filled her pipe and began to smoke. "What about yours?"

Carson chewed over the question. "Sunshine," he said.

"I like it." They began to ride together, Annie puffing on her pipe, but she soon screwed up her nose and put the pipe away. "This really isn't agreeing with me today. Maybe I should have eaten more at breakfast." She put the pipe away, and they began to ride together.

Sven had given them all the information he knew about the valley and about how best to reach the entrance to the mountain's interior, where the Red Kingdom lay.

They rode into the valley, a vast snowy expanse populated with towering evergreens that were barren and needleless. From within the dense forests, there came a sudden chorus of howls. The familiar bellowing roar of the great wolves brought into the world by the ritual that was half-completed in Chicago.

Annie slashed her eyes over to Carson, but he was not worried.

He felt them, even from far off: the dark threadlines ran from the brutal pack toward the center of himself. With a simple gesture, he silenced their sound. He held them at bay so that they never even came out from their hiding place. But with that gesture, the cold seemed to deepen, and the light of the eclipse dimmed, so that even the white of the snow could barely be seen.

They set to light their lanterns, hung them from their horses' tacks, and rode on.

When they approached the cleft of the rock within the Astolat mountains, they found, standing very still in the darkness, a single figure.

"Welcome." The voice was smooth and dark, unknown to them. The figure was of medium height, though they could not see much else. "You are the envoys, yes?"

"Yes," said Annie. "We are here to meet with the red king."

The figure moved slowly toward them. "And here are you met with him. I am King Kristian, and you now stand at the precipice of my kingdom. The house that shelters my people. Your horses will need to stay here, but you may come in and enjoy my hospitality."

Annie looked to Carson.

"You know what will happen if you betray us," said Carson.

The king made a grand flourish. "I am Kristian of the Red Kingdom. My promises are a sacred thing. There is no need to threaten me, Carson Ptolemy."

Carson felt a pressure fill the air around him, a pressure orders of magnitude and wholly superior to that which Sigurd used to dominate the will of others. That invisible pressure touched Carson's mind, but he tossed it away, and sent his own will to touch the mind of the red king.

Kristian inhaled sharply. "My friend Sigurd spoke truly to me, I see."

"Don't do that again," said Carson.

"My apologies," said the king. "I assure you, I was merely testing that which has been spoken of so fearfully to me."

"And now you understand."

"Most fully, Mr. Ptolemy. Please, come inside, away from the cold and into the light."

They left their horses and followed the king, Carson poised at the ready for any sign of trickery or guile. But none came. They were taken through slender caves that opened wider and wider, and yet wider still, until they reached a precipice overlooking the most incredible city he had ever seen, bathed in the red light of lamps burning on every winding street and within towers near as tall as the mountain itself. And standing within those streets were thousands, perhaps tens of thousands, of vampires, all of them hushed and unmoving. At their feet knelt men, women, and children in tattered clothes. They walked among the cowering human populous lined along every street of that red city, the king leading the procession of three all the way to a grand hall where sat a massive throne of blackened stone.

Standing next to the throne was Sigurd of Antioch. He was dressed in a fine black suit, brooding, dark, and powerful, as unmoving as the cavernous walls surrounding them.

Kristian took his seat of power and, crossing one leg over the other, said, "And so we come to it, Ptolemy. Name your conditions, and I will consider them."

"It's not for me to name the conditions," said Carson.

Kristian cocked an eyebrow, curious. "Then who?"

"My name is Annie Miller," she said, stepping forward to approach the throne. "I am the head of the Peregrine Estate, and the terms I am offering are this." Slowly, with absolute certainty, Annie spoke. The terms were simple.

The Red Kingdom would remain in the mountain, no longer to be hunted by any human agent. The vampire nation would be amply stocked and provisioned, not with human life but with that of cows and lambs, and any other livestock they wished. Never again would they make a slave of a single human life, so long as they subsisted upon the Earth.

Kristian's brow furrowed. "And why should we accept to live among humans. . . like humans, creatures to whom we are so vastly greater than?"

Annie turned, giving one eye to Carson.

At that moment, Carson threw himself into the dark, churning abyss of the Nine. His flesh smoked and swirled, turning black as pitch. He opened his mouth and from his singular throat poured a chorus of voices singing the song of the Nine, that terrible hymn that had for eons ached to once again cast its supremacy over all the Earth. The cold, disastrous dissonance that had reigned from a throne higher than Kristian would ever hope to have, that song birthed out of darkness from a time when the universe itself was only in its infancy, rolled out before them.

Sigurd shied away, terror on his beautiful yet terrible visage. And King Kristian's smiling face fell into a mask of horror as beneath him, the stone throne upon which he sat crumbled to pebbles.

The cavern walls shook.

The scarlet lanterns lost their light.

"Cease!" cried the king, cast into a darkness even he with his tremendous power could not understand. "Cease, I demand it!"

Carson withdrew the song. The scarlet lights of the Red Kingdom flared bright and hot.

"This is the power behind the eclipse and the winter you hoped to use to reign over the world, King Kristian," said Annie.

He shook his head. "I. . . I did not understand."

"We are going to end it, here," said Annie. "Today."

"You will wish for me to release your people who have

been my subjects," said Kristian, rising from broken, jagged stones that had once been his seat.

"Right," said Annie. "All of them."

Kristian looked to Sigurd, not unsure but in resignation. Then he turned to look upon Carson, then to Annie. "Your terms," he said. "I accept them. And should I perish, my successors too shall keep these terms, so long as they are upheld by your own kind. So long as"—he dared to look at Carson once again—"so long as whatever is inside this man is never allowed to touch my kingdom again."

* * *

The subjugated people of Colorado were released. Over a series of long hours, they marched out of the depths of the Astolats—a free people. Carson and Annie directed them, the two of them watching as the formerly enslaved first walked and then began to run down the valley. The survivors clutched their husbands and wives, bounding up together in disbelieving joy. They sprayed out of the mountain to follow the Cam River back toward the homes waiting for them in the city from which they had been stolen.

* * *

When they were gone, Carson and Annie stood in the valley, alone together. The eclipse lorded over them, a circle of silver amid the ablating cold. Carson went to Sunshine, and from the saddlebag he produced the Black Manuscript. His fingers were trembling. His heart beat slowly.

All his life had drawn to this moment.

Carson, standing in shadow of mountain and the dim light of the eclipse, led Annie and the horses away to stand at a safe distance. He did not know what would happen once he spoke the word, and he would not risk any injury to the woman he loved.

He kissed her long and deep.

"I—" Annie began.

Carson kissed her again.

He stepped out into a little glade, set near them at the middle of the valley and, taking the manuscript in one hand and a knife in the other, he began to carve the singular symbol of the word he had made. The new, admirable word. The leather of the volume curled away in slender black ribbons, and smoke rose from the symbol. He dusted the peeled leather away and then opened the manuscript for the last time.

Carson opened the book to the page upon which he had written the ritual in the language that had dominated his life. He looked at Annie.

She was crying.

Carson placed his hand upon the page, and looking up to the eclipse, he spoke.

The word, his word, less than a whisper.

All his pain and sorrow were in that word. All his love and hope, all his desire. All the strength that had been stolen by his want for revenge came back to him for half a heartbeat. All the sorrow of loss and the bliss of loving Annie Miller.

All of him was poured out.

And the word spoken. All he was, man and conduit, came rushing out of him. Like poison drawn out of an old wound, the smoking shadow within his heart and mind and soul rushed forth, flowing down the shadow of his arm, flooding into the pages of the manuscript.

And the manuscript fell from his fingertips and thudded into the snow, where it snapped shut.

He swayed, his strength holding fast.

Then he turned, took a step toward Annie, and all his strength left him.

CHAPTER THIRTY-ONE

The Astolat Mountain Range, Black Wells, Colorado

A nnie watched.
Carson's lips moved.
The manuscript fell.
He fell too.
She ran.
The world seemed to shift with each stride. Brighter.
And brighter.
She took him into her arms, knowing before she knew.
There, in Annie's lap, Carson Watts Ptolemy lay dying. His eyes, wet with pain and understanding, lifted to hers. A cornflower light bathed the man's face, turning his green eyes into shining opals. He lifted his hand, straining with exhaustion, and extended a trembling finger to point up past her. "Look," he said.

"I know," she said, refusing to turn. Her tears fell, tumbling to diamonds in the night fire of the rising moon. "I can see the light, too."

She felt his heavy breathing begin to grow shallow.

He closed his eyes, shaking his head. "So stubborn," the words a whisper. *"Look."*

Annie, her chest heavy, pursed her lips. She slid her glove from her hand and ran her fingers through his hair, then set her warm palm against his forehead. "Okay. I'll look."

She followed the trembling line of Carson's arm. The fingers ruined by his enemies were outstretched, as if he was trying to grasp the glowing orb set high above them in a sky full of stars.

The moon, though full, seemed such a small thing amid the vastness of all else. But the moon shined. It shined down to color everything in a tangible radiance Annie had never seen before. That light sublime.

Wind tossed Annie's hair, blowing it over the both of them.

Carson shivered.

She pulled him closer, trying to keep the cold at bay as best as she could.

"I couldn't have done this without you, Annie," said Carson, his voice strong at first but then weakening so that her name was a ghost on his lips.

Her tears, hot on her face, fell into Carson's hair. She pulled him closer, though he was already as close as he could be. "I don't want you to go," she said. "I won't let you."

"Always had it your way. But not this time," he said. "I've gone my whole life keeping my promises, Annie. This one. . ." He closed his eyes. His breathing slowed.

Annie took him in, the scent of his hair sending her drifting down a long river of memories. Memories beginning with a kiss that, so long ago, had been nothing to give. And now, she knew, this one final kiss would take everything.

Their lips met, his cool against her warmth.

A kiss that, greater than the cold, became all she could feel.

And there, diamonds in starlight, their tears collided.

Carson inhaled deeply, as if trying to breathe her in. Annie squeezed him close, holding him so tightly that no matter where he went after this moment, he would never feel alone again.

"I love you, Carson Ptolemy," she said. "I love you. I love you forever."

Carson slid his lips over so that they brushed her cheek, and his voice fell upon her ear. "Always," he said, weaker now.

His head drifted, brow sliding against Annie's neck, so that he came to rest upon her shoulder.

Carson Watts Ptolemy took a deep breath.

Then, another.

Then, once more, and never again.

EPILOGUE

MILLER & SON

EPILOGUE

The Starlight Valley
Black Wells,
Colorado

T he boy, a carefree ruckus of happiness, turned and turned among a spray of sunlit wildflowers clinging to their color against the cold promise of autumn. Dizzy with joy, he laughed, arms outstretched beneath blue skies. It was a sound that ran the length of the valley, up the gray shoulders of the Astolats, where its pure, uncomplicated delight echoed off the stone and tumbled into the ears and heart of his mother. He spun again, fingertips kissing petals of violets, sunflowers as yellow as the star sustaining them, and shoots of dew-kissed grass the color of his father's eyes. And his own.

"George Carson Miller," the mother said, playfully chiding. "You better get over here or I'm going to eat all these lemon drops myself!"

He stopped suddenly, swaying, his little mouth widened in disbelief. "Momma, no!"

Annie Joy Miller lifted an eyebrow at the boy. A dare.

The boy knew this look, had known it the whole short measure of his young life. He didn't hesitate. He ran through the flowers, little arms pumping hard, never slowing. He crashed into his mother, hoping to bull her over. But she was too strong a pillar and caught him in her arms. She kissed his sun-reddened cheeks, giving him everything until he squirmed, begging her to stop, secretly wishing she never would.

"Okay," said Annie. "*One* lemon drop."

"Ugh." George threw his head back as if in anguish. "But Miss Sarah always lets me have five!"

"Well, Miss Sarah may be the mayor of Black Wells, but I'm the mother. And for now, let's start with a little sweetness. Just enough for us to build on." She narrowed her eyes at him. "But, I suppose today is special. . . so I might be persuaded. Not yet, though. After."

The boy cheered, arms shooting into the air, fingers reaching. He wrapped his arms around her neck. "Carry me this time."

"How could I refuse?"

Bundled together, wrapped tight as a Christmas gift, they made their way through the flowers of the valley to the curving rush of the Cam River.

They visited the grave often. Always on this day.

She set the boy down at the foot of the plot. The sun, shining bright, cast the boy's shadow into a long, slender figure. The shape of the man he would become.

"Sometimes," said George, speaking to the simple gravestone, "when I'm lying in bed, I talk to him. Do you think he likes that?"

"Oh," said Annie, "I think he likes that very much."

The boy turned, looking at Annie with Carson's green eyes and spoke with the candidness he got from her. "Do you think he can hear me?"

"I like to think he can," she said, hoping.

"What do you think he would have liked about me?"

"Well, that answer I know. He would have loved everything about you. His love was a very, very big thing. Big enough for everyone, but especially big for you."

The seriousness in the boy's face—his father's seriousness—was carried away as quickly as it had descended, replaced with a smile. "Do you. . ." the boy's eyes fell away in rare shyness. "Do you think I could talk to him now. . . alone?"

"Take your time," said Annie. "I'll go pack-up our picnic and saddle Maple."

Annie turned, giving the two of them privacy.

She bundled up the blanket and picnic basket, then headed for a little copse of apple trees. Maple, now branded with Annie's own brand, swished her blonde tail happily, muzzle chomping one of the fallen fruit.

Annie laughed, remembering, then clicked her tongue.

Maple looked up, then slowly sauntered over to rest her nose against Annie's shoulder.

She took her time brushing the mare as she gazed back through the trees to look upon her boy, watching for a long time. She saddled the mare, then together they turned to see the child kiss the top of the stone that bore his father's name.

George Carson Miller, smiling, began to run toward Annie and mare. Loud as his previous laughter, George, running from the plot, said, "Bye bye, Daddy. I love you!"

He turned back for a moment and, cupping his hands around his mouth, he hollered the words all through the Starlight Valley. "Momma loves you, too!"

George turned, ran again.

Annie hesitated, watched.

The sunlight his father had won, bright and clear, threw itself over the son he would never know. The man Annie Miller had loved, the man she would love forever, had saved that light. And the light kept the cold at bay.

CEMETERY DANCE
EPILOGUE

Upon the Death and Burial of My Father

For Dad

The McKenzie Cemetery is old and dusty, and filled with the sounds of the West Texas chaparral pasture. To reach its century-and-a-half-old rocky fence, you turn off a blacktop Texas highway that rolls on and on, connecting San Angelo and Colorado City. Between those oil-boom towns is nothing but road, barbed-wire fence, and short, spindly grasses that give way to wild, roving expanses of mesquite trees. The trees are of a gnarled shape with cracked, black-brown bark that fans out suddenly into needle-sharp leaves of a green the eyes can only find in this part of the world. It is a color that exists, like the cemetery between the two towns, as a particular kind of treasure only revealed to those whose ancestors have passed along the secret of its existence.

Turning off the road, one passes over the triple-bump shock of a cattle gate, where a powdery dirt road stretches not too far to reveal the cemetery's simple square expanse.

The cemetery is a quiet place. Airless in its heavy silence that is broken only by the braying of Hereford beef cattle grazing, or by the West Texas wind that, when it comes, comes whipping and howling, sharp and sandy. The silence also breaks in this place when mothers and fathers, sons and daughters, extended family and friends find themselves turning off the blacktop to make use of one of the plots. Many of those plots in the cemetery were filled a long, long time ago. So long ago that even the great grandchildren of those who lie there have died.

The morning is the only time to make use of those plots. The time when the Texas dawn is just beginning to lose its velvety purples and scarlets and wildflower pinks. When the sun is the gold of a swollen peach, not quite ripe. Like the cemetery's location, like the unique green of the mesquites, there is a betweenness to the time that is best to make use of this place, before its hard, unforgiving sunlight makes the day too hot for fellowship or mourning, so bright it hurts the eyes.

One of those plots was opened two days ago, the dusty ground and impacted caliche chewed into easily by a backhoe driver, who has no idea for whom he is digging a grave. A day later, backhoe driver nowhere to be seen, the plot is adorned with a canvas canopy under which are set three rows of chairs set atop the bristly green shag of a faux-lawn carpet.

A long white car arrives.

A hearse.

Within the hearse are two men. One of them is a driver. A professional man dressed in a suit who is the last chauffeur his singular passenger will ever have. The passenger lying inside the black and brown casket composed of repurposed tobacco-barn oak, is of medium height. His face made up to counterfeit the skin to that of the healthy, tanned complexion captured in photographs his family will look upon for years and years when they want to remember.

Inside the casket, set upon a cream-colored pillow, the passenger lays tranquil. Still. Eyes closed forever. The passenger wears a blue-white, almost silver shirt embroidered with black diamonds that match the leather belt and washed-out wranglers. The passenger rests inside the hearse for a short time, and eternally, waiting. And then, the people who knew the passenger arrive in the comfort of multiple caravans comprised of his friends, his extended family. Where they wait until the passenger's immediate family arrive, as prepared as they can be.

The passenger is born out of the hearse into the golden burn of the West Texas sun, untouched in that moment by all the light he cannot see, hidden away in the casket. Then, the passenger is carefully rolled toward the grave by two sons, two nephews, an uncle, and a brother-in-law.

All those who knew the passenger are drawn-in by the approach of the casket and the gravity of the man inside. Bundled together, the people stand beneath the late-morning golden light flaring yellow, bringing with it the heat that has forged the hard men of this harsh, rudely beautiful landscape for hundreds of years. The mother, the sister, and the children of the passenger sit, and for a short time, the wind comes blowing eastward, snapping the canvas flaps like funeral banners.

A preacher welcomes the waiting crowd, many of them with lumps in their throats. Ashes where their hearts should be.

A song is played. A George Strait tune about fathers and their children and the hereafter.

The preacher speaks again. Corinthians and Romans and the prophet Isaiah have their timeless words called out. The cattle lowing along with the preacher's message of comfort and peace, Alpha and Omega.

Another song is played. A Willie Nelson gospel tune

about those called, the vellum of their lives rolled up like a scroll.

The second son of the passenger gets up and, taking a deep, measured breath, heart racing, hopes that he can, with words written by his hand, give a voice to all the many feelings he and his siblings have felt over all the many years they have known this man. Because he their brother has, while writing about the father they share, thought wholly upon them. Thought about the illimitable gratitude and largess and mending they have, each of them, provided the rest. The work and the challenges. The debates. The laughter and the tears. The pain they share. And all the unmistakable heavenly glory residing in each of them.

He says:

"We are so glad you are here. We only wish it were under better circumstances."

And with the deepest breath he may ever take he speaks to the crowd, letting them hear the last gift he will ever give to his father.

* * *

My family is worried that my long-winded nature will make a prisoner of all of us in this moment. They are afraid, and rightfully so, that I will go on and on, spilling over with stories and voices, jokes and metaphor and similes, like so many tumbleweeds blowing through the West Texas chaparral flats where we, all of us, came to know this man.

But they don't need to worry, because how much time could I take to tell you? How much time could I spend? To tell you all that you already know about this man.

He was born Max'sl Karl Humble on September 23, 1960. He was a part of the graduating class of 1979 from

Snyder high school, and to hear him tell it, he was the fastest son of a bitch to ever run the 400 m hurdles.

He was a hard man raised on this unforgiving landscape, by other hard men, who were hardened by the times and circumstances they grew up in. A man who cowboyed through life, always riding hard, and cutting a lean, beveled silhouette against the Texas skies that only his forebearers knew better.

He was a son. He was a brother. A husband. He was a father of four children, who called his eldest son Bubba, his first daughter Sis, me he called son, and having what might've been the singular prophetic moment of his life, he named the last child after himself, always calling her Max'sl.

Dad was beloved by many people. Those in his younger heavy-haul–trucking years knew him as 'the mule.' Those who worked underneath him while he was a truck pusher, the best truck pusher to ever shit between a pair of boots, called him 'boss.'

To his many female admirers and girlfriends and paramours, he proved, with eyes the blue of sunlight kissing the topmost spindle of a glacier, to be the most charming rake they would ever know.

And this, his charm, along with his deep, personal definition of fidelity to his friends, was the part of him that shined the brightest.

Dad was uncommonly likable.

Even to those who argued with him, those who fought with him, those who were once his enemies, all of them, found it very difficult to never become his friend.

Dad's love was a rough kind of love, unvarnished. Always direct. Here at the end, it is a love, seismic in its power and utterly unique, that will stay with all of us in different and impactful ways.

And he was a man, more man than any man who came before, that proved true the troubadour words of Waylon

Jennings and Willie Nelson, "Cowboys ain't easy to love, and they're harder to hold."

* * *

Words said, the airless silence of the cemetery returns, and he sits.

Another song, "I Come to the Garden Alone," comes pouring out over the friends, the family, the father in the casket, down into the empty, waiting grave, and then up and up and up. On and on, past the cattle, the gate, over the brush and the mesquites. All the way to the singular blacktop highway that provides the only road whereupon the McKenzie Cemetery can be found. Her newest occupant, resting within a casket, within a vault, within earthen tomb, laying quiet.

Resting, finally, now that his hurried, hot-hearted life has come to an end.

About the Author

C.S. Humble is the award-winning American novelist of the Amid the Vastness of All Else Saga. He is also a screenplay and short story writer. He lives in East Texas.

A Note from Shortwave Publishing

Thank you for reading *The Light of a Black Star*! If you enjoyed this book, please consider writing a review. Reviews help readers find more titles they may enjoy, and that helps us continue to publish titles like this.

For more Shortwave titles, visit us online. . .

OUR WEBSITE
shortwavepublishing.com

SOCIAL MEDIA
@ShortwaveBooks

EMAIL US
contact@shortwavepublishing.com

AN EXCERPT FROM

TO CARRY A BODY
TO ITS RESTING PLACE

THE PEREGRINE ESTATE, #1

To Carry a Body
to its Resting Place

The Blind Crow Saloon
St. Louis, Missouri
January 8, 1845

It was in the winter of Ashley's Sutliff's nineteenth year when his brother, Willow, walked through a set of snow-powdered St. Louis saloon doors and, without offering salutation amid the low, smoky lamplight slanting across saloon girls and card-holding gamblers and cowhands alike, said simply, "Daddy's asking you to come home."

Ashley Sutliff, in mid-hand and absent of all desire to travel back to the hog farm, much less speak to his father, drew out his rejoinder, long and dramatic. "Well, hello, dear brother. As you can see, I am currently preoccupied with success." He looked up from his cards, the rest of him unmoving, giving his brother a hot-eyed stare. "Winning at the life Daddy said would only lead to ruin. So, you will understand me when I say: Fuck off. Go home. Let me gamble."

Will, half-a-head taller than any other man in the room, reached up and removed his ridge-top hat. Like the man, it was powdered with snow, rumpled, marked by more than the weathering of its years. And Ashley saw what the shadow of the mud-speckled brim had been hiding. What he had not heard in his brother's voice. There were tears in Will's brown eyes. Tears and the silent resignation only seen in the absolute surety of an oncoming tragedy.

Ninety-nine times out of a hundred, Ashley would have japed his brother and cussed him in front of this gambling cohort. He was that kind of man, priding himself on his meanness and brusque manner. But, made a witness to the pain in his little brother's face, Ashley was compelled toward that one in one hundred moment. An unwritten compact, composed by the blood in their hearts, bridged the silence between them, altering their lives forever.

Ashley rose and said to the gamblers surrounding him, "Gentlemen, I have urgent business at home. But I assure you, I will be back, expecting my due from this full house you all thought I was bluffing."

He splayed his cards among the mess of chips: two kings and three nines, set before four groaning men and a dealer grinning like a Jack.

"Put it on my credit, Charlie," said Ashley to the dealer, a smooth-shaven man wearing a French silk shirt and red vest, fancy as you please. "I'll spend it all on whiskey and gals soon enough."

"Ain't no way," said a beady-eyed elephant of a man seated to Ashley's right, gripping his cards so tight they seemed to wither like flowers in a drought. "There ain't no goddamn, motherfucking way you slow-played a full house. Not the way you've been throwing your chips in with deuces and fives and stole a pot on a goddamn pair of threes."

"And yet..." said Ashley, smirking, palms up. He realized he'd forgotten the man's name. Was it Wilbur? Willard? No, it was Walter. He was sure of it. There was no need for things to get crazy, no reason for tempers to flare. And so, Ashley put a hand on the big man's shoulder and squeezed. "No hard feelings there, Walter, I—"

The corners of the man's mouth lifted, exhuming an expression set between a snarl and the nose catching the aroma of horseshit. "Who the fuck is Walter?"

"Ashley," said Will, still standing in the cut of the saloon door. "I will not suffer to wait."

"You'll fuckin' wait until I get what's owed me," said the big man. "This little shit is a cheat if I've ever seen—"

"A what?" Ashley snapped.

"Ash—" Will started.

"A fuckin' cheat, I said."

"Aw, shit," said Will, resigned.

"A cheat," said Ashley, nodding. Eyes widening as he accepted the inescapable detour set before him and his journey home. And thus, Ashley sprang from his seat while cocking the right hand that had broken noses and shattered the eye socket of a Louisiana mule-skinner not six months back, and let it fly with all the destructive power living within him.

The blow struck the big man in the face. The other two gamblers at the table scrambled, the dealer, too. Ashley threw himself as a pile of fury atop the man, smothering him with blows—overhands and hooks, slaps and eyerakes. Ashley might have given up a full grain-sack worth of weight to the gambler, but when it came to the melee distance between them he refused to give an inch.

When Ashley was a boy, his father had educated him on the tempo and insistence of violence. "Once you get on top, you waylay until they lay still. Don't quit if they beg.

Don't stop if they're hurt. Unless someone pulls you off, you hit a man enough times so he can't remember the fight but will never forget what you did to him."

The big man had wagered to call Ashley a cheat, and that gamble would prove—

"Ashley," Will's voice called from a far-off place, calm and cold, cutting with command.

"Christ," cried the big man, toppling out his chair, his face slapping hard against the grimy floorboards. He lifted massive balled fists around his head, wailing for the help of a god that would not answer. Would not intercede.

Every eye watched. None of the witnesses moved.

Ashley kicked one of the man's hands away and, knee first, dropped his full weight on the man's wrist. There was something like the sound of an old tree limb giving way. The big gambler howled.

Satisfied with the sound, Ashley howled right back, eyes and mouth stretching wide, a jester made a lunatic by a joke that has driven him mad.

"Ashley," Will said again.

Undeterred and wild with rage, Ashley set one thumb over the other and wrapped his fingers around the big man's throat. Though he had been away from the hog farm for two years—away from the setting of fence posts and the tossing of hay bales and the hammering of ten-thousand nails that sunk head-deep on a second strike—the holding of cards had taken none of the laborious strength vested in his grip.

Then, there was the sound of something metallic sliding loose from a smooth place. Followed by a peal of thunderous gunfire and panicked shrieks from the smooth-shaven dealer and St. Louis saloon pikers.

Ashley, snatched from the maelstrom of his killing rage by the heralding of gunfire, defensively reached for his revolver.

There was a ratcheting click. The sound every gambler

and gunfighter knew. A double-action hammer drawn back in warning or finality.

Ashley, drawn erect in alarm, hand frozen for fear of what punishment drawing his pistol would bring, looked up to see Willow Sutliff's eyes glaring down a gun barrel at him. Confidence and surety, stiff as the December wind outside, whipped an unhappy smile on his brother's face. And through the lips came a tone colder than the spindles of ice dangling from every saloon house from here to the frozen Missouri River. "Daddy is asking you to come home. I, however, will not ask at all," he said. "Get up. Grab your shit. Let's go."

* * *

To Carry a Body to Its Resting Place is out on July 15, 2025 from Shortwave Publishing.

www.ingramcontent.com/pod-product-compliance
Ingram Content Group UK Ltd.
Pitfield, Milton Keynes, MK11 3LW, UK
UKHW040305170625
6427UKWH00001B/17